Jo-Anne Richards comes from the Eastern Cape and now lives in Johannesburg. She is a journalist. *The Innocence of Roast Chicken*, her first novel, was an instant South African success, topping the bestseller lists for fifteen weeks.

Praise for *The Innocence of Roast Chicken*:

'Jo-Anne Richards displays a wonderful feeling for place and period . . . her prose is sharply evocative, and she conjures up the child's powerful feelings with a vividness intensified by nostalgia'
Margaret Walters, *The Sunday Times*

'A rapturous and tactile evocation of dust, food, noises and a childhood domain, rendered with a marked empathy for the child and the magical properties of a child's stamping ground'
Elizabeth Buchan, *The Times*

'A fresh and memorable addition to the literature of apartheid'
Observer

'Jo-Anne Richards' writing seems effortlessly expressive and flows with an unerring feel for authentic detail'
Wendy Woods

'Is niet alleen een belangwokkende roman omdat hij zo goed geschreven is'
Het Parool, Amsterdam

D0725292

The Innocence *of* Roast Chicken

Jo-Anne Richards

review

First published in 1996
by HEADLINE BOOK PUBLISHING

First published in paperback in 1997
by HEADLINE BOOK PUBLISHING

A REVIEW paperback

10 9 8 7 6 5 4 3 2 1

ISBN 0 7472 5931 3

Typeset by
Letterpart Limited, Reigate, Surrey

Printed in England by
Clays Ltd, St Ives plc

HEADLINE BOOK PUBLISHING
A division of Hodder Headline PLC
338 Euston Road
London NW1 3BH

The Innocence *of* Roast Chicken

Everyone should have a farm like that in their child-hood – too idyllic to be real outside the tangible world of a child's imagining. And it really was like that, the perfect background for a charmed and untouched childhood. The farm itself was untouched: by ugliness, unpleasantness, poverty, politics. Or so it seemed to me. Until that particular year, when it was spoiled. Everything was spoiled.

As an intense teenager, years later, filled with angst and misplaced sensitivity, I wrote a poem about my childhood. I wrote of a white sheet hanging on the line on a summer day, rippling and flapping in a gentle breeze, warmed and dried by the cloudless heat of the day. Then I showed it fallen, a graceless heap on the grassless ground, soiled by filthy footprints which could have been mud, but which looked a bit like blood.

Don't think badly of me. Everyone is filled with self-pity at fourteen. And for many years I carried the full guilt of that year. I lugged the intense, silent burden of having caused everything that happened by doing something very bad, or not standing in the way of the bad things – to field and divert them from us, from my

1

farm. I had too much faith in the way things would continue, in the beauty of before.

When I was older, I realized that, after all, I had been just a child, powerless to deflect the horror, not strong enough to be chosen as the cosmic goalie. Then I felt sorry for myself, until I was older still, and the guilt – more collective this time – settled again. That was when I locked myself away from all the perplexing ugliness of life, and from any taint of hurt or violence.

But I didn't set out to tell about 1966. I don't want to talk about it. I want to describe how it really was, how it was before – before the ugliness. I want to tell you about the soft, lilting nature of my holidays there.

This is how it really was. Each morning at five we awoke, my two brothers and I, to the same sounds. The drowsy sounds of hundreds of chickens, interspersed with the sharp crow of awakened roosters. Lying very still in my bed I could hear the grating beat of the belt-driven generator. From the bedroom next door, the early news on the Afrikaans service, and then my grandmother's soft-intoned, Afrikaans-accented reading from the English Bible, before my grandfather's deep English voice joined hers in the Lord's Prayer.

The *skree-bang* of the fly-screen door into the kitchen, and the cleaning noises in the lounge – invisible cleaning, for we never saw it being done. When the smells of bacon and Jungle Oats finally reached us, we catapulted noisily from our three beds, just in time to join my father heading for his unfailing early morning swim.

Before the full sun of the morning heated the dusty path through the orchard, I trotted barefoot alongside my father while my brothers raced for the pool. We joined them only after my father and I had stood to eat still cool figs from the tree. And he invariably said: 'The only way to eat figs – straight off the tree before the sun's properly up.'

The swimming place was huge and old fashioned – a reservoir built in the war years, now used only for swimming. Moving hand over hand along the sides in the morning, one could be sure of finding a bullfrog or two wallowing in the small square holes just above water level.

Shivering and chilled, we would make for the warmth of the kitchen, where we dried off before the huge coal stove, pinching cinnamon-flavoured *soetkoekies* from the china jar on the dresser. The admonishments this would draw from enormously fat Dora, who ruled the kitchen, never managed to outlast her chest-quivering, almost toothless laugh.

Breakfasts were huge, lunches merely a welcome interruption to an otherwise totally unfettered day, in which the grown-ups remained satisfyingly remote from our adventuring, but comfortingly near at hand for my little-girl needs. Ouma, solid and practical, had a face which brooked no nonsense and truly softened and sweetened only when she looked at us kids. To my kind, literary Oupa – so civilized and impractical – she spoke always in a hectoring tone, which he answered meekly, but with a wink at me. Once, while I sat on his knee being read to – *A Child's Garden of Verses*, I think it was, though I can't be sure – he told me it was Ouma's way of showing her love for us, the dreamy impractical ones, her way of chivvying us into coping with the harder side of life.

But it never worked. She always called me *pieperig*,

and Oupa always sat reading or writing in his library, his soft, persistent cough and constant wisp of pipe smoke betraying his presence. Ouma, whom I never saw with a book other than the Bible, was out on the farm, supervising the feeding of the new chicks, the nailing of sacking over the chicken *hoks* before a threatened hailstorm and, of course, the killing – which I was never aware of, and never went curiously in search of, as my brothers did. And when the crunch finally came, when the hardness of life finally came home to me, I wasn't strong enough to deal with it, and my grandmother's attempts to toughen me were no defence against the events which caused the collapse of my life and the devastation of my childhood – or so it seemed to me at the time. Even if, in retrospect, and with adult consciousness, you smile cynically and think me melodramatic, I can describe it in no other way. Anyway, I wasn't going to talk about that time.

I was going to talk about Ouma's boys – William, her right-hand man, and Petrus, and the others who smiled at us and loved us and carried me over the dusty ground when the sun heated it too much for my small feet to bear. They let me plunge my hands into the barrels of feathers, and gently hold the tiny yellow chicks among the deafening chitter of the new arrivals. And each morning after breakfast I would sit with William and Petrus in the boys' room, drinking forbidden coffee from a tin mug, poured from a large can boiling on a brazier, and sweetened with their ration of condensed milk.

And I haven't yet described the glory of the long lawn rolling from the front of the house, the wonder of Ouma's pride: the flowers that caused travellers to stop and ask if they could buy an armful. Ouma would generously fill their arms for free, and when she had done so, the plentiful garden looked no different, no emptier. The enormous spreading wild fig tree at the bottom of the garden provided the shade for the long summer evenings when my father would carve up a watermelon, and we would gorge ourselves, the sweet, sticky flesh causing rivulets of juice to run from our chins and down our arms to our elbows.

This is where I should stop, leaving the impressions of long, adventure-filled, dusty days of swimming, exploring, climbing trees. Of lying full length on the library floor with a fluttery, exciting feeling of reading some never before discovered book. Of the wildness of the veld and the magic of the people there. I shouldn't go on to tell you about that holiday, the one I have clutched silently to myself for all these years. What good will it do to bring it out now?

It was 1966. I was eight years old, in Standard One in Port Elizabeth. In this small coastal city of the Eastern Cape, where everyone knew my family, I grew up believing I was something of a princess. The youngest child and only daughter, I attended a girls-only school where we wore panama hats and regulation bloomers. There they stressed the importance of turning out 'young ladies'; of deportment, and of climbing the stairs one at a time.

The cataclysmic political events of the 1960s had, for the most part, passed me by. But I did know that blacks, or 'Africans' as I was instructed to call them by my enlightened, English-speaking parents, were badly treated and poor. 'Don't call them natives, dear, they don't like it.'

But I knew that we were on the side of right, as my parents treated Africans with kindness. They were early 'Progs', and weren't scared of arguing with their friends, not all of whom were so sure that Africans were capable of exercising the vote – qualified of course. 'But don't you see,' my father would argue, 'your argument doesn't stand up. According to the Progs' policy old Joseph, your garden boy, wouldn't have the vote, but the educated African would, and he's probably more capable than some of the poor whites who have it now.'

I knew that if we had our way, and got those damned Afrikaners out of power, everything would be OK. And maybe the Progs would win one day. I had a fantasy of taking a ragged child from the street and dressing her in nice clothes and giving her books and money for school. In those days, the days when the fanatical Dr Hendrik Verwoerd was prime minister, we felt bad that we received a good, free education, while blacks had to pay for theirs.

But of the inferiority of Bantu Education I knew little. I remember only that my mother would lecture me when I complained about going to school. 'Education means so little to you because you have it so easy,' she would say. 'Some African child would die to be able to go to school as you do.' So I thought of giving this chance to some child, who would weep with gratitude, and her parents would clutch my hands with tears in their eyes, and I felt so warm and good.

Of course, like everyone else we knew, we had a maid. She loved us as her own, hugged us, read to us, dressed us each morning and carried all three of us on her back until we were too big to fit. Margaret cooked for us and cared for us and I couldn't imagine life without her warm presence and love. She was the first person we all three scampered to greet the moment we heard her comforting clatter each morning.

But I can also, still with a smarting clarity, remember how I hurt her that year. And for no explicable reason other than the ease with which I could do so. This is an unpleasant story, and it puts me in a bad light. But I've decided that if I am to speak of that year and that life, if it has to come out now, I have to tell it all no matter how badly you might think of me. And somehow, I think that if I speak of everything that happened that year, and all that I did, it might help me to understand what happened later.

I don't think it would ever have occurred to me to use the word 'native' when addressing black people. It wasn't used in my home or at school. But when I was warned against using it, I can remember that quite suddenly it became a 'forbidden' word, unbearably enticing in its wickedness.

'Native,' I taunted Margaret, running guiltily through the kitchen. 'Oh no,' she said, dropping her head while her face became, it seemed to me, frightening in its desolation. Of course she forgave me, never mentioning it again. But for ages it would come to me, that cringy, sweaty feeling of regret, of wondering if she could still love me. And then, of course, I hurt her again. But this time it was worse, because it was a rejection of her.

Dawdling and dreaming, I would fairly regularly miss the number eight bus, which carried us Mill Park girls home from school. I relished the stomach-trembling adventure this gave me, of having to walk to my father's office across the Donkin Reserve. I loved the imaginings aroused by the gracious buildings lining this humpbacked commonage.

A slight detour took me past the delicate metal lacework of an old gate, which had once swung romantically open to admit butterfly ladies in horse-drawn carriages. Gazing through the gates into the sash-windowed hotel, tracing the filigree with my fingers, I could so easily believe that I lived in that grandeur outside of my allotted time.

A zigzagged wander took me to my second lingering ritual, which was to run across the grass to touch the red-tipped lighthouse and gaze over the top of 'downtown'. Beyond town, which squatted comfortably at the foot of the hill's steep bump, were the wind-whitened tips of the waves – a startling blue in sunshine, muddying to dirty green under clouds. And the ships moving inexorably past me to the harbour wall.

Just beyond the terraced houses which snaked their way down the swelling bulge of the hill, was my father's office. Here, I could play with rubber stamps and be spoilt by beehived office workers who looked so similar I would get them confused. 'Will you take me up and down in the lift again?' I asked one, only to find it was another dark beehive with fluttering false eyelashes who had taken me on the trip in the metal-caged lift.

My mother would usually arrive at the office within ten minutes of my phone call. In her miniskirt and upswept glasses, she would breeze in efficiently and carry me home in her car. But on that particular day, sometime in 1966, my mom was out when I called. Margaret came instead, using her own money to catch the bus into town and struggle up the hill to the office. When she took my hand for the walk back into town, I was humiliated at the thought that people would think me baby enough still to need a nanny, and one whose hand I had to hold. Petulantly I flung myself away from her and spat out that I didn't want people to see me with her. She never spoke a word of reproach, but held firmly to my hand, telling me the streets were dangerous.

1966. I hated school that year. Removed from the comfortable sub-Standards, we were now part of the real school and no longer permitted to hide behind our infant status. But school was such a small part of my life, and I was, in any case, such a daydreamer that I could float free any time I felt the need. To escape the mean vitriol of our pinch-mouthed teacher, Miss Harper – eternally make-up free behind her pointy blue glasses – I would picture Margaret in the kitchen and my mother taking her afternoon rest. Tea and Salticrax to the sound of the children's programme and *Woman's World* in the afternoon.

That was the year Prime Minister Verwoerd was killed. There was no sorrow in our family and I remember it only because of two things. Miss Harper, her *crissy* hair pulled tightly back from her face to make it straighter, told us that 'our leader, Dr Verwoerd' had been murdered by a madman. But the silence of her created solemnity was broken when she announced a half-day holiday to mourn his passing. And on a Friday, a special bonus.

That I remember most of all. My friend Jackie and I rode our bicycles to the local newsagent to collect the *June* and *Schoolfriend* comics which they held for us each Friday. Only British weeklies, of course. We weren't allowed, on pain of tearing up, American comics like *Caspar* and *Richie Rich*. With our comics and an early picnic lunch, we retired deliciously to a tent we had pitched in our garden and read them from cover to cover. That's the only reason I remember the assassination at all.

But on the Monday it was back to school, without another thought for Verwoerd or who would come next. Each day we hung our hats and lined up outside the school hall. At the first piano-thumped strains of march music we would parade in. There, at the piano, we would see the dead-straight back and teased bouffant of our one glamorous, pancake-smooth teacher. After the hymn, psalm and prayers of assembly, monitors inspected our bloomers, fingernails and hymn books and closely watched us file from the hall to check for stairs taken two at a time.

But I had another life. Each morning at half past five my father would wake me by staring silently at my sleeping face. As the sun was rising in summer, we would be stepping on to the chilly sand in its warm early glow. The first shock of the water always gave way to the fresh cleansing of salt and the exultancy of being the first people in the world, or so it seemed, to squint over the gold sparkling water and imagine where the ships were going and what they were carrying. Tide-walkers, we would find treasures like false teeth or money, or more wonderfully, signs, boxes or bottles from faraway places, washed in from exotic ships. If we had time we would drive to the steep point of the aloe-stalked hill, where we would revel in the full sweep of the golden bay. Or to the harbour, where my father would talk to sailors, and, just sometimes, get us invited onboard to look around. After that, how could the restrictions of school seem harsh?

When school was over, there was adventure. Perched on opposite hilly points, our suburbs plunged, in their centre, down to the wild scrub bush of the Valley. With its small river and sheer rock cliffs plunging headlong, it spelled a questing excitement. On its rough forbidden paths we could dash through monkey ropes and gnarled, bandy bushes. We could bundu-bash through the adult-tall reeds along the river and shriek at the surprised *tuk-tuk* of the thrashing guinea fowl and the yell of the hidden hadeda. Mimicking the piercing *ah ah* of the peacock, we would disturb them into flustered flapping and indignant cries.

'Don't ever, ever go into the Valley,' we were told, I more forcefully than my brothers who were boys and impervious to danger. 'There are bush-dwellers down there.'

It didn't stop us from following the little-used paths from suburb to suburb to visit each other, or to go adventuring. But it added spice. We never saw a bush-dweller, yet the throat-tingling fear of possible watching eyes gave us the *grillies*. What they would do to us if they found two or three exploring little girls we never could imagine. But once, when we found a rough, abandoned bush dwelling, roofed with bendy saplings, we scrambled and ran, screaming deliciously and giggling, up the overgrown, nasturtium-strewn hillside to the safety of houses and streets.

I remember the music my brothers played that year: 'Eleanor Rigby', 'Nowhere Man' and 'Yesterday' — played one after the other on our portable

11

gramophone, with a clunk as each stacked record dropped into place. I, following the example of my mother – 'But they scream so, and they look so nasty with all that long hair' – hated the Beatles, to the noisy derision of my brothers. Sometimes one, sometimes both of them – when the elder could be shaken from the scornful superiority of his advanced years – would chase me and hold me down. One would tickle me till I wet my pants, while the other would hold my head to the thump of 'Please Please Me' on the wireless. I would scream futilely and hold my hands to my ears.

My favourite seven-inch single was 'Telstar', which I played into scratchy submission. But my absolute best was *kwela* music, which my dad would play on his mouth organ before supper in the evenings, thumping his foot on the carpet. He had all the Spokes Mashiyane records, which my mom would never allow him to play. 'All that African music is so repetitive, it drives me mad,' she would say. But she never stopped him playing it on his mouth organ. He held it the wrong way round, the way he had taught himself as a child, away in the backveld.

My most urgent memory of that year is Snowball Scratchkitten. 'If you to go school without crying and moaning, your Ouma says she'll send you a kitten from the farm,' my mother told me. Oh, the waiting for this kitten to arrive, the anticipation which plunged into despair each time I cried and was told the kitten wouldn't be sent.

But he came, a beautiful, clean, pure white piece of the farm, into which I could bury my face each day after school. I loved him and played with him, but he was always that little bit wild, never quite tamed into easy domesticity.

As the year drew to a close, with my first school exams and the smell of jasmine plunging my room into holiday anticipation, my excitement about Christmas on the farm grew. My friends couldn't understand why I would look forward to spending summer holidays away from the beach – and I couldn't explain to them. I didn't have the words to tell them that I longed for the sights, smells and tastes of the farm: the smell of coal smoke, which to this day wrenches me unwillingly to an earlier place and time, the clustered clucking of the fowls, the taste of those unbelievably huge free-range chickens, roasted for us nearly every day, and the *skree-bang* of the fly-screen door. So I told them only of adventures to be had, of the huge pool and exciting grounds to explore.

On the last day of school at the end of the year, we were all given free tickets to the circus, which had just arrived in town – or perhaps they were half-price discount vouchers, I can't remember. On the school bus, the full load of excited little girls in their school gyms and panama hats was chittering with anticipation at the prospect. I, who would not be in town to see the circus, fantasized about giving the ticket away to a poor African child, who would weep with excitement and gratitude. As we stepped off the bus, I saw my opportunity.

Parked in the street was the dust van, from which the dustboys loped, lithe and long-legged, into our gardens to empty our dustbins into the huge baskets they carried over their shoulders. We usually kept a slightly fearful distance between us as they were always running, leaping for the back of the van as it moved off. They never smiled or stopped to chat, as the nannies and garden boys did, with a 'Hello, little missus' and a respectful duck of the head. And they carried the tainted smell of the open garbage in which they had to ride.

This time, one of the men had sat down briefly under the *kaffirplums* on the wide, grassy verge. He was cutting the front off his worn *takkies* with a penknife. 'Here,' I said, holding out the ticket. 'Take your children to the circus.' He stared at me with so little warmth in his eyes – with none of the indulgence I was used to from the Africans I knew at home and on the farm. Then he ran, without a word, for the van which had begun to move. 'Don't worry,' said one of my friends. 'He was mad. Did you see, he was even cutting holes in his shoes.' I felt humiliated and rejected but, even then, knew it wasn't as simple as that.

My end-of-year excitement and shivery joy were gone, and I didn't quite understand why. Perhaps he didn't speak any English, I thought. When I consulted my brothers, of course they crowed. They jeered at my childish gesture and said I was stupid for not knowing that Africans weren't allowed to attend the circus.

So I didn't tell them about his shoes. But I held that memory in my head where it worried at me. Only years later I managed to work out for myself what he was doing, that he was cutting the fronts off his *takkies* to free his constantly running feet from their constraints; too small, he had probably just discovered them in the rubbish. And his eyes – those blank, cold eyes – they followed me too. And afterwards I saw them as an omen. But of course, that's just silly.

That was the start of it, the holiday which caused everything in my life to change colour, smell and taste. But, please remember, it was an aberration. That holiday, which imprisoned me in the glass of my adult reclusiveness, wasn't what the farm was all about. So why couldn't I have stopped it? Why couldn't I have done something to prevent those inexorable events which moved us all into disaster and despair?

1989 . . . 15th October

We fought again last night. I with my glassy silence, he with the rage of a sudden hailstorm. As usual it was hope – or rather my lack of it – which started it.

I married a patient man, comfortable in his large, warm security. I think it is only I who, constantly testing in my imperturbability, can drive him to the wild savagery of last night's fury. And somehow I just can't seem to stop myself. Safe in the secrecy of my glasshouse, I even feel a heart-twisting sense of satisfaction. It is my belief, you see, that human beings are inherently violent, perverted, cruel creatures. It amuses me, in my remoteness, to demonstrate this so graphically with the mildest person I've ever known.

Oh yes, hope! I am incapable of it, you see. I see no point to it. No, I think I should be honest, now at least, and say that it's more than that. It twines around my neck and chokes me. I can't provide God – that rancorous Spirit who created Man in His own loathsome image – with that kind of weapon.

I feel it a bitter cosmic joke that I, who am entirely without hope, should be doomed to live through a time that is so full of it. We're at the end of 1989 and I am in my early thirties, married but childless – by choice, or rather my choice, I should add. I live in one of Johannesburg's nice suburbs, dark with tree-shaded old houses. The village, as the suburb and small cluster of shops are referred to in that twee northern-suburbs style, is populated by young executives. So new age they are, in their identical polo shirts and baby backpacks, and their wives, with clothes carefully chosen so as not to betray their affluence. The older residents, those brown-skirted women with short grey hair – their cracked heels pressed to flat leather – ride their bicycles or walk their Labradors, retrievers or collies, and behave with public and uncompromising liberalism.

But now has begun a time of a great sparkling euphoria, delicately balancing on the very verge of change. For most of those charming executive families, negotiated happiness and non-racial heaven seem tantalizingly close as they stop to chat outside the Spar shop. Some of them now daringly sport ANC T-shirts, still illegal, but of course carrying little danger of arrest in these days of hope and glory. And those same grey-headed dog walkers, who have always voted Prog (even when it became the Democratic Party), discuss whether to join the ANC when it is unbanned – 'Of course, it's inevitable any day now, my dear' – or whether to stick with the Progs from loyalty. That great shining unbanning feels imminent. And I know that, after today, I will have to suffer even more 'any day now' conversations with earnest, glowing faces.

Today, as no one could have missed after a full week of 'jubilant crowd' stories in the newspapers, is the release date of eight jailed heroes of the struggle. Jesus! All this week the 'jubilant crowds' have been busy, it seems – jubilant crowds marching, jubilant crowds singing, jubilant crowds dancing ... That's what caused our latest little storm in the tranquillity of our marriage teacup. My husband is desperate for us to form a little jubilant crowd.

He's finally been overtaken by the general euphoric hysteria. It's everywhere. It's everywhere! Right in the middle of our supper last night, he burst forth. Should there be a rally in Johannesburg to *toyi-toyi* our welcome to the leaders, he said in all seriousness, he thought we ought to go. Apparently, the word around – if you're in the right circles of course – is that a rally is likely within the next couple of weeks.

I gave him my look – I'm very good at it now – half mystification, half amusement.

'What is your case?' It erupted from him as if it had been waiting there all the time, hovering in the wings behind his tongue.

I remained silent. I'm expert at it at this stage of my life. It's probably the only thing I have truly perfected. His hands were shaking and he'd thrown down his fork. I could see the gravy dripping in great brown globs on to the table. It was his idea that we eat at our beautiful yellow-wood dining-room table every night. Years before, he had triumphantly 'discovered' it on a sortie through Graaff Reinet and carried it exultantly home to the Transvaal on his roof-rack. I stared at his shaking hands and remembered how he had lovingly scraped the generations of paint from it and ruined his hands with paint stripper and steel wool. I carefully placed another forkful on my tongue and consciously savoured it. It was remarkably good actually, a roast chicken from Woolworth's. It's funny how so many moments of consequence in my life have been marked by roast chickens.

'Can't you, just once, respond to me? Can't you shout or rage or tell me something about what you're thinking? I just don't think I can cope much longer with your fucking superior smile and your absolutely vacant expression.'

That hurt, of course. I don't mind the 'superior' bit. That's what I've perfected so well. But vacant? I didn't answer. I never do. Finishing absolutely the last grain of rice – that's my curse from childhood, my inability to leave a speck of food on my plate – I pushed my delicate *riempie* chair back roughly to watch him wince. And then I spoke. I very often save my most cutting comment for the moment when I'm on my way out, a parting shot while I'm already retreating to safety.

'It's funny how the times we live in seem to have sucked the brains from all you former "bright young men". And, unfortunately, it's me that must continue living with you as an empty-headed zombie. You never did have much in that department, but now it seems you're left with nothing but faith, hope and glory and an idiot smile.'

I thought he'd given up as I ran the bath in my favourite retreat – he stayed away so long. Our fights never last long. He batters against me with cold fury while my little glasshouse remains impervious. It is our unspoken code that when I return from my retreat in the bath, I speak as if nothing has occurred between us. And he, well, he recovers more slowly, with aching sadness. But he never speaks of it again. What would be the point?

But this time was different. He's really got it bad, this hope thing. It's even overflowing into our marriage. That makes me distinctly unsettled. I think we have a very workable marriage. I'm comfortable with it and I don't like it messed with.

I heard him knocking on the door but I had to turn off the taps before I could hear what he was saying.

'What is it that causes you to be so bitter?' I could hear the tears in his voice. It was a matter of pride to me – but also, if I'm to be honest now, a very deep-down shame – that I could bring his agony, so raw and bloody, to the surface so quickly in aching sobs, while I remained unmarked by the battle scars of tears.

'What on earth was it that made you feel so unworthy, that makes you hate yourself so much? Why do you always act as if you don't deserve anything, not even a small bit of happiness?'

'It must be a terrible burden to you to be a failed Psycho One,' I replied.

'Fuck you, just fuck you!'

Retreat at last. Did I feel a sense of triumph? I don't know. I don't think I ever feel much of anything. I lay and gazed at the soap dish, with its mushy damp soap lying in the small puddle of water which never seems to escape entirely. And the razor, that absolutely safe modern twin-blade razor.

I think about suicide a lot. In a very abstract way – I wouldn't like you to think me melodramatic or over-the-top. It's just that I look at that razor and consider how impossible it would be to use. I think of all the sharp knives in the kitchen and imagine the strength one would have to use to force the blade through unyielding flesh. It's all very theoretical. I run through all the ways there are to do it. I could sink my head beneath the surface of the bath – the ultimate retreat – and take a long, last, considering breath. I think that merely contemplating all the ways there are to make myself disappear calms me. I don't have to do it, but the option is always there. It makes it easier for me to face the next bout of life.

I stepped silently, nearly invisibly, into the bedroom pyjama'd and gowned. That's my choice of sleep clothing. He likes to be naked in bed. Of course! It is only life's most confident fools, its innocent dupes, who need so little in the way of defences.

'You always make such a big deal of the fact that I failed one lousy year at varsity.' He rolled, fully clothed still, on to his back to catch me. In the full glare of his very blue, spotlight eyes, I felt very visible, uncomfortably conspicuous.

'But I'm not going to let you get to me any more. You may have got your lousy MA *cum laude*, but what do you expect? What else could you have done – you were nothing but a bloody swot who never said a word in tuts or moved from the library for your entire university career.'

I sat gingerly on the edge of the bed and looked down to avoid his riveting gaze. My hands were shaking.

'And what have you done since then?'

I shrugged. He knew I hated my job. He knew I was incapable or unwilling to do anything about it.

'Nothing. But what do any of us achieve, actually? A job is a job. Most people on earth are put here just to get through it. I'm not conceited enough to think I could actually have made a real mark on the world. And

what's the point of that, anyway? You still die, whatever you do, and people forget you.'

'But at least I enjoy what I do and really believe in it,
in its worth. I actually feel a satisfaction in doing the
best I can for my clients and, believe it or not, I actually
still believe in justice.'

'Oh, my God. I don't believe this shit I'm hearing. No
one really believes that, do they? Not in real life. And
certainly not in your snooty Wasp law firm. All they
believe in is money.'

'Shut up, I'm trying to get through to you here. Can't
you listen to me for once without sniping? Now things
are finally happening in this country. And I've finally
broken into labour work. With this union as a client,
and consulting during this strike, I really think I'm,
well, part of things, of the change that's happening.'

'*Ja*, sure, so you've got your snotty Establishment
firm's token "public interest" client. You really feel like
the white knight, don't you? You really think you're
doing something – as if you play an important role. But
you're really nothing but a useful little tool. And if your
stuck-up senior partners had given you management as
your client, you would have been equally useful to
them. Just don't expect the workers to fall neatly into
your naive, liberal "noble savage" mould.'

He sighed a long, choking sigh, and rolled away from
me to gaze into the darkened garden. Our high white
wall was just visible through the gloom, but the pool
had already disappeared. The bronchitic gargle of the
pool pump was very loud through the wide-flung
summer windows, which welcomed in the drone and
clatter of suicidal rose-beetles and the suffused sweetness of jasmine.

I relaxed and pulled back the duvet, beginning my fussy ritual of placing my pillows. I thought he'd given up, you see. How wrong could I be. The worst was still to come.

'I want to go to the coast this Christmas.' He meant the East Cape coast, where we both grew up.

'You know I don't go to the Eastern Cape, ever.'

'What is it about that place? What happened to you there?'

'Nothing!' I bellowed, cornered now by the tightness of the duvet, held down by the weight of his body. 'It was perfect. It was a perfect childhood. It's the most wonderful place in the world. I just don't feel like going back. One can't travel backwards. We've left there. Why can't we leave well alone?'

And it *was* perfect, I thought as he finally gave up and slammed into the bathroom. The perfect place to grow up, to be a child.

The smell of the jasmine, that youthful harbinger of Christmas, of end-of-year holidays, began suddenly and inexplicably to suffocate me.

1966 . . . Seventeen days to Christmas

I was carried, coiled in sleep, from the car, too dark and dreamy to join in the half-heard greetings and embraces. My cheek against his jersey, I could smell my father's strength in the comforting, sweetish sweat of his body. But the chill of the night air feathering my hair carried, inevitably, the essence of the farm – that fetid mixture of soil, coal smoke, chickens and pigs.

Warmth embraced me as we passed from the veranda, my father's feet shushing on the smooth stone, into the wooden echoes of the old house. In its musty smell of old books and excitement I could discern our passing through Oupa's library. And then the passage, with drifting aromas of newly warmed bread and vegetable soup. Yes, surely it must have been soup – that full, wholesome smell. It was always soup. The smell of welcome, of murmured greetings in the sleepy darkness.

And then the smell of sleep in crisp, clean cotton and woolly blankets, soon to be kicked off in the closed-in heat of the shared room.

I awoke early, in the brisk clarity of just risen light. I sat up quietly, rejoicing in the stomach-coiling excitement of the crowded *kip kips* and the strident, competing call of roosters. The other animals, the few cows and pigs, were too far away for me to hear. But I strained to catch – I could picture them grunting their greeting – those wriggling pink piglets, born just before our previous visit. Bigger now, I was sure, but not yet gross and unsympathetic in their scaly-skinned imperviousness.

Standing on my bed I could gaze through the window at the constant, grating belt of the generator, stolid in the settled dust of the yard. Curtains were never drawn in our family – my father believed in the rightness of waking with the morning. But here on the farm, we children would always wake earlier than he, to his chagrin. Built on to accommodate the first grandchild nearly sixteen years before, our room now contained three narrow, spring-based beds beneath the largest windows in the house. My father's sleep would be broken only when the strangled early sun could force its way through wood-framed panes to reach the bed. In our room it burst unrestrained through the wide, modern metal windows, which were Ouma's pride.

The squealing creak of my bedsprings brought my brother, Michael, instantly upright in the bed. 'We're here, we're here,' he yodelled, bouncing on his bottom and flinging his pillow at me. Just as suddenly he subsided, with a sigh of ennui and a glance backward at the other bed. My elder brother Neil, superior in his almost sixteen, teenaged status, was groaning exaggeratedly and shaking his head, wearing his grown-up-bewildered-by-puerile-antics-of-siblings expression. Michael, at twelve, swung wildly between unrepentant childhood and unappreciated attempts to emulate the exalted age and behaviour of his brother.

'Oh my God, can't you *piks* run outside and make that noise?' Neil's groan betrayed the slightest catch at the end, a faint memory of childhood's piping squeals.

'Oh shut up, you're not so grown-up, you *vrot* backside.' Michael's humiliated fury was transposed into motion as he leapt from the bed and raced from the room, grabbing one of the pile of swimming towels left for us by Ouma.

I can remember the sudden quiet return to the room and the distant *skree-bang* of the screen door. It's funny, I can still remember every feel and smell of that holiday. Every minute has the clarity of a glass-encased specimen. I often think of it as one of those ornamental snow-filled domes with a castle or church inside. I never thought, until now, that I would be leading anyone inside that dome to taste the bitterness trapped, hidden inside the castle. But now that I have begun, I must do what I have been avoiding for so long, and finally confront its ghosts.

I often wonder when exactly the awfulness began. At the start, everything was as it always had been, as it should be. And I do want you to feel that, to know that that's how it really was. It's just that now, knowing what happened, it seems to me that the violence didn't just collide with the peace of my world in one gigantic crash. From the moment we arrived, it seemed to slither insidiously into the joy of the prosaic everyday, into the innocence of roast chicken and the happiness of baby chicks. But perhaps it's only in hindsight, in knowing what was to come, that I feel as if a malign force was festering all the time we were there. Perhaps it's the memories of that suggestible, fanciful child, who died that holiday and was replaced by this dark-filled shell, that makes me remember it as a grub nestled in the heart of a perfect pear.

That morning, the first morning, all I wanted was to feel the farm, to touch it with eager eyes, to smother my face in its smells. Standing on my bed, I thrust my head through the small rectangular hole in the meshed-metal burglar bars where the window catch was intended to fit. My bed being the one directly below the window, I used this hole every year to catch my first-morning sight of the farm. This year I revelled in being tall enough to stand, rather than having to kneel on the window sill to peer through the gap in the bars. It was a small ritual of mine to see if I could peer past the side of the generator and spy some of the chicken *hoks*. Yes, there was Petrus emblazoned in the bright early sun, doing something in one of the *hoks*, I couldn't see what. I twisted my head that little bit more but he moved, disappearing from my field of vision. Oh well, I'd give up there, I thought, tugging my head backward.

I can remember quite clearly the suddenness of my lazy happiness flooding away, and the horror of being trapped. Cold, nameless panic washed the taste of vomit to my mouth as the strangling clutch of the metal, grown monstrous now, appeared to grow tighter. In the child that I was, everything receded but the panicked need to rip my head from its crushing band. I can't remember if I screamed, but I know I was fighting, scratching, kicking to free myself from this snare. Suddenly, the calm of a rough bear-hug held, then quieted me and the world took on again its more familiar and manageable human proportions.

'You raving bloody idiot,' said Neil. But his fingers

were gentle as he pushed and prodded my head straight and guided it back through the hole, my rough, boy's haircut pushed upward around my head. 'Can't you see you've got too big to do that?' he said, laughing now in his exasperated grown-up way. But he hugged me roughly as my shaking sobs increased. Then, embarrassed at his sentimentality, he gave me a swift slap across the cheek. 'Oh, foolish, foolish idiot,' he said, sighing and settling himself back into bed with his book.

I wiped my face and my smeared nose with my pyjama sleeve and sank back down on my bed. But it wasn't the same. Somehow I no longer felt like wallowing there in that first-morning-on-the-farm feeling. My legs were still shaking and I felt like a fool in front of my awesome older brother. But it was more than that. While the room had shrunk back to its reassuringly ordinary size, the terror of its sudden trap would not leave me. Now I just wanted my Oupa. Slinking from the room I could hear, behind their closed door, the sounds of Ouma and Oupa rousing.

'Come in quickly,' said Ouma, with her quick, no-nonsense smile, as I wavered at the tentatively opened door. Oupa held up the side of his bedclothes and I ran to be embraced by his enveloping eyes and smile.

'Have you held me in your dreams, Oupa?' I asked in our small ceremony of welcome and leave-taking. In many ways, the strands of my childish reality were stitched together by my vital little rites, carried out with great seriousness and intent.

'Every dream has embraced you and held you to my heart,' he replied with his dreamy, poet's voice.

'*Ja*, but that's now enough of the nonsense of the two of you,' Ouma said, her voice brusque, her eyes warm. 'It's now time for the Lord's words. And I'll have no whispering and wriggling from the two of you, you hear? If you stay in here,' she said, her brisk features set in my direction, 'you will show respect and hold yourself still. And you, Johnnie,' she said with the exasperated frown she used to mask her love – I think she feared mawkishness above all things – 'try to remember you are an old man, not *mos 'n kind.*'

'Yes, my dear.' This was Oupa's standard reply, chastened and meek. But Ouma never quite managed to harry the twinkled glint of a smile from Oupa's eyes which brought him, as reply, Ouma's scowl of suspicion, in constant vigilance against his affectionate mockery.

I loved the soothing sound of her rough Afrikaans voice reading aloud the psalms from the Bible. As an unspoken expression of love for my Oupa, she always read from the English Bible although he could have understood the Afrikaans perfectly well.

'The righteous shall flourish like the palm tree: he shall grow like a cedar in Lebanon. Those that be planted in the house of the Lord shall flourish in the courts of our God. They shall still bring forth fruit in old age; they shall be fat and flourishing; To show that the Lord is upright: he is my rock, and there is no unrighteousness in him.'

I'm almost sure those were the lines that concluded her reading. I remembered them and later paged the psalms searching for them – psalm 92. The Lord's words, which at the time filled me with the joy and certainty that comes from control over the universe. For

I knew, with the sure knowledge of absolute belief, that nothing really bad could happen as long as I was good and loved God.

'Let us pray,' intoned Ouma, and I joined in fervently, sure and steadfast in my role as the righteous cosmic goalie for all whom I loved. 'Our Father, which art in heaven . . .'

I missed the early morning swim with my father that morning, but joined Michael and Daddy in the overwhelming warmth of the coal-stove-heated kitchen as they rubbed themselves dry. Michael, as usual, was kidding Dora, and whipping forbidden-before-breakfast *soetkoekies* from the jar on the Dutch dresser. Dora, her vast bulk heaving and shuddering, never showed displeasure. Her mouth, with only a yellowed tooth stump here or there, was always smiling. Her laughs began in raucous descent from her wide-flung mouth and travelled like a quaking avalanche down the great, swelling mountain of her body.

'I'll smack your bottom,' said Michael and darted forward, Dora's vast bottom creating an unmissable target. 'Can't you catch me, Dora? Can't you?'

Her mountainous bulk heaved and wobbled with mirth as she took one plodding step towards Michael, whose skinny legs moved coltlike around the scrubbed kitchen table. In his black school bathing costume he reminded me of the stick insects I liked to collect. His knees were the only rounded part of his angular, prickly body and while he looked awkward, he moved astonishingly fast.

'Hai, *klein* Master. You!' she gasped, leaning on the table to rest.

'Now don't you children drive Dora mad,' said my

father, intervening at last, but indulgently. 'She has the breakfast to see to. How are you, Dora?' he asked in the hearty, slightly louder than usual tone he used for our Africans. 'You're looking good as usual, even more *mafuta* than last time. Your husband must think you're a fine figure of a woman.'

Dora collapsed into shuddering, coy hilarity, one hand still supporting herself against the table, the other covering her downcast face. 'Thank you, Master,' she said at last. 'But my husband is dead now, these three years.'

'Oh, yes, sorry, Dora. I forgot. But do you mean a fine, *mafuta* girl like you hasn't found another one? Shame on you.' He retreated while she shuddered some more, shook her head and wiped the tears, of laughter I thought, from her face with the edge of her spotless apron.

Breakfast was eaten, all of us together in the dining room, dark but for the wide stream of sunlight illuminating the sparkling motes and fairies dancing in the air. The smell of newly applied polish, hot porridge and bacon mingled over the white starched tablecloth, which was already showing signs of my having breakfasted at it.

'Do you want to go round the farm with me – see the changes?' Ouma asked me. '*Ja*, please, Ouma,' I said eagerly. 'Can I have some more milk, please?'

'Not *ja*, say yes,' interjected my mother, holding the milk jug just beyond my reach. 'And for goodness' sake say milk, not mulk.' She poured it for me.

'Nothing wrong with *ja*,' replied Ouma, looking sharply at her. 'It's your language after all. Don't think you're too good for the first language you could speak.'

'Oh, Ma, don't start that again.'

My mother's mouth was set in anger but as I watched her, a welling sheen leapt quite suddenly to her blinking eyes. I had never seen my mother cry – I didn't think mothers did. And I had never seen real anger between her and Ouma. But then, as the silence stretched around us, Oupa slipped in a silly joke – something about sheep I think – and everyone laughed.

'What do you mean, changes?' I asked suddenly.

'Well, *my kind*, we're getting old now, you know. We couldn't keep up this huge old farm ourselves. We've got enough to get along with, with the chickens and a few pigs. And a cow or two for milk. We didn't need to struggle with all those sheep.'

'Where exactly have you sold from, Ma?' asked my father.

'You've sold our farm?' The realization suddenly clutched at me. I stared at her, disbelieving. 'Nobody told me.'

'Well, you didn't need to know, *my kind*. It was our decision,' said my Ouma mildly.

'*Ag*, it's that hard land, from where it runs into the Zuurveld,' she continued, turning to my father. 'We never really kept enough sheep to make it pay. A man called Van Rensburg has bought it – a stock farmer. He's started clearing some of the bush and trees. He thinks he can make a go of it with cattle and sheep. He seems a good farmer, experienced. And, *dankie God*, he took on the boys we couldn't keep any more.

'*En nou, kind?*' she asked, turning to see the silent tears dripping unwiped off my chin.

'How could you do that, Ouma? It was our farm – our special place. You didn't tell me.'

33

I couldn't explain to her. I couldn't express what I wanted to say; that we loved that part, the dusty part where the sheep grazed; that it was my secret place; and that sometimes we could see little buck there on the sharp edge of the world at nightfall, or coax the guinea fowl down to scratch at the chickenfeed we threw for them.

'*Magtig*, you are a funny child. Imagine being sentimental about that great dustbowl.' She finished on a sigh, her mouth clamping tight in exasperation. Yet her eyes had softened. 'But I tell you what, you can still walk over there. Go introduce yourselves to Mr Van Rensburg. I'm sure he won't mind to see you on his land, now and then.'

'It won't be the same though.'

The fever of grief had passed, but my heart still felt clutched by a rough sadness. I couldn't have put it into words, and I'm not even sure that I can now. You see, it had nothing to do with avarice, or with an 'our farm is bigger than your farm' feeling. It was that wild expanse – it touched and fed a wildness deep inside me. Like a small animal, I had the feeling I could gallop for ever. It had a sense of freedom that smoothed all concerns, and was salve for all my city wounds. Whoever had refused to be my best friend, or wouldn't sit with me at breaktime or whatever, evaporated into insignificance on the farm, beside the exhilaration of racing across that grassy, scrubby land, an aura of soft dust rising around me while the hadedas called eerily, plaintively, overhead.

'Come now, I'll show you we still have more than enough land,' said Ouma practically, reaching for my hand.

The Innocence of Roast Chicken

Afterwards, after that holiday, I couldn't lose the thought of how bad I'd been. I could never confide in anyone – how could people continue to love me if they knew how rotten I really was? But it was bad and wicked to be so selfish, to have felt such virulent anger against them. One should never feel such anger against people – it always oozes out somehow, malevolently, to do harm. Why can't I, even now, free myself from the thought that it was me, and all my unharnessed anger, who set off everything that was to follow?

'Kati, Mikey,' called Ouma, before we stepped off the stoep, the heat apparent even in the shaded early morning. A slight breeze whispered through the stoep from end to end, rumpling my short hair. In response to Ouma's call, two bounding horselike dogs appeared around the side of the house and threw themselves at us. Laughing, I was knocked from my feet and rolled and romped, licked and slavered on. Two years earlier these Ridgeback *Boerbuls* had been roly, rumpled, fleshy pups, named by Ouma in an uncharacteristically sentimental moment after my brother and me. Walking beside them around the farm, I put my arms out nearly horizontally to keep a hand on each back.

Ouma walked me first across the lawn, pointing out her flowers, striking in their effusive display. But, characteristically, Ouma's garden was a practical spectacle, regimented from the smallest, most delicate blossoms in front, to the tallest towering majestically behind.

Reaching the flower beds at the very bottom of the lawn, we turned towards the farmhouse, but paused before starting back. Over my head lurked that gentle giant, the wild fig tree, its powerful trunk astride, its thick branches all-encompassing, its shade generous.

Only here, on this cultivated lawn, did the grass smoothly carpet the rolling earth. It spread before us frilled with flowers to the stoep, where I could see Oupa wisped with pipe smoke. As usual he sat on the wooden *bankie*, patched with sunlight. Inexplicably, he preferred it to the stuffed chairs lining the wall, which grew more enfoldingly sunken each year.

Tucked into the crease at the foot of two small hills, the farmhouse was cosseted by the landscape. The nurturing, rounded hillocks behind the house rippled and undulated, fluffy with greenery, fired with aloes.

To the side of the house lay the dusty yard where the generator stood. And that's where we made for, trailing dogs, I dawdling and scampering through the pattering dust of the yard. Beyond it stood the chicken *hoks*, rows of long concrete structures barred, like cartoon jails, with thick vertical bars. The smell was as familiar as it was delicious – that smell of mealies and fowl.

'Hau, it's *klein* Missie,' said William, removing his cap and holding it with both hands below his waist. '*Môre*, Miesies,' he said to Ouma, ducking his head. '*Môre*, William. Yes, how do you think the *klein* Missie has grown?'

'Hau, she is grown very big, Miesies,' he said, flashing his quick grin. He stood quietly then, waiting for Ouma's instructions for the day. He never picked me up and threw me in the air when she was watching. He and Ouma began discussing the chickens, but they spoke Afrikaans, and with a speed and vocabulary which were quite beyond my three years of school. I wandered from *hok* to *hok*, sniffing the smells, watching the hens dart and peck frenetically, the combined *kip kips* deafening close to. Walking down the line, I found smaller and smaller fowls, coming at last to the 'teenag-ers', those scrawny, long-necked, half-grown chickens, endearing in their ugliness.

'We're expecting some chicks one of these days,' said Ouma, catching up with me. 'I know you love those. You can help unload them from their boxes when they come. *Kom nou*, run and ask Dora for a pot of that soup on the stove, and for the aspirins in the cupboard. William's wife is sick again. *Ag*, that girl is not hardy. She is always sick.'

I ran to the back of the house, my bare feet slapping and pluming dust, followed by the roistering dogs, their tongues panting for the large bowls of water in the kitchen courtyard. The *skree-bang* of the screen door propelled me from the smell of coal smoke, familiar and heavy in the courtyard, into the porridgy, soupy smells of the kitchen. It was uncomfortably hot waiting for Dora to ladle last night's soup and warm it over the range, and I was happy to be out again, walking this time, so as not to spill the soup. The dogs disdained to follow, panting in the shade of the house.

I wandered past the fig tree and through the orchard, filled with peach, apricot, plum and loquat trees, fol-lowing the route I knew Ouma would have taken to the boys' quarters. It was cool under the trees and I stopped at the edge of the shade to eat mulberries. Cramming the ripe fruit into my mouth, my hands and bare feet stained a dark red and I could see a spreading droplet – that was going to mean trouble later – crawl-ing down my T-shirt on to the vest which habitually hung out over my shorts.

When my elder brother had been younger and less

disdainful, he and Michael had once covered my face, neck and thighs with mulberry juice from this tree. Screaming 'Help, she's fallen', they had carried me into the house, causing my mother to turn white and jerk upright from her chair, dropping the transistor radio which she'd been holding on her knee. My father beat them, if I recall, but I went unpunished. I think they had thought I was merely a prop to their cruelty.

Beyond the orchard and the lines of squat citrus, the open land lay scattered with trees – some gums, some wild figs, and many whose names I never knew – and riotous patches of uncleared bush. To the side of one I could see, some distance from me, a small cluster of chattering, clicking women and yelling men – their voices muted by distance. I wondered, but thought they must be beating to death some unsuspecting snake which had been foolish enough to emerge.

Passing a similar patch of bush, I carefully placed the enamel soup bowl on the ground to delve in my shorts pocket. Finding the greasy scraps of egg and toast that I had sneaked off the breakfast table, I carefully placed them just beyond the edge of the undergrowth. I sat for a while in the dirt, hoping to tempt a tentative meerkat to emerge just long enough to drag it away. But when guilt overcame hope, I picked up the bowl again.

The ground, aloe-speared, dropped away to the swimming place where I could see Michael bomb-dropping into the water, drenching Neil lying reading on the side. As I skirted the reservoir and its shushing line of gum trees Neil, with the shiny grace of an otter, slipped into the water to duck Michael again and again till he screamed for mercy.

Beyond the water, on a rise, were the boys' houses.

Here, small children played around the cluster of vari-coloured wattle-and-daub huts, smoke pouring from their chimneys. Doors were open to the trampled area of hard earth where women hung washing, scrubbed clothing in bowls, called, laughed and sang together. Babies cried and were shushed, jiggled on blanketed backs. In turn, their mothers would unpin the blankets and sit in the shade of the huts to thrust tired breasts into nuzzling mouths. Their knees grey with callus and dust, six children of ranging size played on the ground with a car they were fashioning from bent wire. A knobbly boy, his face shiny with the crackle of dried snot, pushed an old tyre through the clusters of women with squealing brake noises and *uhr-uhrm uhr-uhr-uhrm* sounds. Two other children squelched and quietly moulded patches of mud.

The children stopped as I passed, silent and watch-ful. '*Molo*,' I said to William's small son, sitting on his doorstep. He was about my own age. '*Molo*, Miesies,' he said and scrambled to join the other children. The children were always wary of us. If we approached them, they silently scattered and regrouped elsewhere, their large eyes watching. I suppose we never stayed long enough on the farm to get to know them, and communication was impossible – we spoke no more than a few words of basic Xhosa, while they spoke a few words of Afrikaans and next to no English.

It was dark in the hut after the blinding light reflect-ing off its pale blue walls. I stood for a moment until I could make out the metal-legged kitchen table and the magazine pages which served as wallpaper. The floor, of packed mud, was newly swept and partly covered by a ragged remnant of red carpeting. The hut smelt of the woodsmoke which always clung to the clothes of the boys and their wives. On a kitchen chair beside the bed sat my Ouma, speaking in her quick, rough Afrikaans to William's wife, Mary.

'*Ag*, here she is. Thank you, Kati,' said Ouma. 'This will make you feel stronger, Mary. But you should really strengthen yourself up, girl. Too many children, that's what it is. And the last one so weak it couldn't survive!' Ouma clucked.

The room darkened and we turned to see a tall young man ducking his head to enter the small space.

The light which had gently silvered Mary's face and haloed Ouma's pure white hair was shut off with the dark suddenness of his entry. With his back to the door he stood, dimly blocking out the warmth.

Squatting on the dirt floor beside my Ouma's chair, I squinted up at him, thinking that I knew him. But not this anger. I didn't know this rage which billowed about him in his sombre silence.

'Is dit jy, John?' Ouma had half turned on her chair and raised her hand to shade her eyes. 'Kom nou,' she said in her impatient tone which I knew so well. 'Staan waar ek jou kan sien. Is jy nou klaar met die skool?'

So it was William's son, the boy who had once lifted me down from the roof of the chicken *hok*, where I had climbed and promptly become smeared and tearful in contemplation of the height and the climb down. But he was unfamiliar now in his silent, seething pride.

'I am back, but I am not yet finished with the school,' he said in English, his gaze direct as he moved alongside the bed. A flicker of disquiet touched the nape of my neck as I sat unnoticed on the floor, picking at my bare toes. Unlike the boys, he didn't duck his head to look down at his shuffling shoes or chuckle into his cupped hand. And he hadn't called Ouma 'Miesies'. I was anxious that he shouldn't make Ouma angry. I had seldom seen her angry, but I knew it was frightening in its fiery eruption. I knew it would go badly with him if he angered her.

'Your father says you are finished now,' she continued gruffly, in English. 'You are nineteen – a man. You should be doing a man's work. Here is your mother, sick again, and with five children after you.'

'I see that while I am at school I am called a man,' he said, his mouth twisting but his cool eyes unchanged. 'But if I work, I become a boy.'

Quietly, his mother spoke for the first time. 'Hai, *sonalwam*,' and then I couldn't understand what she said, but she frowned and shook her head.

'*Molo*, Mama,' he said, unsmiling, but with the slightest inclination of his head acknowledging her for the first time. '*Uvuka njani?*' How are you feeling?

'*Andilalanga kakuhle.*' Not much better.

'*Ja*, you can see very well your mother needs you at home now,' continued Ouma, in her rough but not unkind voice. 'What have you completed now – Standard Six?'

Unanswered, she continued. 'For what do you want more? It can only make you unsatisfied and angry with life, as I see you are becoming. You should speak to the new Master on the next farm. I spoke to him about you and he said he can always use another good boy.'

I was watching his hands, hooked loosely on the top of his pants just above me. As she spoke they clutched convulsively at his belt. He freed them and crossed his arms over his chest.

'Hau, Miesies.' Using the term for the first time, he shook his head. 'I am not made for that kind of work.'

'*Magtig*, what now? You think you are too good for farm work – the work your father and your grandfather did before you? Or are you not man enough to get down to some hard work?'

'I am man enough for work,' he said, his eyes glaring. 'But am I to work for someone like the new Master, who will beat me like he has beaten Albert's son?' His fists clenched and he dropped them to his sides, his mouth a thin tight line.

'Albert's son was beaten?' Ouma asked him. I think only I, sitting with my bent head level with her lap, had noticed her almost imperceptible start. 'What did he do to anger the Master so much?'

'The new Master, he say Albert's son look at the *ou Miesies* in a bad way. And he say he show no respect. He is not a good Master, that one you have given your boys to.'

'I am sorry for Albert's son,' said Ouma quietly. 'But new Masters sometimes have new ways. I cannot interfere with his discipline – he is now their Master. But I am sure he would never beat them for nothing. If you work hard for him and you show him respect, he will treat you well – he would never *mos* hit for nothing.'

I, trying to remain unnoticed by Ouma's chair, was still anxiously picking at the hard skin on the yellowed soles of my feet, stealing glances up at the two of them. I heard John give a dry gasp, or perhaps he was taking a deep breath after holding it in anger. But as my anxious eyes grasped for his face, wanting understanding, wishing for reassurance, his eyes caught and held mine. But there was nothing in them but desolation.

'You were wrong to give your slave boys to that bad Master.' The words burst between his tight lips. He wasn't looking at Ouma now, he was holding me, my unwilling eyes caught by his agonized gaze.

'Do not dare question me or my actions, John, or things will go badly with you.' Her voice was still quiet, but her coal eyes flared. When I was older, and could recall the look and the sound of her anger, I thought that it was then that she most showed, in those glowing dark eyes and taut, high-cheeked face, the French peasant blood of her forebears.

'My boys have never been slaves, and you know as much. Your father has worked here for me loyally since he was a young boy and that is the only reason I will even listen to your nonsense. My people are treated fairly and well, you can ask your own parents. But I had no choice in this. We are old now, too old to run that whole farm. Where else were those people to go? I thank God he agreed to take them. You know their families have lived on this farm for generations.'

Without a greeting for me, or a word for Ouma or his mother, he turned abruptly and, stooping, left the hut.

Ouma sighed in the bitter silence he had left. 'Miesies,' said Mary, her eyes glistening with anxiety. 'He is a good boy really, Miesies. He just wants too much.'

'Mmm. Sometimes, Mary, it is dangerous to have a boy who wants too much. Life is hard for all of us . . . *Magtig, kind,*' she said, noticing me crouched by her side, clutching my legs to my chest. 'Are you still here? *Kom nou*, Petrus's wife tells me some kittens were born in her hut.'

Stretching her hands to her back, she rose from the stiff chair and moved towards the door.

'Drink that soup now, Mary, and make yourself strong for the sake of all your children.'

I clutched for Ouma's hand as the blast of sunlight exploded in our squinted eyes. We stood a moment in the heat before making for the open door of another hut.

A few of the women – about four, I think – left their bowls of washing water and their mealie-meal to follow us into Petrus's hut. Petrus's wife greeted Ouma with a brief bob and smiled as she led me to the small pile of rags under her table. A thin tabby cat with wary eyes lay suckling four squirming, closed-eyed kittens – two of them pure white.

'It's your Snowball's father, you know – he's the father of all these cats. I hope you see him while you're here. But he's wild, he seldom comes near the house. *Ag*, but he's a menace,' said Ouma with a small chuckle, 'the way he makes all these new kittens for us to deal with.'

'Oh, how I wish I could suck . . . I mean hold one,' I said. But the correction of my tangled thoughts was drowned by the spontaneous convulsions of mirth from the women. They laughed, bending double and clapping their rough hands together. Their merriment seemed to go on and on as my face burned and I tried to be heard above them.

'I meant "hold",' I said to Ouma, my eyes filling with tears now at the humiliation, at the thought that they must all think me a baby still.

'I know, *kind*,' she said, her arms folded. She seldom touched those she loved. 'It doesn't matter. You can't hold these, they are too young. Tomorrow we will search for the bigger kittens I saw near the pigsty. There is another white one there like your Snowball.'

As we turned to leave the women parted, still rippling and bending with graceful mirth, like the chuckling reeds near the dam when the wind blew. My face was hot and I smeared my dusty hand across my running nose. I didn't look up at them as we were hit by the full force of the sun.

Ouma walked purposefully along the deeply sluited farm road, rutted like a dry river bed from the rains which came with such power and such force – when they came at all – to the dusty ground.

'Tomorrow the family will come for tea,' she said as I trotted and ran beside her. 'Uncle Frans is bringing us a Christmas tree. I think you will decorate it, like you did last year.'

My heart lightened and I smiled up at her. I suddenly remembered what I had forgotten in coming to the farm, and all that had happened since. We had begun the shiveringly exciting countdown to Christmas – counted out each day in small rituals and tasks like wrapping the presents I had bought with my pocket money, and opening the small, glittering windows on my Advent calendar each morning as I awoke. All the unchanging family ways, held to year after year in the preparation for Christmas, guarded the safety of my world.

I smelt and heard the pigs for some way before we reached the pigsty. Laughing at their disgruntled noises, I ran ahead and climbed the sticky creosoted planks of their enclosure.

'Where are the little ones, Ouma? The ones that were small last time?'

'Why, those ones are to the market already,' she said,

glancing at me in surprise as she joined me at the fence. And as she saw my face: 'But old Nellie is pregnant again. She'll have her litter any day now. I'll call you when they've been born.'

'No thanks, Ouma.' I climbed down from the fence and turned away, plunging my toes savagely into the soft earth. 'I don't want to see them.'

'*Magtig*, you are a funny *pieperige* child,' I heard her exasperated voice say behind me.

1989 . . . 22nd October

The smell of vomit slowly winces into my consciousness, just before the pain pounds into my tentatively shifting head. Oh Jesus Christ, not again!

I squint through my eyelashes to see Joe sliding off his window-side of the bed, his face set whitely in disgust. He only uses that expression on me; I've never seen him aim it at anyone else. By the quality of the light flinching its way through my eyelashes, I judge it to be still early. And it's Sunday; no need for him to get up except to get out of range of me.

He moves quietly, for such a large man, into the bathroom and dresses without re-emerging. I suppose he is as anxious as I to keep up the pretence that I am still asleep. Tender from a knotted, dream-filled sleep, like a cringing snail, I cannot bear to start a conversation until I am strongly battened down for the day, my armour in place.

I keep my eyes closed – the light is less painful that way – as I stop blocking my thoughts and allow the slow tendrils of last night to slime their way into my mind.

'So, when do you think FW's going to release Mandela?' That was the 'bright young man' – ex-student lefty –

who works for Anglo now and wears pink shirts. He had been talking when we entered the room, late again. A largish child had opened the door to us and then raced away, his flannel gown flapping. Listening to Pink Shirt, our host had waved to us silently and gestured to the couch, while Dressed-all-in-Black had leant over Joe's lap to pass us the bottle of Chardonnay.

'Hi, you guys.' That was Mark, our host, a lawyer friend of Joe's, as Pink Shirt finished talking. The other people in the room smiled or said howzit or – this was Dressed-all-in-Black – lifted a languid arm. No one bothered to introduce me.

'Well,' said Mark, turning back to Pink Shirt, '*The Star* says they've actually been having talks. Apparently he's been negotiating his own release. Isn't it extraordinary? Five years ago, change seemed impossible bar a bloody full-scale revolution. Who would have thought we'd see the day when Mandela would negotiate his own release?'

His girlfriend, a silly girl who took herself very seriously, shook her artfully wild curls back and gazed at her pink fingernails. 'Hey, this whole week since that gorgeous Ahmed Kathrada and the others were released I've been so happy, I can't tell you. There's layk just so much layk goodwill on the ground. People are, layk, mixing in the streets.'

'You mean the "jubilant crowds"?' I spoke for the first time. The room fell silent and everyone looked at me.

'Layk what *do* you mean?' asked Pink Nails.

'Well, if one is to believe people like you and the newspapers, the whole country is filled with jubilant crowds. I understand a few more people were

48

jubilantly killed in Natal this week.'

Everyone shifted uncomfortably. And then Dressed-all-in-Black said, rather sneeringly I thought, with a sidelong pitying look at Joe (I wonder if she works with him?): 'Well, of course there'll like still be *violence*. Like, it's a tragedy but it's because of apartheid.'

'Oh, don't give me that meaningless "struggle" shit,' I said with a laugh, rather contemptuous, to counteract her pitying look. I swallowed my Chardonnay and reached for the bottle. It was empty. 'I'll open another,' said Mark.

Expertly pressing the two arms of the corkscrew down with one hand, he changed the subject – he takes his host role rather seriously. 'How's the strike going, Joe? Any signs of a settlement?'

'Not as yet,' said Joe, his face changing from set to animated. 'Management's not budging. But I've been quite impressed with the union guys. And they've got a helluva strike going; eight thousand workers out.'

Frowning at his twirling glass, Leather Jacket, sitting with his long-haired wife or girlfriend leaning against his knee, tried to look knowledgeable as he expounded: 'But tell me, Joe, I hear the word is that this strike isn't all that much about wages. I hear it's got a lot to do with the political climate, and about the union maintaining its political profile?'

'Oh, that's shit – management propaganda.' Joe shifted forward, coming into his own now. 'This is a big company we're talking about, making huge profits. Their packages may not be bad compared with some smaller companies, but you have to look at them in context. They can *afford* to pay better.'

He paused, and then added: 'This is a bread-and-butter issue.' He placed his empty glass down in emphasis.

'Oh, here comes Comrade Joe again, trotting out the dinner-party line,' I said nastily, rolling my eyes.

'You really can be a bitch sometimes,' Joe said under his breath.

Pink Shirt quickly jumped in to fill the uncomfortable silence. 'Well, I'm not sure if that isn't a slightly simplistic analysis,' he said to Joe. 'They learn quickly, these lefty bright young men. Anglo's been very clever – the company line sounds so much more, layk, relevant when spouted by an old lefty. I don't think you can entirely put it down to bread-and-butter issues. The unions have certainly had their positions and agendas overshadowed by the ANC releases.'

'But the thing that's been bothering me a bit is this talk about intimidation. What're your clients saying?'

'Well, I understand that management is largely exaggerating some strong picketing,' said Joe, leaning back and crossing one leg over the other. 'The company's known for that, you know. But, as my guys say, they can't control eight thousand workers completely. But I believe them when they say they're opposed to intimidation.'

We moved through to the dining room then, at the coy, waving behest of Pink Nails, pink-faced now from the kitchen. She was still very conscious of her position as just-moved-in girlfriend and practising stepmother. Publicly fond, she flapped the child off to bed on the way through the passage.

Sitting down to our pâté starter, Pink Nails flashed her expensive linen jacket open and, giggling, asked how we liked the ANC shirt she'd found down in Newtown. Everyone thought it was cool, or they politely said so, anyway.

'So,' she said, flashing her heavily mascara'd eyes round the table, 'when do you think they're going to lift the emergency?'

'And wouldn't we all just hate it if they did.' I should have kept quiet, but I was just dying to see her pert face crumple in horror.

'What do you mean?' she asked, unattractively show-ing some masticated melba, another piece of toast poised in mid-air.

'Well, everyone can enter the "struggle" now that it's safe to do so. Even you. Why weren't you wearing that ANC T-shirt five years ago?'

'Well, I couldn't find one before,' she stammered, her face crumbling and turning pink again.

'And everything's still conveniently black and white, if you'll pardon the pun,' I continued, mercilessly prod-ding at every holy cow in sight. 'Conveniently for you, there are still things to fight against: the old regime is still in place, apartheid laws still on the statutes. Lucky you, you still have time to feel like a hero of the struggle – now that more political prisoners are being released than detained.'

'That's appallingly cynical,' drawled Leather Jacket, as Pink Nails rushed from the room, gulping: 'I must just see to the main course.'

That was about all of it, I think, except that Joe fell silent and tense and wouldn't look at me again. Neither would anyone else, mind you. So I concentrated on the companionship of the Chardonnay. I shouldn't have concentrated so hard, it seems, since I vaguely remember vomiting over some seedlings near the gate as we left. Joe didn't help me but sat in the car, drumming his hands on the wheel and watching the Mercedes and the black BMW (maybe Dressed-all-in-Black is an attorney, after all) drive away.

Oh God, I feel awful! But I must arm myself, put my squirming soft flesh inside some samurai steel. Part of my armour is my clothing, those grey invisible skirts and brown shirtwaisters that I carefully choose to conceal myself. And my glasses, the thick lenses of which hide and shrink the large dark eyes which sometimes, when I gaze myopically into the mirror, remind me of someone else.

'You know,' says Joe, making me jump as I put the hairdryer down on the bed, 'when I met you I thought you were funny, and I thought you were bright, and I thought you were like a kicked puppy that I could nurture. I really thought that, if I gave you understanding and love, you would open up and trust again.'

He takes a deep breath. Here it comes.

'Something happened to you in the Eastern Cape – I don't know what. After all these years you still deny it. But things are happening now, in the country and in my job. I feel like we're really and truly moving into a period of change. I want you to come with me . . . but I don't, quite frankly, know—'

He breaks off, taking a deep breath and shaking his head. 'I don't know if you're alive enough in there to come out. I'm starting to lose faith in there being enough live "you" in there to save . . . Oh, Jesus Christ, Kate,' he says as he contemplates my blank face.

'Even though you're a rampant bitch and you humiliate me in public, I actually still love you. I'm begging you now, I'm begging, damn you. Let's go back there – you'll never heal otherwise. I'll face it, whatever it is, with you. And . . .' His large hands lift to rub at his agonized eyes. 'I want to go home. Since we married, I've never gone home – I've humoured you, hoping it would go away.'

'Oh for God's sake, don't be so dramatic,' I snap, lifting my brush to my hair. 'I'm not avoiding anything. It's just a creepy little place. We left. We came to the big city. I just don't believe in going backwards.'

'If it was so idyllic, as you always insist, then let's go back . . . this Christmas.'

'And even if there was something horrific in my past, how do you expect to face it with me? You can't even cope with the shit I dish out to you. With your hopeful face, you can't even conceive of there being evil in people or places – you're too idealistically liberal.'

I stop brushing and snigger, looking at him in the mirror. 'You're like a gambolling lamb at the start of spring. You'll be led to the slaughter soon enough. Why should I be responsible?'

And while he is still opening his mouth, I close it for him again by saying that of course, we are talking hypothetically and there is nothing remotely skeleton-like in my closet. 'You'd just love there to be. Then you could be the great hunky saviour you've always wanted to be.'

'I've begged you now, I'm not going to do it again. You've got a month and a half to decide. And then I'll have some decisions to make, too.'

He walks towards the door and pauses, turning: 'You're beginning to sicken me, you know.' With a small gasp, he continues: 'And I couldn't bear that – I'd leave you first.'

1966 . . . Sixteen days to Christmas

I heard the shouts, but mutedly, as I lay stretched to my full extent, my ears half submerged in lapping bathwater. I dropped my head lower, venturing into the calm of the sensory bubble which lay below the surface. I floated in this half-world, wallowing closed-eyed, until shockingly I was plucked suddenly upright, back into the bathroom. I streamed water as my father mouthed soundless words at me. Throwing a towel over my head he made a bundle of me, which he tossed on to his shoulder, and jogged from the room.

'What?' I spluttered. 'What did you say?' My voice skipped in time with his body, bounding through the house. At last, holding me right way up on the veranda, he silently pointed. The day was just a faint glow now – a recessed light giving emphasis to the dark splendour of the harsh horizon.

And then I saw him, in all his wild pride and pure white lustre. Picking up the incandescence of the sun's last rosy rays – Snowball's father. I gasped, and a small shudder just touched my shoulder blades with goose bumps. Poised on the very knife-edge of the horizon, there was nothing gentle or homely about him. He was the harsh embodiment of the very wildest, primal aspect of the farm. And then his head turned, drawn perhaps to the lit tableau of silent adults and children, standing, drinks in hand, at the veranda rail. For just a second, our eyes met in an almost tangible joining – and then he was gone. Streaking white across the land he was effortlessly beautiful, unreachable, untouchable.

The dimming horizon was suddenly dull and bereft. But I was charged, my limbs flooded with a raging, wild joy, which could be expressed only by chasing across the darkening lawn, my towel flapping and soaring, my voice raised in a joyous yell. Everything was OK. God had sent me a sign, a wild omen of wonder; of the unchanging certainty of the farm with its ephemeral glimpses of life's eternal miracle.

The group on the veranda was laughing now, made ordinary by their prosaic clinking drinks and chatter. Backlit, they were settling into seats, my mother holding her ankle out as bait while she poised her hand to trap and destroy the next mosquito to land. A rose-beetle tapped its hard little carapace in sharp metronomic clicks, flinging itself suicidally at the glory of the veranda light.

I watched my father Pantene his hair, his hands cupped and smoothing his head. His comb slicked it straight back, cutting sharp tooth-shaped runnels in the shiny hair.

We had left early for our swim, I having woken him with a touch as soon as the morning light rushed through my wide window. Conspiratorially we had left the dim silence of his room and stepped into the morning's gentle cool with that familiar *skree-bang*. The smell of coal smoke and fowls had mingled mustily in our nostrils while we, as was right and fitting, had eaten figs off the tree before diving into the sharp cold of the water.

I was dressed now, in carelessly pulled on shorts and T-shirt – my vest grubby and hanging halfway down the shorts. My father wore shorts too, long shorts with fly and belt, matched with long white socks and slip-on shoes.

'Your mother's family's coming for lunch today.' He paused and I saw him struggle to articulate what he wanted to say – this man whose strength and warmth were expressed through his body. His body spoke for him, in his games, his tickling, his great, outstretched, protecting arms. His voice always sounded gruff, unused to communicating.

I sat on the edge of the bath, watching him continue unnecessarily the precise marking of his already dead-straight parting, a startling pink stripe in his dark hair.

'They're making the effort to come from all over the District . . .' He paused again, but would not look at me. Finishing with his comb at last, he began to rinse it, very precisely, under the running tap.

'Ah *hrum*,' he cleared his throat, but his voice still sounded rough, unused, like someone who has spent some years in enforced silence. 'They're coming to see *you*,' he said, speaking faster now. 'Please make an effort – for your Ma and your Ouma's sake . . .'

I rolled my eyes. A hint of exasperation crept into his tone – he must have seen me in the mirror. 'For good-ness' sake, use some of that Afrikaans that we send you to school to learn. It wouldn't kill you to say a nice "*Goeie môre, Tannie Marie*" now and again.'

I wailed exaggeratedly, flinging myself to the

bathroom floor, my face screwed into an expression of melodramatic agony and distaste. 'I ha-ate speaking Afrikaans. At school the girls say I sound like a *plaasja-pie* when I speak it. And here, they always make comments about how *Engels* I sound.'

'I don't care what the kids say at school. Now is a good chance for you to practise – to speak it properly.'

'In any case, how can you tell me to speak nicely to them in Afrikaans? You hate the Afrikaners. You're always saying so.'

'That's the government I'm talking about – and you know exactly what I mean. This is family. It's different with family.'

He turned off the tap and finally turned towards me, sitting up now, cross-legged on the floor. Pointing his thin black comb at me, he said gruffly: 'You just see that you behave nicely to them. If you upset your mother or your Ouma, I'll tan your backside. And the same goes for Michael. You'd better tell him so, from me.'

I felt suddenly depressed at the thought of the family coming. I was dying to see Great-Aunt Marie, but she never seemed Afrikaans to me. She spoke English, as Ouma did, and never made a fuss over whether I could speak the language or not. Oom Frans and his Tant Anna were altogether different – they seemed more rigid somehow. Even their accent was harder, more strident. I could never feel close to them, or feel that they were family to me.

I slipped past my father and slunk from the house. The ground was heating in the dusty courtyard, where Dora was warming herself on an upturned box. She shuddered with her silent, convulsing laughter. '*Molo*, Missie,' she replied to my mumbled 'H'lo, Dora.' I trotted past her and stole into the chill of sudden concrete darkness.

'*Molo, klein* Missie.' I recognized William's voice but could not yet make out the faces, dark against the dank walls. I could smell the scents of the boys' room, smoke on the blue overalls, coffee, the smell of the brazier.

The wide white grins of William, Petrus and Albert slowly emerged from the gloom. William's son was there too, a half-smile on his face. Wrapping his hands in rags, he poured an enamel mug of coffee from the tin standing on the brazier. He was generous with the boys' ration of condensed milk before handing me the sweet, milky mixture. I liked it unstirred so that, when I had slurped the coffee – holding it between two hands as the boys did – I could run my grubby fingers around the mug and suck the dripping condensed milk from my hands. The boys didn't speak to me, but accepted my presence companionably as they murmured and clicked in their fast Xhosa.

'Will-i-am.' Ouma's voice rose and her footsteps padded closer in the dust of the yard. 'William? Is jy daar?' She stopped just outside the doorless entry to the room.

William had already stood, carefully placing his coffee on the concrete floor. Plucking his hat from his head, he ducked through the entrance clutching it in both hands.

'*Ja*, Miesies.'

Ouma's face was squinted in the sunlight, reflected from the whitewashed outer wall of the room. 'How is Mary this morning?'

'She is better, Miesies. She is very pleased for the soup and the *muti*.'

'Good. But I really wanted to talk about John. What

are you going to do about the boy?'

Hidden in the gloom, I watched William's son take a slow sip of his coffee, his face hardening as William's voice reached us from outside.

'*Ag*, Miesies, what can we do? The young people nowadays, they don't want to work.'

Ouma waited while he scuffed the toe of his gumboot in the dust. 'He was always a good boy . . . a strong boy . . . but he makes his mother sad now. Hau,' he said, shaking his downcast head, 'he is my first-born son but he is a sorrow to me.'

I heard a snort beside me, or perhaps the first-born choked on his last gulp of coffee before clanking his cup to the ground. The other boys continued sipping with their gentle slurping noises. John rose and stepped from the room. He looked very straight beside the hunched figure of his father.

'*Ag*, there you are, John,' said Ouma briskly. 'What have you decided to do? You are causing your father to sorrow, *jy weet*?

'I will do what I think is right,' he said, again not using 'Miesies'. As he turned suddenly towards the darkened room, I could see that fury had hardened his features, glistening now in the sunlight. 'But why don't you ask your boy Albert . . .' He gave the word 'boy' an inflection which caused Ouma's head to jerk back and her eyes to flatten. William, still gazing at the dust, gently shook his head, murmuring 'Hai, hai, my son.'

'*Ja*, why not ask your boy Albert how they had to pull his son's shirt off the cuts on his back when the blood from the beating had dried it on him?'

'Your father has worked for me since he was a young man like you. But from no one will I take that tone of voice,' said Ouma, her voice quiet. 'And don't try to change the subject either. It isn't me that has beaten the boy.'

She paused, and then continued: 'You must do what you have to do. Why should you be different? There are five to come after you – who must pay for them if you don't work? Your poor father? *Ag*!'

She took another breath, slowly expelling it. Her voice was louder now, and stronger. 'You have already more education than is good for you. I don't like the sound of you. You are starting to sound like those political natives up there in the Transvaal. But I won't have that attitude on my farm.

'You will work or you will leave this District. There is no room for layabouts here, causing trouble among my boys. And you know very well, John, that I have always treated my boys well.'

Her tone and her anger had shocked me into frightened stillness, clutched by my dark corner. But it was John's eyes, turned momentarily in my direction, which brought the fear of a world crumbling, a haven violated. Unaccountably, in their cold, blank darkness, they brought the spectre of the Port Elizabeth dustboy into the gloomy room.

From where I sat, I watched John turn and stride through the blinding sunlight, his worn shoes puffing dust.

'Albert? Is jy ook daar?' called Ouma, squinting into the darkness.

'I am sorry to hear about your son,' she said as Albert stepped out to stand beside William, his hat in his hands.

'*Ja*, Miesies.'

'I am sorry this new farmer has hard ways. It is not my way, as you know. But I'm sure he wouldn't beat for nothing. You must tell your son to work hard and to curb his cheeky tongue. Aai . . .'

She sighed. 'All these young people, so insolent to their Masters, so hard for their fathers to control. What is to be done with them?'

'*Ja*, Miesies,' said Albert again. It seemed he would stop there – I had never heard him say much more – but he spoke again: 'It is hard for him to work for that Master. He is a good boy, Miesies, but . . . so much anger. His heart is filled with anger and that Master turns it to hatred.'

'Anger and hatred will get him nowhere with that Master . . . *Ag, magtig*, Kati. Why do I always find you crept into some corner where you have no business? Come out of there now and we will go find those kittens. *Kom, kind.*'

As I stepped from the darkness, the blaze of sudden sunlight began to smooth the goose bumps which the dank walls had brought to my arms and warm the chill which had unaccountably settled into my bones. Ouma let me stand, silent and shivering, in the sunlight, while her brisk movements and vigorous voice brought Michael racing around the side of the house. Stopping with braced legs, he slid forward on the dusty gravel, the *ee-ee-ee-ee* of a skidding racing car on his exultant lips. Still waiting for Ouma I squatted on flat feet, fingering dust drawings into the ground and examining small stones. I couldn't have said anything to Michael, even had I tried. I didn't know what it was I had witnessed. And I could never have put into words my disquiet, or the reason for it.

'Come now, you kids. Let us go.'

I stood at the sound of Ouma's voice and was instantly shuffled and bumped by the sloppy loping of the two dogs. Michael raced ahead in short bursts, his arms aeroplaning sideways, his mouth simulating a helicopter's *shook-shook-shook*. I walked alongside Ouma, falling behind as her energetic stride lengthened. My arms were horizontal, one hand on each warm-flanked dog. Their pale tan flesh was loose, and it wrinkled comfortingly in the clutch of two small hands.

Scattered prickly pears were spiked along the rain-rutted road that led to the shed where Ouma had seen the kittens, not far from the pig enclosure. So succulent and fleshy the fruit seemed, such a thirst-quenching green – but so harsh in the cruel thorns which could rip a T-shirt and tear the skin which ventured too near.

Flitting to the ground on the very edge of my peripheral vision, I saw a flash of orange. Halting the dogs with a squeeze of their shoulder flesh, I stopped to watch the fearless orange of a majestic hoopoe bobbing its crowned head just two adult strides from my feet.

'*Ag, kind*, don't dawdle,' called Ouma.

With a flash of orange-black wings the bird fluttered away. Minutes later I could see its flittering landing just ahead of me – waiting for me, just to the back of Michael's wild zigzag and Ouma's firm stride. As I drew softly level, it fluttered up again and forward. Regal and triumphant, it led me along that farm road, a euphoric emblem of the farm in all its gentle sweetness.

The wild buzzing and chirping of insects sang from the scattering of tall grass and stunted bushes on each side of the road. Disturbed hoppers tapped against my legs as I diverged from the road and thrashed through the grass to follow Ouma.

The shed was tumbledown, its walls crumbling and cracked. Large stones held the flat corrugated iron roof in place. Loose and sagging on its hinges, the opening door grated on the concrete floor. Light from the door-way revealed the tableau in the spilt bag of sawdust. Three curled kittens, spotlit in the surrounding gloom of tools and piles of wood, lay coddled in the fragrant shavings.

As Ouma stepped back to allow Michael and me inside, one pair of dazed, dreamy eyes turned gently upon us. Set in a pure white face, with a body whose white expanse was endearingly flawed by a yellowish patch, the eyes blinked in the light glowing around them. The three soft bundles rolled, tongues pink in yawning mouths – as silky as down, as the softest wisps plucked from farm chickens.

Slowly, the sinuous kittens awoke into tentative, paw-stretched roistering. Long sensuous necks extended, already gawky in the awkwardness of growth. The eyes of the white kitten followed my hand's longing reach.

The tearing teeth and claws which ripped my small, rough hand into a bleeding gash were far from playful. My pain was momentarily blunted by horror and I stood unmoving, unable to shake the wild predator hanging from my hand. I heard yelling, but Ouma and Michael seemed very far from where I was caught in a sticky web of panic.

I became aware that Michael, shock struck deep in his dark eyes, had clutched at the scruff of the animal's neck and flung it from us. I heard myself whimpering as we backed away from this violence of coiled fur. Outside the door we stood, all three of us silent. The abhorrent transformation from soft, fluffy pet to primeval hunter had been too sudden – there was a horror to it, a dread of finding this primitive savagery in the very heart of tender warmth. And there was nothing soft about these kittens, reared in the comforting familiarity of my gentle farm. They were wild, totally wild, with the innate and unaware cruelty of the untamed.

Michael's face was white, his dark eyes and eyebrows vivid. Blood dripped from a long scratch on his arm. As numbed senses began to return, I reached instinctively for my wounded hand, finding it viscous and slippery. The sight of the blood was what caused the scream, the child's desperate fear at the sight of her own mutilated flesh. I screamed and screamed, hearing my high-pitched fright momentarily silence the insects and soft-voiced doves.

I was finally squeezed into calm by Ouma's sensible arms.

'*Kom nou, kind. Toe maar*. It's OK. You've got a bit of a cut, but you'll be all right. We'll go back and bathe it.'

Michael was sniffing now, ducking his head and lifting a straight arm to wipe his running nose on his T-shirt sleeve. His mouth was twisted and a single tear was smeared with the dust from his hand.

'William?' said Ouma, as she located a tissue in her sleeve and began to bind it around my hand. Glancing behind, I saw William and two of the other boys – bidden by my screams – all three breathing hard and glistening with sweat.

'William, please deal with those little *bliksems*. We have too many cats on this farm. They're a menace. Of course, it's the fault of that great white tom – we should have shot him long ago.'

'Oh no,' I whispered. My voice rising, I pleaded: 'Not him, Ouma, please. He's special. Please don't hurt him. It's all my fault, it'll all be my fault if you kill him. Don't kill him because of me.'

An unreadable message was signalled from Ouma's eyes to William's, which quickly flickered down again. Shuffling a greeting to Ouma, the three went on their way at an easy jog across the rough grass.

'*Toe maar, kind*, we won't discuss it again.' Giving me a rough pat and a push, she set off, swishing through the grass towards the road.

Michael and I were subdued, quietened by the enormity of our reactions, almost more than the wild kittens themselves. Brushing through the long-stalked grass and *khakibos*, Michael's short pants were suddenly spiked with blackjacks. My world was returning to normality and, to hasten its ordinariness, I plucked a blackjack from his shorts and pricked the exposed neck below his school short back and sides. In the relief of the everyday, we scrabbled and pushed with an intensity of giggling. Curling his foot around my legs, he tripped me on to the rough, spiky ground and sat on me. Plucking the top from a wild 'liquorice plant' which waved above my head, he crushed its liquorice-smelling juice into my hair, my face and my mouth.

Ouma ignored us, walking briskly ahead. She surveyed her farm as she walked, her hand shading her eyes, which were deeply wrinkled from years of squinting into the harsh sunlight. As we stumbled and tripped, giggling and squealing behind her, she halted, her attention riveted. We paused, suddenly still.

She was staring at the area of uncleared bush to the side of us. Its entwined clutter of gnarled trees and shrubs clambered over a small rise to our left. Branches were bent in twisted tension – a repression of growth which permitted no straggling, no winsome tendrils.

'What did you see, Ouma?' I asked, insinuating my hand into her grip.

'I saw something move. I wondered if it was a snake.'

And then I saw, just a glimpse of what it was – that hard, withered shell and leathery skin, that gloomy ponderous crashing through all obstacles and pausing lugubriously to munch a leaf.

'It's a mountain tortoise!' I shrieked, my bare feet moving towards the bush.

'Watch for snakes,' warned Ouma, but Michael and I were already ducking between branches and swinging over brush.

The tortoise was not yet overly large, and between us we could lift it out and carry it towards the house.

'Please could we keep it, Ouma?' I called over my shoulder as we trotted ahead, moving our hands to avoid the stream of tortoise urine.

'I suppose you could ask William to paint his name on his back. Put him on the lawn under the wild fig. On the other hand, I'll kill him if he eats all my flowers.'

But I could hear that she was smiling.

1966 . . . The same day

'Laat ons bid.'

Oom Frans stood before the window, the sunlight harsh against the austere lines of his face. His voice raised, he lifted his clenched hands to his chest, his face almost angry with the intensity of his conviction. Beyond his upright length, I struggled for a glimpse of the garden's vibrant profusion of flowers and the bulk of the fig tree.

'Here, ons dank U . . .'

He paused. I willed him to speak, to have done with this dark silent praying. But on and on his hesitation dragged, till it brought a smile and a just held giggle to my lips. Glancing around at the quiet, prayerful family, my eyes were captured and held by the locked glare of my mother. Holding me there a minute, her eyes forced mine finally to drop and close.

'Dank U dat ons a 'n familie weer bymekaar kan wees. Waar ons binnekort die geboortedag van U seun, Jesus Christus, sal vier . . .'

He paused again, his voice having gently caressed and lengthened the name of Jesus. Through my swept-down eyelashes, I glimpsed Michael begin to kick his heels against the couch. My mother's hand swooped from its clenched supplication to clutch at his knee, her fingernails digging his flesh. Pain was instantly communicated by his face, but not a sound left his mouth.

'. . . ura ons dat U liefde en vergewensgesindheid ook in ons alger se harte sal woon. Amen.'

Amen, said Ouma. Amen, repeated Tant Anna and Tant Marie, whose light blue bulk was pressed to my side. She smelt powdery, especially when her face – heavy with powder and covered in light hairs – drew close to mine. Small damp droplets had gathered now on her upper lip and a slight smell of sweat mingled with the sweet talc in the air about her.

Clearing her throat, Ouma took Oom Frans's place, her large black Bible held open in her two square hands. But with a glance at Michael and me, she smiled and moved to one side of the window, where our longing gazes instantly swooped. She read for a long time, while my eyes darted and flew to the dragonfly, which briefly hovered its greeting just outside the window. And to the praying mantis, betrayed by a tiny movement on the green of the gently swaying curtain. I remember little of the chapters she read, except for those verses which wormed their way into my mind as signs, or omens, or messages from God. Call them what you will, I was always on the lookout for them – those little missives, intended just for me – to tell me that everything was good in my world, or to warn me of possible harm.

' ". . . For wickedness burneth as the fire: it shall devour the briars and thorns, and shall kindle in the thickets of the forest, and they shall mount up like the lifting up of smoke.

' "Through the wrath of the Lord of hosts is the land

darkened, and the people shall be as the fuel of the fire: no man shall spare his brother." '

In the stillness of my sudden disquiet, this warning from God beat in my chest. Its hammering was calmed only several unheard verses later, when He sent His orange-black reassurance fluttering past the window in the sudden glimpse of my hoopoe.

' ". . . For behold, the Lord cometh out of His place to punish the inhabitants of the earth for their iniquity: the earth also shall disclose her blood, and shall no more cover her slain." '

Ouma closed her eyes briefly and slowly closed the flaking leather of the large book.

Years later, I searched the Book of Isaiah to find the words which had stayed with me. Those words which had lived in my churning thoughts as the final warning from God that He expected of me the goodness that would hold the baying, circling evil from my farm and my family. But the full force of His warning, I think, exploded in me only much later that holiday. At the time, with the family's love centred on the chicken-laden table, I knew it only as a sign from God. I hadn't yet fully recognized the omens in the little things. It was only later that I recognized how early the gathering awfulness had begun, and how clearly it signalled the closing in of the sinister forces.

That day, the warmth of the vast, gravy-covered chicken shimmered above the starched white cloth of the Sunday lunch table. But, encircling the table, it was there also in the eyes, the smiles, the soft laughter of conciliation and family affection.

'Jy praat vlot Afrikaans,' Oom Frans said, opening his eyes after I, as the youngest, had stumbled and

71

raced through a short Afrikaans grace that my mother had once taught me.

Oom Frans's planed face softened into a surprisingly kindly smile. 'But, in honour of our *Engelse* family – you are not included in that, Elaine . . .' he added with a rumbling chuckle which gentled his sardonic nod towards my mother, '. . . we will now speak some English.'

I felt my father's pride across the table in his almost imperceptible nod of approval. My mother's tensely bitten lower lip and darting eyes relaxed slightly as the rites of the carving began. My Ouma stood, her strong arms bracing to lift the large bird to a small table alongside her. She never relinquished this duty and careful ceremony of the dinner table. Now she brushed an escaping white curl from her forehead to concentrate on the line of her slice.

'You can't trust the carving to an *Engelsman*.' I was waiting for her to say it, and she, probably realizing as much, fulfilled my small ritual expectation. Laughter, the uniting laughter of love and released family tension, poured around the room as Dora entered with a gravy boat. Placing the gravy shakily on the table, she indulged in her inevitable mannerism of deferential silent laughter, and quivered from the room again.

'We none of us *Engelsmanne* would dare wrest that knife from your hand, my love,' said Oupa with a soft smile. 'We know how dangerous an Afrikaner *vrou* can be when thwarted or threatened – particularly when she's holding a knife which looks as dangerous as that.'

'*Ag*, Griet, is that our old card table you're carving on?' asked Tant Marie suddenly, her round, glistening face eager, bent to one side. Without waiting for a reply from Ouma – frowning in damp concentration at the chicken – she burst into boiling, excited speech. Her voice was startlingly high and childlike, and, sometimes, the child that she had been and her status of cosseted youngest sibling broke free from the confines of her age and bulk.

'*Ag, weet jy*, Kati, we used to play whist at that table – even on Sundays,' she said with a bubbling giggle and a blushing bob of her head. I had heard this story so many times before, but I loved its certainty and its place in the family rites.

'*Ja*, Tant Marie?' I encouraged her.

'It was my job as the youngest,' she said, her hand stroking my fingers and her eyes seeking conspiratorial affinity in mine, 'to watch for the Dominee. I had to sit on the window seat and watch the gate. As soon as I saw him,' she giggled again, 'I had to shout, and up they would jump.

'Oh, that table would disappear so fast behind the couch and the cards would go under the cushions . . .'

'*Ja*,' interrupted Oom Frans, laughing with his entire shuddering body, 'and by the time Mams was saying: "*Môre*, Dominee du Preez", at the door, there would be everybody sitting silent in the lounge, their hands in their laps.'

Ouma was laughing too now, her lines of brisk disgruntlement softened into plump white smoothness. She was moving around the table, placing portions of chicken on plates without asking our preferences. I was hoping against hope, willing her to assign a wing to me, and she did, without looking at me. And the gravy-coated egg, so delicious and redolent of the chicken – which we traditionally fought over and whose progress we children were following around the table – was delved from the flesh and reverently placed on my plate. Michael's quick look of indignation and protest was dealt with swiftly by Ouma, who said: 'Kati said the grace, Kati gets the egg.

'Do you really remember that old farm in Swellendam, Marie?' asked Ouma, forking delicate slices of white meat on to her plate. 'You were very young when we left there.'

'Of course I do.' She was indignant suddenly, her veracity questioned, her story brought under scrutiny. 'I remember that old wooden gate which squeaked, next to the great old oak tree, and I remember the stoep where Pappie sat and smoked his pipe.'

'How did you lose the farm again, Ouma?' I asked. As the youngest, I was the expected Greek chorus in the ceremonial family play – the questioner, the prompter of plot.

'Pappie was a kindly man,' she said, 'maybe too kind for his own good. Do you remember how I told you that he worked as farm manager on La Rochelle? That was before he married the farmer's only child. She was a beautiful girl, our Mams, much younger than him. *Nou ja*, who could have resisted her?

'The farm was ours then, of course, when Oupa died, and Pappie was very proud of that land. But he was too kindly to neighbours and often – as a man of substance – he was asked to stand surety for people. Anyway, one day he stood surety for his neighbour, Van Zyl, who wanted to buy more land . . .'

'*Ag*, come on, Grieta!' Oom Frans's exclamation burst from him, with a laugh which erupted from deep within his shaking chest. 'That was Pappie's story . . .

he lost it through a bet, gambling – though of course his precious daughters will never admit to that.'

'*Ag, nonsens*, Frans,' Ouma barked. 'Pappie didn't gamble.' Bending her head slightly to one side, she gazed at him speculatively for a moment. Her face broke suddenly into a half-smile, almost sardonic: 'But of course, you like to think so. It makes you feel so good and righteous, just because you've never touched a card since you married Anna.'

'Hha,' gasped Tant Anna, 'Griet, I should think he wouldn't! *Onse Here* is not forgiving about gambling. And Frans, don't talk nonsense, I'm sure your father would never have gambled. You just like to annoy the girls.'

Oom Frans looked slightly chastened by the un-adorned Calvinism of his wife. Smiling wryly at Ouma, he allowed her to continue.

'Anyway, as I was saying, when we lost the farm, Pappie loaded us all into the wagon and we trekked very slowly down the Langkloof to the Eastern Cape. It took us years. *Magtig*, those years were hard!'

She stared into space for a second, then shook her head. Briefly she gripped Oupa's hand – the gesture of love not quite reaching her stern features – before lifting her knife and fork.

It was clear to me that she, as undisputed head of the family, should be placed at the table's starched white end, but she awarded this distinction to Oupa, who sat now with an expression of infinite sweetness for Ouma. On his side plate was a leather-covered book, which he riffled through and peeped into throughout the lunch that he hardly touched.

The silence was broken again by Tant Marie. Her

giggle trilled as she curled her plump hand over her mouth. 'Oh, Grieta, it wasn't hard at all. It was the best fun.'

Turning to me: 'You would have loved that wagon trip, Kati. The oxen would *stomp* in that slow way of theirs, and we – that was Frans and me – we would jump off and run ahead through the veld. When we tired we could sit on the wagon again. I remember being so free ... I'd never felt so free before – before that trip I'd always had to act like a lady. No one can really be so strict about that when you're travelling by wagon.'

'*Ja*, of course,' said Ouma, impaling Tant Marie with her look of withering scorn, 'it was lovely for you. You were the youngest. Didn't you realize what we were doing while you and Frans were racing around being children? Every morning we had to load up the wagon for travelling, and every afternoon we unloaded for outspan. And every day Mams insisted that I wash one set of clothing for all of you because she said we had to show people what we were. She wouldn't have us in dirty clothes, ever. You remember, we only had two outfits each. But she said we weren't *bywoners* and we wouldn't look like them.

'Every night, us four girls crushed up to Mams to sleep in the wagon. The boys slept under it with Pappie. And we were so poor we were happy to get one piece of fruit between us. We didn't go peeling it, like you spoilt children do.' This with a frown aimed at Michael and me.

'What? You ate banana skins?' asked Michael, collapsing into wild laughter and slipping from his chair with the glory of his own wit and hilarity.

My mother reached across and slapped him so that he slid upward again, just a small giggle still escaping.

'No, of course not,' Ouma snapped, but a small chuckle rumbled from her throat. 'I meant apples, of course, and pears and peaches. You knew perfectly well what I meant.'

'So how did you finally get this farm in the Eastern Cape?' I asked, anxious to keep the ritual on track.

'*Ja*, well, *my kind*,' said Ouma, brushing a damp curl from her forehead and reaching for empty plates, 'Pappie worked for farmers along the way. We'd stop for long periods while he worked on farms or even sometimes loaded and carried. Menial work, which he wasn't built for. But he did it, and he made money along the journey.'

Oom Frans was smiling mischievously: '*Ja*, Griet? Is that really what happened?'

She stared at him a moment. Her voice quavered with the slightest hint of amusement as she glanced at Tant Anna's unsmiling piety. 'What is it, Frans? What did you want to say? Speak up and tell us what you think.'

'*Ag, nee*, nothing really, Grieta. Just that us boys sleeping under the wagon didn't always stay there all night. Pappie had other ways of making money besides labouring on farms. He was lucky on that trip. *Magtig*, but I remember how lucky he was.'

'Frans, watter nonsens praat jy nou?' snapped Tant Anna, her agitation ousting her English. 'Moenie dit sê nie. Ek wil dit nie hoor nie.' She had placed her long, unpretentious hands over her ears. With her unaffectedly cut fingernails, she showed her single adornment – her plain gold wedding band.

I could see slight smiles all around the table. Even my mother's unexplained tension seemed to have evaporated during lunch. Ouma and Oupa looked down to hide their amusement, while Tant Marie shook and quivered behind her small white hands. Michael and Neil grinned unrepentantly.

And that is really all I remember from that lunch, that wonderful communion of roast chicken and love. I think we had a hot pudding, which my father refused. 'Hot pudding reminds me of boarding school,' he often told us. Michael and I lapped up the home-made custard. I'm sure we must have. We always did.

'I just love custard,' I told Ouma – well, I think I did. I usually said so on the farm as I poured great globs and dollops from the jug. 'We never have custard at home – only cream.'

And Ouma always turned to an invisible audience to comment: '*Magtig*, the child complains about being fed cream.'

I do remember the full, lazy move outside, Oupa slapping his pockets to find his pipe and opening his book again. Scrabbling for his glasses which had fallen down the side of the lumpy couch on the stoep, he settled there. The rest of us wandered in the slow, buzzing heat towards the fig tree, stopping to admire and to comment on Ouma's flowers. Laughing, my brother Neil had to rescue a shrieking Tant Marie with flapping arms from an enveloping cloud of *miggies* which settled on her hair and her face.

A scattering of upright chairs and a blanket had been spirited beneath the tree during lunch and we collapsed there now, Michael and I lying full length, lazily picking at the grass and sucking stalks. In an unusual show of solidarity he rolled over and opened his grubby, damp hand. Gesturing with it, he allowed me to choose a wilting clover from the clump he had unearthed in Ouma's flower beds. I smiled at him and we munched our clover leaves, chewing the stalks with quick little bites.

My father came then, running around the side of the house with a watermelon tucked under his arm like a rugby ball. Shifting it into both hands for a pass, he ran past Neil who was dawdling on the lawn. He gestured the melon towards him and the two began running side by side down the lawn in our direction. Daddy passed and Neil, laughing, had to leap sideways to catch it, falling on his elbows and rolling over to protect the melon. My father slapped him between the shoulder blades when he rose – the only form of touch he allowed himself with his boys – and left his hand there while they sauntered, laughing, towards us in a togetherness of men.

In the deep, cool shade of the tree, Daddy knocked on the watermelon and listened for its hollow signal. 'Sounds like a good one, Jim,' said Ouma, while Mom, her long legs curled under her, tugged at her mini and nodded, smiling at him.

The afternoon lazed into shadows while we lay or sat, waving arms lethargically at flies which buzzed and landed, buzzed and landed. Tant Marie dozed on her straight-backed chair, her plump chin dropping towards her chest. Jerking awake, she looked around and brazened her pretence of not having slept.

We talked of the bioscope – Neil had seen *Khartoum*, while Mom and Dad had recently seen Sophia Loren's latest, I forget now what it was called. Daddy was loud in his disappointment at having read somewhere that she was expecting a baby. 'Lovely popsie that, just lovely!' he added admiringly.

Tant Marie said she hadn't been to the bioscope for such a long time, but she was very keen to see *Dr Zhivago*. 'But I just wish I could get to Johannesburg somehow,' she said, sighing. 'I would do anything to see Maurice Chevalier while he's here ... it's that accent of his. It just does something ...'

And the cricket. A hotly disputed discussion about how good the sides were, and who would win the Test between Australia and the Springboks being played in Port Elizabeth.

Oom Frans smilingly teased my dad about Britain's treatment of Rhodesia. 'So which *Engelse* are you supporting this time? Harold Wilson's boycott, or Smithy's boys?'

Oom Frans knew my parents had voted against a republic in South Africa and still spoke of the 'union' – but I think he suspected that they supported Rhodesia's UDI.

My father smiled and sliced more of the watermelon. My mother's eyes began their darting again. Oom Frans held on, reluctant to let a good teasing point drop.

'Sanctions won't bring Rhodesia down, you know! Those blimming Brits can't think they can keep telling us what to do in Africa. And now the Americans are getting in on the act.'

My father wielded the carving knife like a panga to swish down on the blood-red slices, cleaving them in two. He smiled and made as if he hadn't heard. My mother's eyes were fixed, anxious and searching, to his face. Seeing his smiling imperturbability, she relaxed slightly and put out her plate for another slice.

'Those Americans,' Oom Frans said, sighing and shaking his head, letting the subject drift into the indolent heat of the afternoon.

Tant Anna turned her anxious gaze on Neil. '*Ag*, my boy, your Ouma tells me you're applying to go and live with them for a year. Is this true?'

He rolled over and sat up, facing the old people.

'*Ja*, Tant Anna. I'm applying for an exchange scholarship to go to America. I really hope to get it. I'd like to see how their country works and look at their democracy. But really . . .' He leapt to his feet and, shaking off his earnest demeanour, laughed raucously. Bending forward to twang at an imaginary guitar, he continued: 'I'd like to go to California to see the Beach Boys. And I hear there's some real groovy surfing over there.'

Laughing still, he flung himself back to the blanket.

'But I hope you're going to be a good ambassador for us,' continued Tant Anna, looking perplexed, and anxious still.

'*Ja*, Tant Anna, I'm going to tell them how terrible apartheid is.'

My father's panga-knife faltered, and his arm dropped quietly. In the sudden silence I saw my mother's eyes freeze and, beyond her, I caught a sudden flitter of my landing hoopoe. But it was my last glimpse. I don't remember seeing another hoopoe that holiday.

Oom Frans's eyes had hardened. To me they seemed, frighteningly, to have developed the consistency of glass. His lean body had stiffened on his upright chair, his tie still firmly knotted to his collar.

'How the *donder* can you possibly sit there and tell Tant Anna you'll be an ambassador for South Africa, when you have views like that?' His voice was very quiet, with a sibilant quality. But we all heard him, with the clarity of shattering glass.

'Well, obviously, Oom Frans,' said Neil. He tried to appear unconcerned, but his shoulders had stiffened and hunched. And his fingers fiddled with the blanket, weaving the tassels between them. 'How could anyone possibly justify apartheid? Ask my dad. It's like trying to justify the Nazis. The only way I can be an ambassador is to let them know that not everyone thinks like the hairy-backs do.'

'Neil!'

My mother's cry held a depth of anguish. Her eyes were squeezed closed and her hands, white-knuckled, clutched at each other in her lap. Her whole body, with her legs tightly tucked beneath her, appeared to bend into itself. My father finally dropped the knife from his loose fingers and shifted across the blanket to place an arm around her.

'*Ag*, I'm sorry, Ouma, I don't mean you. You know I mean the government,' said Neil, glancing anxiously at my mother's face before gazing pleadingly at Ouma. My Ouma sat, her hands held loosely, palm up, in her lap. She stared bemusedly at them and didn't look up when Neil spoke. But she sighed a long, shuddering sigh.

'*Ja*, Neil, I know that's what you meant.' Her sadness, like a watercolour wash, stained away all the brisk stern lines from her face and left a soft, slightly sagging whiteness. Tant Marie, her eyes darting between her sister and brother, gave a small giggle which ended in a tiny catch.

That sound acted as a switch to Oom Frans, whose sprung body flew upright from his hard chair. 'I can't sit here and listen to this kind of talk. And in front of my wife too.' His wife sat transfixed, her mouth slightly open.

'Griet, we've always tolerated you and your damned – *ag*, excuse me, Anna, but I'm angry – Sap views and your *Engelse* pretensions. Why, for the blessed goodness, did you have to create a little English girl? Now see what you've done. You've created a monster.'

Turning on my mother, whose face was turned into my father's open shirt-front, his hand stroking her hair, he rasped: 'You're *volksvreemd*, my girl, you always were and you always will be. But just look at what you've produced – a pack of *rooinek* savages who have no more idea of *volk*, family or *nasie* than hyena cubs.

'Kom, Anna, laat ons nou gaan. Ons kan nie hier sit en luister na hierdie soort ding nie. En ons kan nie hier sit saam met hierdie soort mense nie.'

He stood under that great, achingly joyful, embracing tree, and burnt us with his rage and hurt. His anger and rigid conviction consumed his age as he marched, long-limbed and sure, towards the house.

1989 . . . 28th October

His thick, sinuous sliding makes me flinch in my softest innermost self. Above me his alien, frighteningly engorged features dance in their primitive rhythm. And beyond . . . beyond I can just glimpse the chirruping morning sunshine. The day breezes in the jasmine to mingle with the hot smell of sweat and last night's wine.

Raising his body on freckled, almost hairless arms, he lifts his head in the proud exultancy of conquering manhood. Then his eyes drop in admiration, not of me, but of his veined, glistening lunge.

His wet, pressing insistency rubs unwilling sensation through my quivering belly. But my cringing, secret being feels battered, desecrated by his impervious hip-flexing – his slow, unrelenting plunge and withdraw, plunge and withdraw. Between my two tight-clenched fists I hold, in safety, my soul.

The dance moves faster and my detached gaze holds and frames, for an instant, his slackened mouth and eyes that are beginning to roll back. My guard, I suppose, loosens slightly as I feel a film of contemptuous revulsion spread over my eyes. Suddenly my frail wrists are manacled in the imprisoning grasp of his hands. Panic flies, hot and acrid, to my mouth as my hands are roughly pinioned above my head.

'Stop it! Let me go!' I can hear the high-pitched fright in my voice.

But the dance, relentless, is in its frenetic death-throes now. In his grunting, inhuman state I doubt he even hears me. He gives two final, violent thrusts – thrusts that, had he been wielding a sword, would have been death strokes – and collapses, trapping me beneath his heavy, wet weight.

'Fuck you, get off me,' I gabble, pushing my released hands at his shoulders.

Slowly he raises himself, perplexed now, the familiar hurt spreading over his open features. Rage smothers me like a hot blanket. How could he never understand? How could it never be brought home to him how close sex brings him, and all men for that matter, to the totally primitive, the bestial? Even gentle new-age men lose their thin veneer in this act of conquering, which so closely resembles a wrestled fight to the death.

'You know I hate that.' My voice is almost a shriek. 'You know it. We've been through this. How dare you hold my hands like that? You did it on purpose to scare me, you bastard.'

He rolls off me, his hands and feet entwined in mine, withdrawing as suddenly as if he has found himself embracing a cobra. He rolls to the edge of the bed and sits, his feet on the floor. He makes no effort to cover his damp, withered self. He is always like this – totally comfortable to fight with me in his nakedness. Unselfconsciously he raises his arms to rub at his face and neck. He feels no vulnerability in his unclothed self. I, in contrast, have obsessively mummified my body in the twisted duvet and sit now, gazing at his back.

Faced with his lack of response, I quieten. Breathing is difficult, my indrawn breath almost a sob.

He breaks the silence, his voice quiet but darkened with the agony I know so well. 'I don't know how much longer I can take this. Kate, tell me truthfully, have you never enjoyed our lovemaking? Never? Not even in the beginning?'

'This has got nothing to do with sex!' My voice is high, far louder than his. 'I didn't say I didn't like sex. You bastard. You know – you knew a long time ago – I hate having my hands held like that. I hate it.'

'But Kati, for God's sake, that was years ago. You reacted so badly to it because you hardly knew me. You thought I was going to hurt you. But we've been married for years now. You must know I would never hurt you. You must surely have some trust in me and our relationship.'

'I'll never trust anyone that far!'

He flinches as my rasped comment hits him.

'Then what have we got, Kati? You tell me, what have we actually got to show for all these years?'

He turns towards me and now his eyes bore into mine in angry despair. Mine drop to watch my hands picking and picking at the small balls of cotton formed on the duvet cover.

I hear, as usual, that his voice has changed with his easily softened emotions: '*Ag*, Kati, don't you know sex is my way of giving you love on a platter? It's the only time I ever feel at all close to you – for me, it's a sharing.'

'It's got nothing to do with love, or sharing. You men, you glorify your primitive urge to conquer and control.

I shouted "Stop it" there at the end. You never even heard me. You couldn't have stopped if I'd been crying or bleeding to death. I don't say that I don't feel sensations – I do, so don't think you can get into that male defence that I'm frigid. I just can't stand the domination involved. You use me, you use me like a plastic doll. And that's another thing – you talk about trust. That's one thing I hate about sex. It needs trust only because it's so close to hurting. You wouldn't need trust if you couldn't glimpse every man's raw brutality when he's pounding away.'

'Oh, Kate, that's such a perverted way of looking at love and lovemaking. I wish I knew how to help you. I wish I knew that I still wanted to help you.'

He sighs.

'Sometimes I think it would be easier to give up on you, although there are times when I can still just feel or catch a glimpse of that vulnerable damaged child in you. There're still parts of you I love. But they're retreating, Kate, they're retreating. You seem to be getting worse – more tightly bound, more desperate to hold yourself in . . .'

I sit, my forehead burning. I resent him and his gentle insights. I hate the fact that, no matter how I've protected and guarded myself, he knows things about me – he can pity me. I am what I never wanted to be. I'm vulnerable to him. I resent him for it, more and more as he knows me better and better. And I find I have to punish him for it more often as time goes on. But, at the same time, it ties me to him. To protect myself, my vulnerable coiled self, I have to keep him close by for my secret snail soul to be truly safe.

'Don't think you can make everything my fault. No

one could be turned on by you. You think you can twiddle my nipples a bit, like you're tuning into a radio station, and then leap at me. And then you practise being a scrum-half – quickly in and quickly out.'

He knew his punishment was coming. He took it without flinching, his mouth twisted into a smile.

'It's sad, you know, Kate, that we've come to this. I loved you so much at varsity I thought I could protect you for ever. And I really – shit, I was naive – I genuinely believed that my love would open up your pitiful, damaged little psyche and that one day I'd know what it was that did this to you.'

I think of him as he was, that enormous boy-man, with emotions that flashed uncurbed across his innocent face. I remember when I first noticed him, when he smuggled his pathetic white rat from the psychology class to protect it from being dissected by biology students.

He blushed when my eyes caught him slipping the disgusting feral creature – its nose twitching and its bald tail twining – under his sweatshirt. 'We've made the little buggers perform so many tricks for their food, I think this one deserves a little rest. After all I've trained him to do, I don't think he should be sliced up.'

But he'd already been watching me for weeks.

'Do you remember when I first noticed you?' he asks now. 'You made the whole tut laugh – it was the first time you'd opened your mouth that year. You told that pretentious little twerp of a psycho lecturer that you thought his "science" was about as exact as water-divining. And you called him "nothing but an advanced spoon-bender".'

He is smiling slightly, but he doesn't look at me. I

think he is working through our relationship for his own benefit, trying in that solid, exact way of his to make sense of it all in his own mind.

'Jesus, you were beautiful. I could see you were beautiful – you still are, no matter how much you try and hide it.'

He glances at me and away again, to the window and the buzzing morning sunshine.

'And so fucking clever. I've always been proud of you, do you know that? I was proud of you skimming through your Masters while I was plodding through my BA, repeating first year, and struggling to get my LL B.

'I couldn't believe it when this beautiful creature actually agreed to come back to my digs with me. And then you unveiled those marvellous, myopic eyes from behind those glasses, and that body from all its wrappings. I'll never forget my first glimpse of those breasts and those provocative legs.'

There is silence for a long time. So long that it seems he has given up his clumsy attempt at communication, at letting me know how he feels about me. I think of him as he was, the gentlest person I've ever known. That's what ensnared me. But, over the years, I've taken such perverse pleasure in needling him into violent eruption. I have a bitter enjoyment in proving to myself over and over again what I came to believe so early – that savagery lurks everywhere, and in everyone.

'And then, against all the odds, you were a virgin,' he says suddenly.

I remember that, of course. I remember that dingy little back room in the run-down, historic house. The scrappy, worn carpet covered little of the dusty floor-boards. His double-bed mattress lay on the floor in the middle of the room from where I could look up and, if my glasses were on, see the titles of his books arranged on rough wooden planks held up with bricks. I remember being amused by his choice of books – interspersed with university texts – so earnest and romantic. D. H. Lawrence, Rod McKuen, E. M. Forster and L. P. Hartley. And on the end, the innocent volume of hackneyed Eastern philosophy by Kahlil Gibran.

'You were a virgin!' he almost accused, that day when it had snowed in Grahamstown for the first time in years. It had seemed so easy, so other-worldly, to slip through the blanketed, muffled town to his digs in African Street.

'Well, for fuck's sake, there's no need to be so awe-struck. This isn't a valuable antiquity you've discovered here. We do exist, you know.' I felt irritated, as if he had something on me.

'No, I think it's great. It's just that you always seemed so contained, so sophisticated, really. This makes me feel so tender – and, like, protective. I'm sorry. I should have been gentler. I just thought that I wouldn't stand a chance if I wasn't a dynamite lover. I'll teach you to like it – I'll be so gentle you won't believe it.'

And at times, I believe he thought he had. I'm a great faker. It's just that lately, in these days of everybody else's jubilation and hope, I grow tired of pretence.

Our courtship and marriage went along just fine, for years it seems to me. It was comfortable. And it was never too deep for my anxiety level. It was an easy arrangement; he laughed at my jokes. I hurt him quite often, with my sniping, and we bickered, but he always seemed to get over it before.

'You know, the real reason I fell in love with you . . .' His voice startles me and I look up to see his rough, gentle face, '. . . was your total, hidden vulnerability. I felt so, well, protective. It made me want to nurture you and – shit, am I stupid! I thought my love could heal you. Oh, *ja*, sometimes I'd give it up for long stretches – I'd think I just had to give you more time. And I could live with that. You made me laugh.

'It's just that now, I don't know how much longer I can stand the agony of it – just as everything else is filling me with such hope and optimism, you're coiling yourself further and further inside yourself. And your jibes get worse. You didn't used to be such an absolute bitch. Jesus, but no one can hurt me like you can.'

'Oh, now I see it. Suddenly you want all your ducks in a row. You think the country's on the up and up, your career's on the way to perfection as far as you're concerned and so, as the perfect complement to the perfect life, you want the flawless, picture-book marriage.'

He sighs and rouses himself, shifting his still naked body. The breeze riffles his dried hair as he reaches for the *Saturday Star*. He fetched it from outside much earlier, with a towel wrapped around his waist. Then he sat on the edge of the bed and woke me by stroking my long, unbound hair – and with his irritating look of wonderment.

I feel a pale pity for him, despite myself. 'Shall we divide some of the pages out between us?'

'No,' he says gruffly. 'It's OK. You read it.'

He is clearly, in his petulant hurt, going to be obstinate about accepting my small shred of contact.

'I'll have another look through the *Weekly Mail*,' he says.

'Oh yes, of course you should. No aspirant labour lawyer should be caught dead without a *Weekly Mail* tucked under his arm. Oh, and don't forget to memorize bits, you never know when you might be called upon to prove that you actually read it.'

He retrieves the paper from his bedside table and ignores me, leaning against his pillows, as close to the edge of the bed as he can get. I lean forward, the duvet tucked tightly across my breasts, and page through my newspaper.

A piece of me, a coiled snail piece of me, wishes to stretch out, naked and raw, and touch his aching body. But I know I won't do it. I know I can never open myself up to that extent, to anyone. The only way I will make contact will be to smash my closed shell against his unprotected flesh.

I fold a news page precisely. 'So, I see that your clients aren't the only ones grabbing the headlines with a strike this week. Look at the terrible crisis the country's in over the Breweries strike: "Panic over beer shortage for Christmas". Now isn't that a prospect too ghastly for the South African male to contemplate!'

He turns a page, but doesn't look up. Oh my God, but he's unyielding when he is in that wounded frame of mind. His great bear jaw knots and unknots as he turns each page with those large wrists and fingers – gently folding each as if it's rice-paper.

I skim over all the 'age of miracles' stories. I am so sick of all this forced optimism sweeping the land. I glance at the articles heralding tomorrow's 'Welcome the Leaders' rally, but they are filled with 'jubilation' and hopes for a peaceful gathering. Joe hasn't mentioned the rally for a week, and neither have I. There is no way he'll get me into an 'expected crowd of 100,000' *toyi-toyi*ing people, all 'jubilant' and keeping 'within the spirit of peaceful action'. I flip pages in irritation.

'I see your clients had to think of something really impressive to be noticed this week, what with the "Welcome the Leaders" rally to contend with: they had to resort to firebombing a child.

'Listen here: "The child of a casual worker is in critical condition following the firebombing of his home."

'Mind you, I suppose we should say "scab", shouldn't we? Maybe you think he deserved it. How dreadful to be the child of a scab.'

I watch him wrestling with his adopted 'silent' position for a moment. With Joe, silence can never win out for long.

'Kate! That's an appalling thing to say. Of course it was a terrible incident. I haven't spoken to them, but I know the union guys will be devastated. They've never advocated violence. But you have to remember there's two sides to everything . . .'

'Oh my God, now you're going to say it's all OK in the struggle for democracy because "look what they did to Biko".'

'Jesus Christ, don't be fucking stupid. Can't you see that spontaneous explosions are inevitable – can't you see that? This is a highly emotionally charged situation here.'

'All I can see is that management must be laughing

this week. They're starting to look lily-white while your guys are looking distinctly scummy. And look here,' I say, stabbing a finger at the page. 'The union's getting all petulant about their image – they're accusing management of telling the media about the violence just to put them in a bad light.'

I watch, with a certain wry satisfaction, as his attitude hardens in the face of my baiting.

'Well, maybe this'll bring home to management that there's going to be trouble if they refuse to budge. They can't just stick on their original offer for ever. And the union can't stop fighting for what is right, just because of some people . . .'

'Oh God,' I say, sighing and rolling my eyes. 'Not the omelette theory, please.'

'Well, management has just refused to be reasonable. If they won't move, somebody's going to get hurt.'

'Yes, let's have it! Now,' I say, addressing an imaginary audience near the door, 'we will listen to Comrade Joe expound on the important role of infanticide in the struggle for a democratic future.'

'Oh fuck you, Kate!'

'Ooh, if only you could do it properly . . . as properly as you adopt the lefty line, anyway.'

'You're not going to get to me that way, Kate. I'm not insecure about myself sexually. You think you're so clever, don't you? You know I don't think like a Stalinist. You just make me so mad with your cynical jibes; you get me to say things I don't really mean. You think it's so funny to manipulate my reactions. But at least I feel . . .'

'Oh, I feel too, Joe. I feel tired of people posturing and using others for power and advancement.'

'Jesus, you're actually a reactionary. You really believe that management line. Do you really believe this strike is only about the union "spreading its political wings"? That's just so much shit about them having to compete for headlines against all the news of political reform.'

'Oh, you mistake me if you think I'm pro-management, Joe. I just have no need to say so in this house. You management-bash enough for two. I believe everyone's out for what they can get. There's nothing to choose between the company bosses and the union bosses. This is all just a ranging of two forces that mirror each other. It's a power play with the workers as the cannon fodder of both sides. When it's all finished the union guys will sit down very easily with the captains of industry – they'll all go hunting together, or visit a game farm, or go trout fishing or something.'

'Don't be ridiculous. I'm in a position to know that this strike is all about bread-and-butter issues. The company is greedy. It can afford to pay higher wages, and managements are going to have to get used to the idea of paying a living wage in the future.'

'I just don't see what the use of higher wages is, if you have to spend three months of every year without pay to get higher wages for the next year – well, I suppose it's OK if you're employed and paid a salary by the union. And it doesn't seem as if the union is getting anywhere.'

'Well, they just have to use more bargaining chips. That's why they've called a national boycott this week – to try and force management's hand.'

'Oh, this is such bad news to me. This means that next week I'll have to sit sagely nodding my head while you try to justify the violence that will follow. I can just see you earnestly explaining why poor little shopkeepers should be punished for not complying with your boycott. And I bet you won't mention the shopkeepers' "bread-and-butter" issues – the families they have to feed.'

'That's typical of you to think that'll happen. These people are disciplined. The union people are committed, intelligent people . . .'

'And what about the picketing of businesses that could put the poor shopkeepers out of business?'

'Well, I'm sorry if it does. But picketing is a legitimate process, just as calling a national boycott is legitimate leverage to use against a management that won't move.'

Joe is standing now, totally unreserved about his nakedness. His hair is wild from the agitation of his large, impassioned fingers. He is breathing heavily as, astride, he gazes challengingly at my hunched, duvet-entwined body. My tangled hair, just touching the newspaper, is my only flimsy screen.

I look up at him suddenly: 'You take this all in deadly seriousness, don't you? This role as labour lawyer to the toiling masses. You actually identify yourself with them – you who were never anything more than a vague, wishy-washy liberal before.'

'Yes I do,' he says. His lower lip juts out as he pauses. 'However you may mock it, I feel that this chance came for me at just the right time. I feel that, by getting into labour work, I'm identifying with the process of renewal. And I've finally got to the point where I can make a stand . . . I can align myself with the forces of change. Things are happening, Kate, if you haven't noticed. No one can sit on the fence anymore.'

'Oh, please! Do you really think that you and your legalistic notions are part of this? You're just momentarily useful. Labour lawyers are the disposable nappies of the struggle – they use you, shit on you, and then throw you away.'

'I told you I didn't care how you mocked me!' He pauses and sits, his eyes warily seeking mine. And are they pleading? I can't be sure.

'That's also why I want us, you *and* me, to go to the rally tomorrow. We have to take sides – you too. And this isn't a request,' he bursts in quickly as he sees my head's slow side-to-side movement. 'It's an ultimatum. I know that you need me in a perverse kind of way. I know you can't just throw our marriage away with alacrity. You're used to me gentling you, and never forcing you, because I always thought you needed time.'

I cannot reply. He grabs my shoulder and adds, very quietly: 'Well, that's all over now! And that's why I'm telling you: if you don't come with me tomorrow, our marriage is over.'

1966 . . . Fifteen days to Christmas

The glittering mystery of the miniature cardboard window lay at the tip of my unmoving finger. My perfect stillness held the anticipation within me – the thought, feathering my stomach, of what might lie behind the gold-speckled shutters.

Tension edged my fingers towards movement. To avoid the opening just that little bit longer, to prolong my delicate balance of expectation, I jerked my finger into a light stroking of the pastelled forest scene. Slowly, ever so slowly, I fingered the oak, ash and elm trees, though I wouldn't then have known their names. Snow-dusted, their homely trunks enfolded tiny glittered doors and windows while, from their roots, squirrels, badgers and hedgehogs stirred and peeped.

This gentle wooded scene was so familiar, so right. It was part of it, my Christmas, as much a part as the dusty heat, peeled prickly pears and watermelon under the enveloping wild fig tree.

A sudden flick and the window opened to my longing eyes. There, suddenly revealed, was the angelic child who had sung in privacy all through the year. She was a well-remembered harbinger, a soothsayer leading us, in joyous expectation, to Christmas.

Leg-tangled, I looked up from the end of Oupa's bed and smiled. Oupa, his tranquillity intact, had waited in silence through my ritual anticipation and elated discovery, as he did every morning, as he did every year, when the Advent calendar was unpacked with the Christmas decorations.

'*Ag*, don't tell me you two are still sitting there with that calendar. *Magtig*, how long does it take to open one little window?' Ouma's tone was exasperated as she entered from the bathroom, but when I turned, I found she was smiling. In her plain blue cotton, her face shining and, as always, free of make-up, she looked fresh, smooth-faced and very clean.

'Well,' said Oupa solemnly. 'It takes a long time to do it properly. You can't rush these things, you know.'

And then the Christmas gladness washed warmth through my chilly limbs and we laughed, Oupa and I, with a solidarity of purpose and perfect understanding. Throwing my head back and flinging my body across the bed, I boiled with raucous laughter. Everything was going to be wonderful, all the Christmas things were still to come – the tree, the baking, the wrapping, the decorating. How could anything possibly spoil that?

I was scurried through breakfast – 'Come on, child. It's time for Dora to clear the table so she can prepare for the baking,' Ouma told me.

Dressed quickly in my shorts and shirt, I left the house with a *skree-bang* and ran barefooted across the chilled dust in search of my brothers. The two dogs trailed behind me in their loping tongue-lolling companionship. The earth felt still. The unwoken insects had not yet begun their buzzing, chirruping accompaniment to the building heat.

Coming to a sliding halt before a still silent clump of bush, I felt the dogs colliding, their ears and legs flopping. Firmly, I pressed a hand to each one's hind-quarters, urging the two to sit. Scrabbling in a greasy shorts pocket, I found scraps of egg white and toast which I had discovered on the stacked breakfast plates on my way through the kitchen.

Nestling the offering between dusty leaves on the very edge of the bush, I settled silently between the dogs, my feet crossed at the ankles and my knobbled, scratched knees poking skyward on either side of my face. We waited, as the dogs and I had often done, our ears aching for a quick scurrying patter. We heard the waking insects begin their buzz in the heat which dampened my neck and the hair on my forehead. Somewhere overheard, the *zee-ee* of the Christmas beetles grew deafening.

The smallest skitter suddenly drew the dogs into tense alertness and shrank the sound of the insects to its usual background hum. I leant forward, sliding my feet through the silent dust into a crossed position. And there she was, collecting the food – for her nestled babies, I thought. Sleek and shiny in the morning sun, the small grey meerkat delicately clutched at a crust and scurried back to safety. I pressed my hands down hard on the two tan flanks, tense beside me. Their noses sniffed and worked the air and, with their eyes, they followed the small animal's return. This time she nibbled neatly at the egg white before skittering away with a larger piece.

Content with the results of my offering, I stood and released the dogs. They dashed side by side into the thick, thorny brush. Futilely swinging their clumsy, excited bulks in circles, they crashed against the impenetrably entwined growth.

'Mikey, Kati,' I called, and heard their dusty padding behind me as I ran. Then, as my bursting exhilaration could no longer be detained, I sprang into the air and began cartwheeling wildly down the centre of the rutted, water-scored track. Crossing the spiky clumps of grass, I saw the pool ahead and slightly below me.

'Hha, *ja jonkie ja-a.*' Michael's chant floated up to me. He was dancing exultantly in the dust, flicking his fingers reprovingly at his elder brother. *'Ja jonkie ja-a.'*

He was facing a frowning Neil, whose mouth was twisted around an unheard retort. A small wisp of smoke wavered from Neil's fingers into the unmoving air above his head. As his eye caught my approach, he quickly staunched the source of the dancing wisp. Waving arms above his head dissipated the remaining wandering smoke.

'Can't I ever be free of you bloody little *piks*? Why do you always follow me everywhere?'

I was hurt that he included me in his scowling displeasure, I who had made no comment about his scary defiance of the forbidden. 'I didn't say anything . . .'

'Yes, well, you didn't see anything, did you now?' he snarled. 'Buzz off, both of you. Leave me in peace. And Michael . . .' He stood in one agile straightening of his long legs and towered over the willowy boy. His large hand closed in a wincing clasp of his shoulder as he bent towards his ear. In a menacing growl he continued: 'Tell Mom if you want to, just tell her and see what happens to you.'

102

The Innocence of Roast Chicken

We escaped, Michael and I, from the moody adolescent disquiet around the swimming place. 'I'll race you,' he said, his spirits unlowered, his body doubling and snapping in perfect Arab springs across the brush-like grass.

He won the race, as he knew he would, with a decisive *skree-bang* of the screen door. We tumbled, wrestling and laughing, against the dresser, scrabbling in the blue and white jar for *soetkoekies*. Our thin arms snaked and twined to be first inside the jar's narrow mouth.

'*Chi-i-ne!*' sang Dora, shaking her head. Her quivering bulk was heaving with inevitable laughter as she stood, sweating arms on hips. Bowls and jars of glacé fruit and flour stood on the scrubbed wooden table beside a great lump of marzipan.

'Is that you, kids?' called my mother from within, as I twisted a pinch of marzipan from the yellow lump.

'*Ja-a,*' intoned Michael, his voice an unenthusiastic down-tone. Slowly, we wandered through to the lounge, Michael pulling a face at my lump of marzipan. He believed the Christmas cake should be made without its generous coating of the sweet almond paste. Before eating, he would always theatrically peel the marzipan free and scrape the cake to remove the last remaining scraps.

The Christmas tree stood, bare and magnificent, brushing the ceiling. Beside it was piled a mound of boxes – boxes which had always held the Christmas decorations and the Advent calendars for as long as I could remember. Outdated advertisements told of their long-ago contents of shoes or shirts in curling old-fashioned script.

'Aren't you going to decorate the tree this year, Kati?' asked Mom, her legs folded under her as she opened boxes and lifted out tangled tinsel strings.

'I was going to do it, Mom. Can't I do it just now, though?'

'No, you'll do it now! Your Ouma doesn't want these boxes here to trip over all day. And I'm going to help you. Just now, I have to help Ouma with the baking.'

My father, summoned from somewhere outdoors, sat meekly in a chair, a long string of lights across his lap. In his hand he held his ever-present silver penknife. He plugged the string of lights into the wall beside his chair and clicked his tongue when no lights glowed. Unplugging again, he methodically unscrewed and retightened each small light. The bulbs, in delicate olden-days style, formed glowing miniature Christmas trees, Father Christmases and wrapped gifts. At his feet, Michael settled to help him with his plodding detective work by plugging and unplugging, switching on and switching off.

Ouma was busy with some farm business, a pencil and a large hardbacked black notebook on her lap. Oupa, a book pressed close to his spectacled eyes, was reading in his armchair, his stick resting against its arm.

Gently dusted light flowed through the fly-screened sash window, embracing my smiling mother, who was now softly laying glass tree ornaments on her open palms. Beyond her, the light held Ouma in its golden grasp – the two of them gentled, haloed, and somehow drawn together.

No scowls appeared, no lips were tensely drawn between teeth, no eyes narrowed. For a moment I held a superstitious stillness, my indrawn breath a talisman against the reappearance of yesterday's ugliness. Then with a tentative return to movement, I realized that there were no reminders here of the awfulness, since no thought of it was welcome in the Christmas-scented room. It was gone – how silly to have believed it an omen.

In my anxiety and hope, Christmas – even the hint of its coming, it seemed to me – had sponged away the dread. The tangled joy of preparation had restored the farm. Smiles, passed from person to person in the tinkering room, seemed to draw each into a charmed forgetfulness.

Only Neil, in his unacknowledged guilt and resentful adolescent anger, remained outside the circle of tacit forgiveness. By his absence from the Christmas preparations that morning, he had not sanctioned the unspoken truce tentatively reached within the home.

'What's the time, Dad? Has the cricket started?' I remember Michael, his clear face eager. He asked the question which I knew at the time to be his own ceremonial talisman to ward off evil and draw the room's warmth tighter.

'Quite soon now, son. Go and fetch Ouma's wireless in the meantime.'

And I, aware of the magic in the liturgy of cricket commentary, remained silent, leaving my usual 'ughs', 'yechs' and 'awfuls' unspoken. The wireless, fetched by Michael, awaited its part in the ceremony, as I spun webs of gold and silver tinsel and charms of bold-coloured balls. Glittering birds silvered the branches in the hesitant sunlight and my father, his practical feet firmly planted, wove an enchanted scene with his strands of sparkling lights.

Last to be unwrapped was the fairy, my favourite, my sorceress. Her lumpy forehead curl had lost its gold, her green net skirt clung to her plump plastic stomach with clumps of gluey glitter. Her gauzy wings were bent into the kinks of age and years of being packed away.

Yet as she – my fairy portent of the joyousness of Christmas – rose to the tip of the tree, my last demon of family disquiet winged with her.

'Shouldn't we just put a star up there?'

My mother, balancing on a chair, was wrinkling her face at the fairy's plain plumpness as she stretched upward to attach her.

'She's really seen better days. She's so ugly now.'

And down the fairy plunged, her head aiming floorward in my mother's hand.

'No,' I shrilled, hysteria pitching my voice higher. 'You can't do that. She's important. I love her.'

And then everyone laughed, a warm drawing-together kind of laugh. It was aimed at me, but for once I didn't pout in hurt humiliation. I felt only relief, even if it was I who had to be the instrument of God's purpose in pulling the family together.

And as my fairy flew again, and was wired to the topmost branch in exalted familiarity, I felt that nothing could be wrong or ugly now that the preordained rites of Christmas had begun. We had moved into that magic, suspended time of preparing a feast for God. For Him to allow awfulness to intrude would be for Him to destroy what was His. It would be like my crushing my birthday cake the day before my party.

But we had to be careful. Everything had to be the same, and I knew it was my responsibility to hold it together, because only I realized how important it was to keep everything as it was before. And to be good. Good enough to avoid His wrath. He'd seen our Christmas before and He'd been pleased because, before, He'd blessed us constantly with unfailing family warmth. And, most important, He'd granted us this perfect place – the farm. The farm was all about Christmas – in some ways I thought it existed for Christmas. The perfect place, God's place, which He'd created for the celebration of His most important ceremony.

'It's time, it's time, isn't it, Dad?' Michael was darting and bouncing.

'*Ja*, turn on the wireless, Michael.' Daddy's chesty chuckle created a balm of togetherness with his younger son. Looking up suddenly, I saw that my elder brother had joined us, aloof in his armchair. I saw my mother take a breath to speak and lift her head in her drawn-up disapproving look. But my father, who rarely interfered, frowned suddenly. I bet he couldn't have put it into words, but at the time I instinctively understood what his frown communicated: let the cricket do its ceremonial job of calming and drawing together; let the cricket have its way.

Mom subsided then, her breath harmlessly expelled.

'Hy kom, en hy kom, en-hy-kom-en-hy-kom en hy BOUL.'

Ouma's radio had been tuned to the B programme, the Afrikaans station.

'Change to the A. Let's hear what Charles has to say,' said Oupa, smiling, his book laid flat, open to his place, on his chest.

'Sometimes I rather like listening to the commentary in Afrikaans,' Neil said, his sudden eagerness wrestling with the entrenched ennui on his face. And suddenly, as Ouma looked up from her notebook and smiled at him, I knew the cricket had already woven its spell, drawn him in, and healed the hurts of yesterday.

'I don't know about you,' he continued, glancing at Dad and Oupa, 'but I like the way they make it into quite a different game. It's not like the cricket we play, but it's ... I s'pose it's more exciting really ... like gladiators fighting it out.' He finished this with a little deprecating laugh. But no one laughed at him. They nodded and strained towards the room's new focal point.

Heads drew forward towards the centre of the room where the wireless sat on the coffee table. Daddy and Michael, who was frantically tuning the radio now, looked suddenly very similar, their expressions achingly eager and ... young. All the faces around the room, except for Ouma's, were gazing intensely at the set, as if they could see the green of the pitch through the dials.

And suddenly Charles Fortune's thick, treacly voice poured into the room.

'Oh what a glorious day this is at St George's Park, this day! The very heavens are crowding above the green and white arena below me. Thirty thousand people are here this morning to see the majestic Pollock wield the blade on this, the third day of the first Test against the Australians ...'

'Oh, get on with it, Chawles,' my father mocked. 'Tell us what's happening.'

'Tell us the score, Chawles,' said Neil, laughing now with my father. But their exhilaration was unmistakable, impossible to conceal behind the camouflage of their mockery of the commentator's plum-pudding speech.

'McKenzie is walking slowly back to the Duckpond end. He's taking his time. This is going to be a long, hot day. I remember just such an occasion back in fifty-three . . .'

It was working, I could see it working. And that's what mattered to me. Even my mother was smiling, cross-legged on the floor, gazing at the transistor as Michael leant forward and pounded her leg before grabbing her wrist in a ferocious 'Chinese bangle'.

'We're winning, Mom, our side's winning.'

'Denis Lindsay is settling in nicely with Graeme Pollock now.' Charles Fortune's voice wafted endlessly through the hot, airless room. All were motionless except Ouma, who – unaware in her unromantic pragmatism of the transfiguration around her – raised her wire-mesh fly swatter and rose to end the lazy buzzing of the lone fly which had found its way past the fly screens.

'You will remember that glaur-rious knock in the first innings . . .'

'Oh glaur-r-ious, Chawles,' mimicked Neil. My father threw back his head and bellowed with laughter. But they loved him. He was part of it, I could see that.

None the less, the bile began to rise in my throat. I couldn't help it. I understood that it was important, but the very sound of Charles Fortune's rich, fatty voice caused dry, heaving retches. For too many endless car journeys I'd sat squashed in the back seat, nauseous with a terrible carsickness, while Charles's voice had endlessly commentated on unending cricket matches. After a while, I simply associated the two.

His voice wafted after me as I slipped from the room. 'Dare we hope he can repeat it now as the Australians gather all their strengths to smash this partnership? Oh! – Good ball that! Was that a chance? I think not. The ball went to ground well before gully. No run. Lindsay stays without a blot on his second innings. And I'll hazard a guess, he'll offer few this quite lovely summer's day . . .'

Cool silence. Dropping into the enveloping leather armchair in Oupa's library, I could smell the slight mustiness of old paper and crumbling leather spines. I gulped twice to allow my nausea to subside and felt, as I always did here, the beginnings of a small twining thrill which crawled up my belly as I considered which shelf or cupboard to explore. Last Christmas holiday I had discovered *King Solomon's Mines*. It had seemed rather too grown-up a book for my seven-year-old self, but I had thought that next year, next year I would be old enough to read it. And I also knew that in the lowest cupboard, hidden at the back, Oupa kept a pile of 'Angelique' books, 'quite unsuitable' for the youngsters.

And so the morning crawled through the pages of Oupa's books as I lay full length on the worn old rug . . .

'Do you want company?' Oupa's voice startled me and I realized suddenly that I was starving. 'Lunch is nearly ready,' he said, dropping into his armchair and placing his stick by his side. 'Shall we read while we wait? I don't have to sit glued to the cricket like the others do. As long as I hear the score once in a while, I'm happy.'

My clumsy, escaping legs held firmly to my body

with two thin arms, I nestled on Oupa's frail lap while he drew out his favourite, placed always within easy reach of his chair.

'No (Oom Schalk Lourens said) you don't get flowers in the Groot Marico. It is not a bad District for mealies, and I once grew quite good onions in a small garden I made next to the dam. But what you can really call flowers are rare things here. Perhaps it's the heat. Or the drought . . .'

And then there were mealies for lunch, hot mealies eaten off the cob, rubbed first with a lump of farm butter held between the fingers.

And after lunch – on that long, lethargic farm day – I think we baked. I can remember the baking, and I'm sure it must have been that day.

The kitchen was hot, with the trapped heat of the afternoon and the coal stove. Ouma stood, damp now, unhesitatingly measuring ingredients into the palm of her hand. She worked fast and practically.

On a further counter, near the stove, Dora also worked, silently rolling out the marzipan – part of the ritual, but not quite part of the sisterhood around the scrubbed centre table.

'Why don't you use a recipe like Mom does?' I asked Ouma, leaning my chin on my upturned hands and my elbows on the table. Mom was perched on a kitchen chair, watching.

'There is no recipe, that's why. This is the way my mother taught me, and one day your mother . . .' This with a sharp, but amused glance at Mom, 'will teach you the Christmas cake recipe.'

'But then you must teach me, Ma,' my mom said, gazing earnestly at Ouma. 'You must measure out the ingredients so I can understand the amounts. You can't expect me to learn how much to put in by the feel of it.'

'*Ag, my kind*, you must *maar* watch. You should have been watching and learning since you were a little thing. But you were never interested in your own traditions or the old ways of your *volk*. You were a citified child from early on.'

I glanced sharply up at my mother, and caught Ouma's quick, floury caress of her cheek – more like a small cuff really – and they smiled at each other. Everything was still OK, but I had to be vigilant. I had to take care of them.

I heard the *skree-bang* of the door and the clicking chatter of two of the boys' wives, as they began to pluck a chicken on the new, metal-rimmed table in the scullery.

'Tea, Dora!' Ouma's peremptory request propelled Dora, in her slow side-to-side waddle, over to the coal stove, where a pot of Rooibos (bush tea my mother called it, with a shudder) boiled perennially. She poured for me and Ouma. Before she could reach for another cup, Ouma, who was stretching her back, brushed a damp curl from her forehead and said: 'Not for Miesies Elaine, Dora. She doesn't drink it. She's too *Engels* for our tea.'

Dora laughed with her then, in great heaving quivers, as Ouma drew her into the joke. My mother smiled without showing her teeth, her eyes examining the painted nails in her lap.

Later, as the cool crept over the land, I walked beyond the sweeping lawn to watch the heavy shadows darkening the eastern side of each glistening rock, bush and hillock.

I walked in a wide sweep, through the silent fragrance of the late afternoon flower beds, and around in a circle to the back of the house.

As I turned towards the house I caught, on the fringe of my peripheral vision, a flash of white. It was gone by the time I turned. But I knew it was Snowball's father, I just knew it. At the end of this exactly perfect farm day, it was only fitting.

I drifted towards the courtyard, wandering around the back of the boys' room. I was dawdling now, unwilling to go inside to the mundane 'getting ready for bed' tasks. I leant against the wall of the room, empty of boys at this time of the evening, and wrote in the dirt with my toe.

Looking up, I saw a large metal pail just in front of me. Solitary behind the room – most of the other buckets, forks, spades and things were cleared away by this time – it was covered by a grubby mutton cloth.

Curious, I approached it and lifted the end of the cloth. At first I didn't recognize them, and I brought my head nearer to see more clearly.

Their plump fluff was draggled now over skinny pink bodies. There were three in there. Lifeless kittens. I couldn't see much of two of them, just their ears and heads below the water. But the topmost one was white, almost pure white, with a yellowish patch on its shoulder.

Their wild, budding lives smothered in a bucket of water. They were dead because, seeing only the kittens' silky fur, I had tried to coddle an untamed spirit. They were dead, because of me.

1966 . . . Fourteen days to Christmas

I slipped out early, alone and insubstantial as a ghost, to the dark of the plucking barn.

There, among the three barrels of differently graded feathers, I knew I could melt silently into the ethereal comfort of that billowy world. I headed, as I always did, for the drum of the softest down. That morning particularly, I yearned for its muffled balm.

Squeezing my eyes closed, I blindly gripped the metal edge of the drum and stretched one tentative hand to barely brush the wispy down. Like the gentlest summer breeze, it whispered against my palm.

I sank my arms into the faint mass, as substanceless as air. They melted up to my disappearing shoulders in the white cumulus. As I turned my cheek towards its touch, my face was pillowed by its drowsy drift.

Suddenly, furry in its softness, it transformed before my darkened eyes into three rolling kittens. In horror I winced away from the evocative fluff and grabbed the biting edge of metal. I struggled to hold my eyes closed, fearing to see a metal bucket filled with water.

Beyond my control, my eyes burst open and the bucket was gone. A half-drum of down, plucked from the secret undersides of dozens of chickens, stood on the packed-earth floor of a barn lit only by the dim light washed through the open door.

As sounds returned I heard deep, roiling laughter. I jerked my head up and saw the boys, who had filled the barn with their presence and surrounded me with their tangible substance of life.

There were six of them I think. In their black gum-boots, they were solid and full of warm, pulsing flesh. Their faces, turned from the door's pale light, were hard to discern except for the wide whiteness of their teeth. They were filled with unfettered mirth, but I knew, in the humanity that poured warmth into my numbed limbs, there was no mockery in their laughter. Joyful and compassionate in its hearty reach, it had taken me into its circle.

I smiled unwillingly and wished to bury myself in this sympathy, this affection. I flung myself at William, whose features had formed themselves in the gloom.

'Chine!' Still shuddering with laughter, he caught and balanced me on one strong arm. I could smell woodsmoke and damp overalls and the coffee which had just been brewed in the tin can on the boys' room fire. Jigging me gently on his arm, he said: 'You go always in those little feathers. Those feathers are no good. You want feathers to take, I give you big feathers.'

Bending slightly to the right, he dipped his hand into a second barrel and handed me two straight white quill feathers. The boys all laughed again, happily, and one slapped his leg with a resounding clap on his high rubber boot.

'You come to the cows, Missie. Is no good you sitting all alone here in dark. You come help with milking?'

I rubbed my cheek against rough blue canvas. 'Mm,' I said.

I watched William's large boots squelch the damp mud into patterns as we strode to the milking shed. Pale sun glistened on tiny drops of rain.

'It's a monkey's wedding, William,' I said, rousing myself from my symbiotic absorption of his body's substance. 'That's lucky, you know. It's raining luck on the farm.'

'*Chin*,' he said, a rough chuckle in his throat.

The milking shed was dry, warmed by large furry flanks and gentle eyes. 'Hello, Klara,' I greeted the black and white cow waiting to be milked. Warming my arms and face against her shifting shoulder, I reached a hand to caress her snuffling nose.

'Do you think cows remember people?' I asked William.

'*Ja*, Missie, she know people. She know you. See, she greet you in she's cow way.'

I squatted flat-footed, as William did, beside her breathing belly and watched him squeeze long streams of hot milk into a metal pail. I didn't want to ask about that other metal pail. I didn't want to know if those gentle, pink-palmed hands had held the struggling kittens under the suffocating water. No one knew I had seen it yesterday. And I still couldn't frame the words to talk about it.

'You want to try?' Rubbing cream on my palms and fingers, his large hands guided mine and squeezed, tugging my hands downward on the slippery teat. We laughed and I glanced triumphantly up into his smile-wrinkled face.

'You make milk from her, see? Now you can taste.'

Skimming a tin mug over the foaming surface, he gave me it to gulp the warm, bubbling milk. Rubbing a bare arm across my milky moustache, I said: 'Thanks, William. I think I'll go now. I want to see if the new chicks are here yet.'

'New chicks no come yet. They come any day now. Missie must wait.'

The droplets had stopped, leaving a rain-washed sun to dry the newly cleansed farm. Nothing stirred in the jewelled bush as my bare feet slapped through clear puddles. Joining the rutted farm road, my toes squeezed deep brown mud between them in its water-formed depressions.

Spiky clumps of grass held tiny mirrored spots. Passing beneath two leafy pepper trees, I looked up to see a perfect spider web caught between two reaching branches. Each undamaged strand was highlighted in its perfection by sun-sparkled droplets. On the side sat its motionless yellow and black spider – I never did know what they were called, those spiders that were everywhere, that trippled on your face if you walked unwarily into a bush-spun web.

I squelched my bare feet back towards the farmhouse and the chickens. I knew the baby chicks had not yet arrived, but I had in mind to visit the 'teenager' chickens.

Through my farmyard inspection, I think I was reassuring myself that the farm was still there, still together, and that all the things I loved were in their place. In the loamy, cleansed smell of the soil, I wanted to know that all death and ugliness had been washed from every part of my farm and left it refreshed, scattered with the luck of the monkey's wedding. As omens went, the morning was doing well for me. Two crows had kraaked in the gum tree behind the house as I had made my way to the feather barn this morning. From my magical, portent-filled discussions with Dora on many mornings spent squatting in the kitchen courtyard, I knew that sight of a single crow was ominous. Two crows together were another matter, a sign of good things to come, of happiness returned. The farm was the same, and with each reassuring familiarity, my confidence returned to me in joyous floods.

Standing on the low, whitewashed wall of the chicken *hok*, I clung to the thick bars which sprang from the wall and reached up to the overhanging roof. They made me laugh, those frenetic, scrawny-necked chickens. Even in the heat of midday, they never had the drowsy look of full-grown hens. Squawking and flapping their half-grown wings, they rushed frantically from side to side, following each other in waves of movement.

I dawdled there for a while, watching their untidily feathered bodies sweep to and fro. Desultorily, I threw a few dry mealie pits into the cage, amused by the flurry of life behind the bars. I always liked to get to know these chickens – I could tell a few of them apart by their markings and feathers. I watched as a black-speckled teenager took the lead again and again in the surges of movement around the cage. And my heart reached out to the small pure-white, who was trampled and squashed at every turn.

Warmed and entertained, I turned from the chickens and ran out of the luck-sprinkled yard. Through the orchard, my feet slipped and squished in the fallen fruit under the dripping overhang of the trees. The overripe smell was sharp in the freshly washed morning.

As I broke through the last of the fruit trees the dogs joined me, roistering in panting bounds. In twin stretched leaps, they pulled ahead of me only to stop in tandem, waiting for me to catch up. We passed the swimming place. Ahead of me, Kati's ears flopped about her face as she lowered her head and shoulders to her straightened front legs in playful, puppy attitude. I ran forward to see what had attracted her and saw both dogs bounding in floppy leaps around a great, hunched bullfrog. The bullfrog was puffed in indignant belligerence.

I shushed at the dogs' hysterical barks, laughing at their silliness, and pushed them both away, leaning my weight against their large flanks.

'You can't bite it, your mouth will froth,' I said, gasping from running and laughter. I ran from them, calling: 'Come, Kati, come, Mikey,' in an animated staccato. Lifting wrinkled, eager faces, they were fooled for the moment into thinking something far more exciting was just ahead.

They raced after me and stopped in a joint skidding motion in front of my leaping legs. Sniffing the air, they half turned back towards the frog. But by then it had disappeared to safety through the swimming-pool fence. Mikey scrambled back to sniff madly at the fence before giving up and running in high puppy bounds back to Kati and me.

Walking now, I could see as far as the bank of prickly pears which lined the tumbledown fence on the hill just beyond the boys' houses. I was making for the valley between the farm's two smooth hillocks – the Forest. A place of mystery, of silence, of beauty, of adventure. A place to imagine magic, to play spy games, to climb monkey ropes, or just to moon in the dappled shade.

I shaded my eyes with my right hand, held by a glint of movement on the hill. Her willowy, upright walk poised, one of the wives appeared from the huts. The sun was caught once on the metal bath she balanced on her head, her hand stretched up to steady it. I watched as she crossed to the thick bank of prickly pears, and saw her swing the bath to the ground.

I changed direction then. I could go to the Forest later. Suddenly, above everything, I wanted to feel a prickly pear's pipped green juice on my chin. My favourite of all fruits, this reminder of the farm, this bringer of Christmas, held summer in its flesh.

The dogs followed me up the gentle slope, but ran ahead to bound and bark at the woman, who stopped and backed against the fence. Yelling at them, I slapped at their rumps.

'Naughty dogs. Stop that. Don't you dare bark at her. It's OK,' I told her. 'They're just being naughty. They'd never bite anyone.'

The woman stood unspeaking, her eyes on the dogs. Pushing and biting at each other's ears, Kati and Mikey tumbled down the hill then, racing and rolling with each other. Only then did she step forward and, still without a word, spread sacks on the dampened dust.

I squatted, watching her movements. In her blanketed grace she confidently gripped the thorned fruit between its prickled clusters and deftly plucked it from the cactus. Each was dropped, rolling on to the spread sacking. Lifting her small metal knife from the sacks, I let my other hand hover and choose one of the fruits. As I'd so often seen adults do, I stretched my palm to hold it between thumb and forefinger, top to bottom. I managed the grip, but my hand was not quite large enough to clear the barbed skin.

I started and dropped the fruit as I felt my palm brush a thorny cluster. Rubbing a finger over the grubby palm, I could feel the bristle already embedded. I brought my sore palm to my mouth, nibbling and biting to staunch the invisible irritation.

Looking up, I saw the woman's eyes, large under her red scarf, watching me. Nimbly, she squatted beside me, her long feet dry and calloused. She smelt of fires and eucalyptus, which I'd seen the women use as a remedy and preventive measure against colds. She had very long fingers, rough and spindly. Spider-like, her hands spread and covered the fruit with the sacking, rubbing and chafing the worst of the prickly hairs from each blanketed shape. Unwrapping, she held one as I had tried to and, with three quick slashes of her knife, split the skin top to bottom in three places. Popping the small green egg-shape from the skin, she gestured it towards me, and smiled for the first time.

Slippery and cool, it touched my hand, and I no longer cared about the elusive pricking in my palm. I bit into the many-pipped flesh, sucking at its freshness. It had the sweetness of summer sunlight.

I sat there for some time savouring the taste of the farm. As the sun warmed the grass, it awoke the hay-like smells in the spiky clusters and the sharp scent of *khabikos*. The insects began their high, keening accompaniment to the day, while in the low, spreading thorn tree overhead, the Christmas beetles sang their *zee-ee* chorus. Birds signalled the end of the rain. My simple favourite, joining in then on that warm, cleansed morning, was the plain grey dove, whose *cor-cor cor-cor* tucked me into the enveloping safety of the farm.

Eventually the woman completed her picking and rubbing and, uncoiling her long legs, balanced the nearly full bath on her head. Still without a word, she started down the hill, weaving around the stalked aloes. Lithe and light on her feet, she walked steadily, ignoring the distraction of two white butterflies which danced and circled just before her eyes.

The lush, moist, life-giving centre of the farm, the Forest was nestled between the two rounded mounds which sheltered the farmhouse. The cleft was scented by the dark, dusky smell of fallen vegetation, thick and fetid underfoot.

I wandered on to the dim, covered pathway, narrow in the entangled growth, and heard the hoarse croak of the Knysna lourie. So near it sounded, but impossible to see its rich, shy beauty in the impenetrable bush.

The sun watered through, greenish and murky. My feet made a *shush-shush* in the leaves, which lay like a heavy brown snowfall, thick and damp. They were slightly threatening to my bare feet, which curled at the thought of snakes underfoot. Above, old man's beard hung limp and musky, swaying in the slightest breeze. Wild figs dominated the cramped acacias. The fleshy grey arms of euphorbias rose above thick bushes, whose stems were lank and twisted in suffocating profusion.

The path twined through the wall of vegetation and I followed it, clambering over the trees bent across the walkway. Cluttering the narrow area were coiled monkey ropes. Sweeping downward they came, through the muted sunlight and the sound of the birds.

I wandered as far as the stream, seeping its gentle tears down the sides of the valley. Blackened stones crossed the path here, wet and moss-encrusted. They must have been set there a generation before, I thought, to hold human feet above the chill stream. Large boulders hulked here, flat and inviting beside the watery lilt. It was an enclosed world with its gentle rustlings, birdcalls and insect songs. If I concentrated hard, I thought I could just hear the grate of the generator, but nothing else of the farm.

As I rounded the path's tight twist to approach the boulders I saw Neil, mooning there in pensive posture. He was hunched on the largest boulder, his arms folded around his legs. A cigarette was dangling from his fingers. He glanced up sharply as I approached, but didn't smile.

'You didn't see me here, OK?' He made no attempt to stub out the cigarette and looked down again, his eyes glazed, at the stream as he flicked ash on the path.

'OK,' I said and crept on to a smaller boulder at his feet. The silence wasn't comfortable – for me anyway. I was in awe of my handsome, golden brother. I wanted him to like me, with a yearning that made me obsequious. But I had no communication bridge for the gulf between our ages. He was largely unaware of me, while I always wanted to speak to him but never knew what to say.

We sat like that long enough for my bottom to grow numb from the seeping damp of the stone. I was no longer aware of the forest, its sounds or its smells. My concentration was centred on the lanky boy-man, curling smoke past his screwed-up eyes.

'Have you seen the new people's farm yet?' His voice startled me when it came.

'No, I don't want . . . I didn't know what it would look like. It'll be different.'

'Of course you don't know what it'll look like if you haven't seen it, idiot.'

He looked at me, his face twisted in habitual disdain. 'Come, fool. I want to see how they've wrecked the place. You can come with me if you like.'

He swung his blue-jeaned legs over the boulder and tramped his *stompie* into the path. Then he strode off over the twisting path without waiting to see if I would come. He was so sure that I would scramble to follow him, as I did, running in little spurts to keep just behind his unheeding figure.

Outside the forest canopy, the midday sun burnt the colour from the sky and created shimmers in the air before us. Suddenly he slowed his stride and dropped back to speak to me.

'Do you know anything about the new people?' he asked me.

'Not really. I heard William's son say he was cruel, that he doesn't treat his boys nicely. But Ouma said they were lucky to get work.'

'Hmph,' he said, reining in his stride to walk beside me.

The grass was clumped. Thorn trees were sparser; stunted, bent and dwarfish. We had reached the rim of the Zuurveld, what used to be the wild outer reaches of our farm. Even slightly dampened by that morning's rain, the landscape here was a dusty tan, a far-reaching, tree-scattered loneliness.

Winding its way across this veld was a new fence.

And beyond it – a wasteland.

Cleared of its sparse trees, the land was bare and grey in the heat of the day. Even the whispering old gum trees had been hacked down and in the middle of nothing, in the centre of a dusty vacancy, sat a house. Low and flat, it squatted with little pretension and no attempt at softening embellishments.

'But it's so ugly,' I burst out, shocked by the bare aridity and the plainness of the house. It was a corridor of windows, each the same as the last, at the end of which was a larger picture window, providing a flat brown view from what must be the lounge.

'*Ja*, well, the guy's cut all the corners, it looks like.'

'But look, Neil, it doesn't even have a stoep.'

'Never mind a stoep. There's no drainpipes, or even a doorstep.'

Without speaking, we followed the winding fence past drowsy groups of sheep. Picking up a small stick, I ran it along the wire fence, producing a *ting ting* accompaniment to our walk.

Ahead of us, on the other side of the fence, we could see a small cluster of square-built block buildings. And there, two shushing old gum trees had survived. This group, of what looked from our farm like a barn or shed and perhaps a dairy, had some sort of simple charm that the farmhouse lacked. Perhaps it was because of the shifting shadows of the trees.

We gaped – I through the fence, Neil leaning on the top – trying to catch a glimpse of life beyond this new great divide. A small *piccanin* was playing in the churned mud beside a small enclosure, similar to our pigsty.

'I s'pose that's where they keep their pigs?' I asked.

'Must be. Can't you smell them?'

The small boy had scabbed knees and a torn khaki shirt. He seemed to be playing with two rounded stones. I waited for him to look up, then smiled and waved.

'*Molo*,' I called.

The child stood, wiping his forearm across his snot-dried face, before turning and running. He ran in a wide circle around the buildings and disappeared to the back of them. We waited in silence to see if anything else would happen.

'Joh-an-nes!' The voice was pitched high, with an imperious upward tone at the end of the name.

From the pigsty a figure rose, wearing a tattered T-shirt and khaki shorts. He ran in a curious jogging trot towards what I had supposed to be the dairy.

'*Ja, Ou* Miesies,' he said. He was barefoot. I was trying to figure out what it was that was different about him, from our boys that is.

'The stingy Dutchmen can't even buy their boys decent overalls,' muttered Neil, answering my unspoken question. He wasn't speaking to me though, I think he was explaining to himself his own feeling of strangeness.

The woman emerged then, holding a bucket. Her hair was a rigid grey, set in a firm hairnet close to her head. She was tall, and she held herself stiffly upright, her neck a taut line to her proudly pursed mouth.

'Have you ever seen anyone walk so straight?' I whispered, tugging on Neil's belt loop so that he would remember his small companion. I wanted to feel part of his adult observations of the place, to feel a solidarity of purpose and superiority with him. 'If she was at my

127

school, she'd earn a white girdle after about two seconds flat.'

I was referring to my school's award for deportment. Neil smiled at that, filling me with happiness at the thought that I'd amused him. White girdles were a family joke. My mother warned constantly that I would never earn one unless I could learn not to hunch my shoulders and gaze at the ground watching for cracks, spaces and omens.

The elderly woman noticed us then, her head tilted slightly to one side as her eyes frisked us. With an imperious uptilt, her head gave us to believe we were ignored, beneath her interest. And to underline her haughty point, she turned slightly away from us.

Standing on a slight rise, she spoke quietly to the figure hunched below her. Her mouth hardly moved as she spoke into the air above his head. I couldn't easily hear what she said, and her Afrikaans was a bit fast for me anyway. But I watched him nodding. With his back facing us, his nod tensed his neck and shoulders into an exaggeratedly subservient bob.

'Shit, but she's an old cow,' exclaimed Neil, gazing at her with venom and shaking his head.

'You're telling me,' I replied, smothering a giggle with my hand. I was pleased to be included in so grown-up a comment.

As the boy turned and resumed his jogging trot, I saw with a sudden shock that he was Albert's son, the one who was supposed to have been beaten. I remembered him from Christmases past, when he'd been younger and we'd taken the traditional photographs of us standing with all the farm's children.

What was it about his desolation, his bleak features,

that made me think afterwards that he'd had a doomed look about him? But that's nonsense of course. I couldn't even have considered the concept at eight. The very idea had never entered my world. But I remember feeling a desperation to reach him. I wanted very badly to communicate with him. The elderly woman had glided slowly back into the shed, her knees hardly bending.

'Hello,' I shouted. '*Molo*, Johannes. Don't you remember us?' I was curling my fingers into the diamond spaces in the fence, pulling myself higher and pressing my mouth through one of the holes. Johannes turned once, his trot arrested briefly. As his dark eyes aimed at us, I felt a piercing cold, a force of hatred so strong that I thought suddenly I might vomit.

That's how I recall it, anyway. I know it sounds a bit much when I talk about it now. But remember, I was a suggestible child, sensitive to atmospheres and magic – evil and good.

'Come on, let's walk back past the house once to see if we can see anything else. I don't think he remembers us. It doesn't matter.'

Neil's casual arm on my shoulder seemed a comforting, protective gesture. I didn't want to move in case he thought I was shrugging it off. I wanted to hold it there to ward off the hatred that I felt was prying at me, peeking into my vulnerable being to get at me. I wonder if Neil felt anything – he never said, and I never asked.

As we wandered slowly back along the sad fence, we both saw the Baas that we'd heard about. He was bending over a sheep not far from our perimeter. He was wearing gumboots, belted khaki shorts and a shirt.

Large-bellied, he was dark and, I suppose, handsome in a big-boned way. He had piercing blue eyes under startling brows, but his hair was shorn to bristles, back and sides. On his forehead it flopped forward in what we derided as a 'Dutchman *kuif*'.

'*Middag*.' His voice was rough, a bear growl.

'*Middag, Meneer*,' I replied. Neil drooped his eyes in his look of veiled animosity and mumbled: 'Howzit'. I think he wanted to proclaim his distance from this man by an inappropriate greeting – but without the outright rudeness of ignoring him.

'Bloody rabid rockspider,' he muttered as we moved from the fence. As if to impress upon himself and me the violence of his feelings, he spat suddenly on to the dust. 'You can see the man's nothing but a hairy rope?'

'What do you mean, "rope"?' I asked.

'Thick, hairy and twisted,' he said. 'You can see what kind of people they are just by looking at them. They're not like us. They're cruel and they treat their Africans badly.'

Pausing to take a breath, he stopped walking and faced me. 'They're the kind that keep apartheid in this country. They vote Nat just 'cause their fathers and grandfathers did and they've got no brains to think that the government's wrong.'

I nodded, wondering if it wasn't perhaps lunchtime. Seeing the direction of my gaze, Neil glanced at his watch.

We were late for lunch, and sprinted back in the direction of the farmhouse. Neil was holding one of my arms and pulling me along with such force that in places I left my feet and soared above the ground, laughing again. I don't remember seeing William's son ahead of us, I must have been concentrating on the flying ground and sky. But suddenly Neil stopped and I jerked to my feet.

'Howzit, John. How's your school going?'

'I've left,' he said abruptly without looking at us. His eyes followed his worn shoe which was tracing a pattern in the dirt.

'But shit, man, why? You'd got as far as Standard Six. Why stop now? You had so many plans.'

'*Ag*, what's the point anyway?' he said, looking up suddenly at Neil, his eyes two flaming points. 'What's the point of going on with Bantu Education? All it's teaching me is to be a boy. And all I can ever be is a boy. It's different for you. Life must be good for the *klein* Missie and Ma-aster.' His mouth was a sneer.

'*Ag*, man, don't be like that.' Neil's face was a mix of boyish hurt and eager concern.

William's son, striding from us again, stopped to throw over his shoulder: 'Anyway, I have to get work now. The *ou Miesies* says I have to get work from that hard Baas next door.' He paused and, his voice filled with bitterness, finished: 'He's full of apartheid, that one.'

Neil didn't reply as John began to trot across the veld, back towards the warm safety of our farmhouse and the happy boys' room.

Neil sighed, walking slowly now, his face scrunched into a tight frown. My stomach had tightened and I felt the spectre of the ugliness approaching again, darkening the threatening day. And this time it wasn't on the next farm.

'I suppose it's hard for him,' I said suddenly, wanting to take away the anger, to put things in perspective for myself. I wanted the farm back in its place.

'But he's lucky,' I continued. 'Not many Africans go to school for so long. And he shouldn't be so angry at Ouma. It wasn't her fault they got too old to run the whole farm. It's not her fault the man next door's a rope. He shouldn't blame her if he has to get work. It's not fair.'

He looked at me for a minute. I wasn't sure what I could read in his expression. His face was a churning mix of quizzical, angry and slightly amused.

'Maybe it's all our faults,' he said roughly, 'for letting things happen. Don't you know that's what the Germans said in the war, that it wasn't their fault and it wasn't fair to blame them? But you know what? They were all guilty, for letting things happen. It's the same here. We're to blame, me and you.'

1989 . . . 29th October

'Long live the tried and tested leaders of the ANC! Long live!'

'Lo-ong le-eve,' roars the massed crowd, thousands upon thousands of them.

I cannot actually believe that I have allowed myself to be drawn into this pandemonium of hysterical hope. I won't look at Joe because I can feel his eyes again, anxiously checking my reaction. I suppose he feels he should keep an eye on me in case my twisted sense of humour overpowers me and I mortify him for ever by yelling something outrageous like: 'Long le-eve the SAP of South Africa! Long le-eve.' That would go down like an Aids victim in a massage parlour. Or perhaps he thinks I'll find this rich and overpowering diet of faith and glory too much for my stomach and that I'll vomit all over the stand.

The force of the heat is pounding down directly over my head. Funny, everyone thought it was going to rain. Ads in the papers yesterday said: 'The Welcome the Leaders rally will go ahead whatever the weather. Bring umbrellas.'

This morning, I dawdled and procrastinated as much as I could. The sun was still somewhat watery when I got up – late – and headed for my wallowing sojourn in the bath. I spent a long time in there, floating naked in my watery womb. And I spent a long time preparing my shell – long drawstring skirt, big T-shirt, glasses, bun to hold the vulnerable wisps of hair in check.

'Come on, Kate.' I heard his voice outside the bathroom door. 'I know what you're doing. Please don't try and hold us up any more. Please, Kate!' His voice broke slightly on my name and he cleared his throat.

'We're going to go, no matter what. All you're going to do is make us miss the most exciting part.'

'What?' I yelled back, as I tucked curling tendrils into clips. 'You expect it to start on time! Come on, Joe, that's taking this optimism thing too far.'

He waited then. I suppose he weighed the odds and decided not to risk provoking me any more. And so we reached Soccer City stadium by noon, just when the 'cultural programme' was meant to give way to the political rally proper. But even from the car park I could hear that the cultural events were still in full swing.

The sun was soaring down on the gravel. Swirls and eddies of dust rose above head height as the crawling, bumper-to-bumper queue reached the parking area. Buses, I'd never seen so many buses in one place, hundreds upon hundreds of buses lined up in neat rows, disgorging thousands upon thousands of people.

We began queueing almost from our car – truly, I could not believe we'd done this to ourselves voluntarily – shuffling along the high link fence to enter the stadium. Film crews and photographers strutted on the inside of the fence, greeting each other and passing clever comments. Oh, they were trying so hard to keep those tough, seen-it-all expressions in place. But the eager excitement kept flaring up on new blasé faces as quickly as it was being damped down on others.

ANC marshals controlled the gate and reduced the queue to a shuffle as they arbitrarily pointed people to places in the stands.

'Very democratic, isn't it?' I muttered as we finally reached the narrow gateway and were wordlessly pointed to the topmost, furthest stand from the platform which stood at the other side of the field.

'Shush, Kate. Stop whingeing. There's such good feeling on the ground here. Don't spoil it.'

'Oh no, it's not that. I don't really care to be nearer all those emotion-struck faces that I'm sure will preach at us from the platform. In fact, perhaps the marshal knew that – he read my mind. Otherwise why would he send the people just in front of us to the main stand near the platform, and us to the furthest, highest possible stand? Ah, well, ours not to reason why . . .'

Warmth engulfed us as we reached the tip of the topmost stand. For one awful moment I thought the smiling ANC-capped marshal at the top of the stairs would embrace us. But he swerved aside at the last moment. I think he saw my face. He and Joe gripped each other's shoulders instead. I can't bear touching at the best of times, but in all this mushy sentimentality it would just be too much.

'Welcome, Comrades!' Two black women – one plump and buxom-breasted, the other gaunt – bobbed down the stand to grip our hands. There was a gushing quality, I thought, to their display of joy at our lily-white presence. I was embarrassed that they were so thrilled to have us, and then I was embarrassed all over again at Joe's effusive gratitude at being greeted so fervently.

'Viva the ANC! Viva!' The voice booms from vast loudspeakers.

'Viva!' roars the mighty-voiced crowd. The litany moves the mass to fling itself upright in religious ecstasy, its many fists flung skyward in an emotion-charged salute.

I have to admit it's impressive, this passionate power. Such strength in the ritual of the slogan, in the fervour of the congregation's response.

Smiles whirl from person to person. Oh God, Joe's wallowing in it. He almost has tears in his eyes. I hunch on to my seat, tearing at my nails, while he shakes all the waving hands behind us with his carefully prac- tised two-handed grip and sliding, three-staged shake.

'Hello, Comrade; Yes, thank you, Comrade; After- noon, Com; Hello, Com, nice to see you here too . . .'

A voice intones from the dais. 'A 'liberation' poet, I think he was called. He has just been introduced, but I wasn't listening.

> 'Welcome the leaders
> The leaders of the people
> Welcome the leaders
> They will free the people
> Welcome the leaders
> Of our land.
> Africa
> Our land.
> The people shall govern
> This land.'

I sigh. The sun is drilling into my skull. Around me I can hear the hum of messianic devotion. Emotion pours its intensity over the sweating crowd. Joe's eyes are on me again. I'm beginning to feel claustrophobic in the heated enclosure of his glances.

I turn on him fiercely, but he's moved his head again, watching the crowd and the faraway specks on the platform, wonderment in his glowing eyes and opened mouth. Momentarily, the eagerness in his face has trounced anxiety, but anxiety again gains the upper hand in his next quick, jabbing glances at me.

I shift on the hard stand, moving my legs from one side to the other, in futile avoidance of the harsh blows of the hammering sun. There's no escape here. People are still pouring on to the stand. I suppose if I get up and wander off I'll lose my seat to someone and, horror of horrors, Joe'll be forced to fight some virtuous comrade for my place and he'll never forgive me.

'I don't suppose generations of students will find it necessary to analyse the deeper meanings in the poetry of this Alfred Tennyson of the liberation movement,' I mumble, but quietly, so that no one can overhear and disapprove of us.

'But he's historically important.' Joe is in his earnest, pedantic mode. 'He's the "people's poet", that's why he's important. But listen to his delivery – it's quite amazing. He has such a hypnotic quality.'

'Hypnotic is right,' I mumble. 'It's an incantation to transform the crowd into the living dead.'

'What was that, Kate?'

'Oh, nothing, Joe. Nothing at all.'

He burns the twisted smile from my face with the fervent light in his eyes. But then, suddenly, he smiles.

'I don't care how you resist it, Kate. You're here, that's all that matters. It'll get to you, I know it will. Not even a block of wood could remain unmoved through this kind of experience. This is the most important event of our times, Kate. Do you know that? Doesn't it make you feel just a little awed? That we're part of it? It must be three or four decades since the ANC openly held a rally in this country.'

'Yes, I feel immensely awed that I'm actually sitting here, the sun burning a hole in my head, while I listen to sweaty poems and heated slogans.'

Joe continues smiling beatifically, infuriating me into flinging my surly frown towards the miles and miles of dusty cars beyond the stadium.

I suddenly remember the giant ants we used to get in the Eastern Cape and how we would trap them beneath a magnifying glass until they began to smoke and cook in the concentrated glare of the sun. I know how they used to feel, those ants. I wonder who is waiting for me to bake before eating me.

There are dancers on the stage now, but they are too far away to see. How long overdue is this rally going to be, for God's sake? It's nearly an hour late already. People are streaming in and out now, bringing peanuts and ice-cream, sharing their goodies with a glowing neighbourliness.

Our smiling marshal appears below the seats, clutching an armful of posters and Freedom Charter pamphlets. Snaking arms cluster in the air, reaching for the prizes he tantalizingly passes to whoever catches his eye. Joe, smiling to show that he thinks this is all great fun and that he isn't in deadly earnest – well, not altogether – makes a quick grab at a poster on its path over his head. But he laughs good-naturedly as it is snatched from his tentative grasp.

'More, more,' yells the crowd. The marshal laughs.
'I'll bring more later.'

Hundreds of flags flash red in the sunlight, or wave green, gold and black in the stands. The two – the red of the South African Communist Party and multicoloured ANC banner – share centre-stage glory behind the distant platform.

'I'm too hot, Joe,' I say suddenly. Perhaps I can enlist his sympathy. 'I think I'll go down behind the stands and investigate all the little kiosks down there.'

Oh, what the hell, I can't sustain the sympathy-seeking for long.

'I want to take a closer look at all those busy workers, filled with entrepreneurial spirit, running the people's businesses. Forward! The people shall trade. Let the people be liberated to employ assistants. Free enterprise for the people.'

I'm running off at the mouth again. But he'd think I had died and become part of the angelic host if I didn't jeer just a little bit.

'OK, I'll come with you,' he says with a quick smile, surprising me. 'It's part of why I wanted us to be here.' He answers the question in my eyes. 'I want to experience it with you. I want to watch you see this rally – all its parts and all its people.'

People are streaming on and off the stands, chatting, buying, laughing, holding hands, linking fingers. I feel more isolated in my protective insulation than I ever have before. That's why I hate hope. I distrust it, and the weapon it gives the great cosmic joke-maker. But it also makes me feel like an empty orange, sucked dry through a hidden seep-hole, alone in a full pocket of juicy fruit.

Slipping, sour and sucked, down the stairs behind the stands alongside Joe, I glance at the fronts of the people I pass, avoiding their eyes, and discover that I can read the entire history of the struggle off their T-shirts. *The People Shall Govern*, says a woman's large breasts, while a man's narrow chest holds the entire policy set out in the Freedom Charter. I pass two worn and scruffy *Organize and Mobilize* chests and, at the bottom of the stair, a *One Country, One Federation* steps aside to let us pass. Large numbers of *Welcome the Leaders* mingle with chains breaking on *Release the Leaders* and *Release Mandela*.

'We're living in the age of catchphrase politics, it seems to me. If policy can't be expressed on a T-shirt, it doesn't exist.'

'Well, it's a good way to make people aware, don't you think? Clever, very clever,' he says, his voice trailing away as he stops before a pair of upturned boxes to finger and unfold piles of T-shirts containing variations on the *Welcome the Leaders* theme. Alongside are further piles of Rasta shirts.

The Rastafarian selling the shirts leans his whole body into a diagonal line against a pole. His dreadlocks are tucked in a thick pad into his crocheted red, green and yellow beret.

'How many you want?'

I suppose this is what's known as direct sales. You can't get more direct than that.

'Ah c'mon, Joe, you're not seriously considering joining the ranks of the self-conscious nouveau ANC T-shirt-wearers in the northern suburbs?'

'Just the one,' he says to the Rastafarian, who shoves himself into a straight line with his shoulder.

Joe looks up and smiles at me: 'I don't suppose you'd be wanting one . . . perhaps a little secret desire deep down?'

'Huh! I don't see why I should fall for this. Look at them all. They're doing a roaring trade in the holy relics of the struggle. I think I'll just manage to content myself with a sucker from the democratic workers' ice-cream cooperative over there,' I say, indicating with my chin the men wandering up and down with polystyrene cooler boxes strung across their shoulders.

Reaching our stand again, we find that our seat neighbour has kept our places by shifting across and spreading his picnic bag.

'Thank you,' I say, remarkably gracious and lacking in sarcasm for me. Joe is still smiling; at me, at our neighbour, at the country, at the world.

White faces scatter our top stand like freckles on the negative of a photo portrait. There is a stir now as a small group of middle-aged whites arrives. I notice the woman for her pale serenity and make-up free face. Of course, she spoils it by wearing the uniform of the ageing lefty: straw hat tied on with scarf, Indian skirt and leather sandals. In the sudden hum of shared information, the people on our stand are all bending towards neighbours, talking about them. I don't make any move to ask, but my neighbour clearly feels I ought to know. He leans over, offers me a bite of his chicken leg and informs me that she's the daughter of some famous lefty from the fifties. Big deal. And now she arrives like royalty, with her small coterie, lifting her hand in mildly waved greeting.

'They're coming. They're coming.'

The noise rises like a wind-whipped moan across the

stands and, in its passing, raises people from their seats. I can feel the joyous frenzy building in the *toyi-toyi*ing bodies around me. Joe joins in but, for God's sake, I'd feel just too ridiculous for words if I were he. Two rows in front, I can see the low-slung jeans of a plump white boy exposing too much pasty buttock as he *toyi-toyi*s madly, clearly proud of his expertise.

'Viva the tried and tested leaders of the ANC! Viva!'

'Long live the tried and tested leaders!'

'Long live the mothers!'

'Viva the tried and tested mothers!'

The hypnotic revivalist litany whips the stadium into a divine passion. Faces are raised to the heavens, fervent fists punch the air. I feel our stand, jutting out over a lower stand, begin to move in harmonic motion with the *toyi-toyi*ing. For a moment, I think I must be entering into a holy 'struggle' experience. The Heavens Moved, that kind of thing.

'A-N-C, A-N-C, A-N-C . . .'

And then they are there, tiny specks emerging from a Mercedes Benz far below us. The crowd's roar overwhelms the stadium, the air, the sky. It loses the consciousness of human voices and becomes the primeval roar of the earth itself.

Joe's forgotten to keep watching me, he's been swirled up by this tornado of euphoric hysteria.

Toto, I've a feeling we're not in Kansas any more. This is surreal, like a different world, for someone like me. I can actually see uniformed Umkhonto we Sizwe soldiers marching in a guard of honour far beneath us – this I never thought to see.

And then we stand, faces raised to the punishing sun,

for the hymn of the struggle, '*Nkosi Sikelel i'Afrika*'. I watch Joe and the plump white boy, who has moved back to his place in our row. Their faces filled with the glory of visions, they fling their voices into the anthem. Joe makes it about halfway into the first verse before he begins mouthing and humming. The plump boy drops his face and looks at his feet, moving his lips quietly. It is, of course, quite difficult to learn a song in a language you don't understand.

Every one of the released men is expected to speak. As I read their names off the back of a T-shirt just below me, I wonder how many of these men we'll ever hear of again. But today is their day. Today we will listen to them.

I think that Raymond Mhlaba, the first unidentifiable speck on the horizon to speak, loses his audience after a few minutes of his pedantic description of the history of the struggle. Slowly the individuals around me emerge from their hypnotic trances and get on with the business of chatting, shouting to friends across the heads of others, eating, sharing bread, sausages and chicken. Small children, the mascots of the struggle, race up and down in front of the first row of seats, tripping over their oversized adult T-shirts emblazoned with *ANC Lives! ANC Leads!*

'I think he should rather show slides of a few T-shirts and have done,' I mutter to Joe, who I notice is breathing normally now and appears to have returned to the land of the sane and the living. He smiles as he brings his head close to mine in the solidarity of the cynical comment. But he doesn't reply.

I feel inexplicably sad, sad for Joe, sad for the gathering. I can't work out why. There is joy in the glowing day, jubilation in the dancing limbs and smiling mouths. And I'm so used to jeering, I thought I'd lost my capacity to feel this sadness for others. But after all, why should I? Why should I feel for these people who haven't yet lost what I lost, so brutally, so young?

It strikes me that there's a shining innocence to this gathering – OK, maybe most have seen and heard too much, lived too harshly, suffered too much brutality. But about this they are innocent. Hope soars above their sweat-glinting heads, hope and the expectation of deliverance. There is a sweetness to the 'Jesus' T-shirts worn below waving communist flags, to Azapo's presence 'in the spirit of comradeship', to the arms outstretched to tentative white liberals. And, perhaps most of all, to the icon purity and saintliness of those just released.

The sadness comes in the pathos of the inevitable – the clay and mud syndrome. Clay feet of real live politicians, and mud-slinging between above-ground political parties. Outside of mythology, very few lions ever get to lie down with lambs. Give them a few months. They'll be brutalizing and stabbing each other in the back with the best of them.

They're all the same. I have no illusions about humans and their nature. Particularly in this country where, it seems to me, human behaviour mirrors its environment. This is too harsh and brutal a land. It has too few rolling contours and rain-washed meadows to breed soft, green sentiments. This is not the country to sustain this dangerous level of jubilant hope for long.

Of course I know my husband's innocence. Its manifestations irritate me, and yet deep down I know that's one of the reasons I chose him. He is my own innocence lost, and perhaps it is this constant reminder which chafes at me and yet binds me to him.

I am amused, in my detached superiority, by his glowing naivety. But this rally has affected me in a way I never contemplated. To see his faith and trust multiplied so many thousand times fills an aching void with sadness. I think it flows for their innocence, still inexorably to be lost. But I know it is also for mine. I feel sorry for myself, sorry that I've been sucked of the juice of my simplicity and doomed to witness the greatest surge of hope the country has ever seen. Great cosmic joke, that!

As the history of the struggle struggles on, fighting its way through layers of heat and lethargy, I lean forward to glance along the rows of faces. Suddenly, in the distorting shimmer of the sunlight, they transmute into the brutal faces of the Eastern Cape, the faces of my shattered childhood, of inexpressible eight-year-old horror vomited on to the thorned ground.

In the next instant they are gone. And with them my sadness. I feel it overtaken by a perverse pleasure at the disillusionment to come. Why should I be the one to carry the burden of this bitter knowledge for so long, and so alone?

'Today we see the apartheid regime facing a deep and irreversible crisis.'

I cannot see Walter Sisulu at all, but his voice wings clearly across the stadium to us. He stresses our unity in this divided country of ours. And with his priestly demeanour he draws everyone in: the workers, the police, young white men resisting army call-up.

Of course, all this saintly goodwill and unity perceived, emphasized so artfully in Sisulu's words, exist only in the presence of a recognized evil. The common enemy is still at large and Sisulu uses it, recalls it to their eyes. The power of darkness, though greatly weakened, is not yet vanquished. The scent of righteous victory is in every nostril on this crusade for godly power. The devil's legions are to blame, he proclaims, for the violence among the righteous people of Natal.

'While we have made many strides, the carnage among our people in Natal is a blot on our noble struggle for liberation.'

He pauses to allow the crowd's assent to pass.

'It is the evil hand of apartheid that is behind the violence in Natal. Reports of police collusion in the killings abound. We know that it is the general characteristic of the ruling class to divide our people.'

Drawing to a dramatic and climactic close, Sisulu flings his oration to his congregation and beyond.

'We must unite in action with the broadest range of apartheid's opponents. We should not allow ideological and other differences to stand in the path of our unity against apartheid.'

'Great,' I whisper to Joe but he avoids me now, my eyes and my head leant closer to his, inviting cynical solidarity. 'Now we're all drawn into this great big laager of love.'

He is silent. I can see uplift glowing in his eyes and in the deep rise and fall of his chest.

'These ANC guys should've been revivalist preachers: they would've made a fortune.'

But I can see he won't listen to any more of my comments. My isolation feels more intense for the tiny leak of fellow-feeling we briefly had between us, and that earlier moment of solidarity we shared.

Ahmed Kathrada continues the process of drawing us all into the presence of good, and of solidifying the force of unity. And he, who has seen the devil, is so good at identifying him for all those at the furthest extent of his beckoning reach.

'We have to persuade our white compatriots that the greatest dangers facing them, their children and their future are not the black people, are not the ANC or the South African Communist Party, not Archbishop Desmond Tutu or Dr Allan Boesak. Their greatest enemy is apartheid, the Nationalist Party, the Conservative Party and all those who still propagate under different names the policy of white separateness and white supremacy.

'White South Africans must know that we are aware of the fears that exist among them. We want to assure them that it has never been in the past, it certainly is not at present and will never be in future the policy of the ANC to drive the whites into the sea.

'We firmly believe that fundamental human rights, including the language, religion and cultural heritage of all our people, will only be adequately guaranteed by firmly entrenching individual human rights.'

Very clever oratory, I have to admit. Very comforting for the softly smiling whites among us to see his vision of heaven, so mistily portrayed and deftly described.

The speeches keep coming, on through the fading afternoon. Yet through them all runs the love-thy-neighbour thread. The crowds grasp at the message and hold it to the end.

The sun is a dusty, tan glow beyond the stadium when we stretch and stir to collect our belongings. The stands are a mess of papers, bones, cans and crushed polystyrene cups as we file, shoulder to shoulder with our many-shaded compatriots, down the stairs and along endless concrete walkways to the shadowed car park.

Joe is silent during the shuffling surge. I'm not going to break his mood this time. We open the car with a beep of disarming alarms and slide into its lung-burning heat. Joe starts the car, sits with glazed eyes aimed at the dashboard and then switches it off again. His head turns.

'I know you felt it, you know. You can deny, you can mock, you can jeer as much as you like. But you experienced it. I wanted you to come, and you did. That's important to me. But more than that, I know you felt the awesomeness of what's happening in the country. Now you'll have some idea why it's so important to me. Why we have to do something about you – about your fears and your refusal to open up. And why we have to do something about us.'

1966 . . . Nine days to Christmas

'Our Father, on this day of our Covenant with Thee, we thank Thee for Thy deliverance of Thy people from the Zulu hordes. We thank Thee for our victory against the godless at Blood River.'

Through one slitted eye I could see Ouma, her portrait-like composure framed by my eyelashes. Her hands were pressed to her beige bodice as she prayed aloud.

'We ask Thee today, O Lord, to deliver Thy people once again. In this time of trouble for South Africa, we beseech Thee to bring about a victory against the godless and the troublemakers. Help Thy people, O Lord. Amen.'

'Amen,' repeated Mom and Oupa. My father cleared his throat. A gruff mumbled 'amen' escaped the imprisoning hands before his mouth. Michael and I, sitting cross-legged on the carpet, held our grubby-nailed hands flat against our eyes, squeezing them closed. We snuffled a giggled response into our hands, embarrassed by this once-a-year prayerfulness of our parents. Neil, sitting beside Ouma on the couch, said nothing. His hands rested at his sides and his eyes showed none of the squinted blinking of those just opened around the room.

There was silence as we all shook off the solemn prayer and wriggled into our social morning-tea demeanour. I was yearning after the white-capped Christmas cake standing beside the teacups on the coffee table.

A fly, trapped between the closed window and the fly screen, buzzed and rested. In two brisk steps, Ouma flung the screen up and silenced it with her wire-mesh swatter. Sliding the sash open to its fullest extent, she abruptly brought the farm into the silent room. The twittering of birds in the wild fig, the grate of the generator and the faint grumble of a tractor sounded through the screen, which she slammed with a sharp *zzz-clunk*.

'Let's have our tea,' she said, turning with a smile to Michael and me.

'But Ouma, why did we have to say grace before tea today?' asked Michael. I, who had been present at Ouma's early morning prayers, already knew and sighed exaggeratedly at him, rolling my eyes at his ignorance.

'It's a special day today.' Ouma was pouring and handing out cups. 'If we weren't here on the farm, we would have gone to church today. Since we can't thank God in His own house, we must *maar* be content with saying prayers in our own place.'

'But Dad, when we were swimming, you said this is Dingaan's Day. Why must we pray for his day? I don't remember praying for him last year.'

'We always pray for people who don't know God,' said Ouma. 'But in actual fact, Dingaan's Day is just what you English inappropriately call it.'

She gave her rough, gravelly chuckle as she lifted the

cake knife and brushed a curl aside with the back of her hand. She lifted her head to look at Michael and I could see her laugh pushing her cheekbones into high-planed relief against her plump face.

'I don't suppose it was really his day at all. There was a great battle and they say the river ran with the blood of his people. I don't suppose he thought it much of a day at all.' She paused while she cut a large slice of the damp, loamy cake and slid it on to a plate.

'You don't remember praying last year because we didn't bother to include you. But now you and Kati're both old enough to join in – you're not babies any more. I know you people don't care much for this tradition at home. But while you're here you'll learn to respect the ways of your forefathers.' Her face fell easily into its usual unsoftened seriousness as she looked around the room, holding her gaze briefly on my mother whose eyes were examining her hands in her lap.

Her gaze completed its circle and rested again on the two of us, our crossed bare feet and raised knees echoing each other on the floor. 'Today we thanked God for listening to the prayers of His people and letting them win the battle. In return, we promised to remember this day each year. That's called a covenant, and that's really what this day is called – the Day of the Covenant.'

'But now, Ma,' said my father suddenly, 'who are these people of His that you're praying for today? All of us, or just your people?' His voice was gruff, but he was smiling.

Mom's head shot up from regarding her nails as she heard his voice. In that instant I caught her air-shivering fear as it arced from her eyes to his.

Ouma looked at him for a moment from under repressive dark eyebrows. But her mouth quirked as she replied: 'Well, I suppose anyone who wants to consider themselves part of His people. It's up to you.'

My mother's shoulders relaxed. She took a deep breath and reached for her tea and cake.

'But Ouma, why did you tell God it was a time of trouble now?' asked Michael. He never did know when to stop, when to shut up and eat his cake.

'Bantu troubles, that's what I meant. It's not like before. There was a time when, if you treated your people well, you got loyalty and hard work. But now, *magtig*, with these native troublemakers in the Transvaal, trouble has spread to the Eastern Cape. I can see the signs of it, even here in the District.

'Nowadays it doesn't seem to matter how well you treat your boys. If the troublemakers get to them, you'll see trouble. So much anger and hatred, it's hard to know what to do . . . Sometimes I wonder if it isn't *maar* better to be harsh from the start like some farmers.'

'You mean like the man on the new farm?' asked Michael. 'Kati said he beat Albert's son.' As he spoke he kept his eyes on his plate, where he was removing every scrap of marzipan and white sugar icing from his cake. I withdrew myself from the gathering, fearful of this conversation which, it seemed to me, skirted dangerously near the rank depths of awfulness. Dreaming of dogs and sunlit exploration, I unearthed the cherries from my cake and sucked at them voluptuously. For once my mother, her eyes on Michael's face, ignored our grubby fingering.

'New farmers have new ways,' Ouma replied. Then she sighed. 'But the Lord says people must work.

Nowhere in the Bible does it say it should be easy for any of us. It's also very hard to run a farm in these times of trouble. I feel sorry for the next-door boys, but then this is their lot. They must *sommer* grit their teeth and work hard. No one would beat a person for nothing. If they keep their noses clean and keep away from the troublemakers, they'll manage all right.'

I looked up to see Michael struggling to swallow a mouthful of cake and, at the same time, take a breath to continue. Across the room, Neil's face was wrestling with his desire to argue. He took a breath to speak but let it escape harmlessly. My mother aimed her tautly strung look and as it caught him, she pulled it tight, binding him into immobility. Coiling it in, she tried to use it on Michael. Missing and rethrowing, the tension in her hunched shoulders grew as Michael avoided her eyes and refused to be captured. Unable to bear it at last, she dropped from the chair to her knees and reached across the floor to pat Michael's thigh. But I saw that her red nails were clawed.

'That's enough, Mich-ael.' Her tone was light, but a slight quaver caused her to pause and swallow as she said his name.

Oupa puffed silently, as he had throughout the teetering blade-walk we'd all been on. Tapping his pipe into his ashtray, as though for attention, he smiled briefly around the listening faces before clearing his throat and composing his face: 'Did any of you hear on the wireless this morning that Walt Disney died?'

Dearest Oupa, always the peacemaker, always the one who stood fearless in the storm and calmed it with his hands and his voice.

'*Ag*, no,' I said. 'Does that mean there won't be any

more pictures made after *Cinderella*?'

'No, my darling Kati,' he said, his chuckle bouncing the down turned book on his chest. 'It's a company that makes them now. It'll continue without him, I promise you.'

'And did you hear, Dad,' Michael broke in, his eyes fired with excitement, 'they say South Africa's developed a new weapon. They said on the radio this morning that Defence man – Botha I think they said, isn't that right, Dad? Anyway, he won't say what it is but he says it's been made from research right here and he says it'll prepare us for the future like they were prepared before Blood River.'

Neil smothered a derisive snort with his teacup, which he held high, draining the last of the tea into his tilted mouth. Dad cleared his throat, his thoughts gathering behind his already moving lips.

'Well, Michael, it is important for any country to have a strong defence force. Especially for South Africa. She has a lot of enemies. But you know, new weapons won't solve all our problems, Michael. I just wish the government would spend a bit more of its time dealing with the African problem.'

'Michael, let's go,' I muttered, giving him a 'boney' on the arm with a quick jabbed finger. 'Let's go outside.' With a slight wheedle I added: 'I'll show you the new farm.'

'OK . . . We're going. Me and Kati're going outside. OK, Ouma?'

'Don't be late for lunch,' Mom added over Ouma's nod. 'It's roast today.'

'Yay, yay,' we sang, scattering dark crumbs as we ran from the room.

The sunlight was a warm hand of benediction on my head as my pent energy burst from me in sideways gallops and competitive cartwheels with Michael. We went a different way this time, plundering through rough bush with a crackle of dry bundu-bashing. Michael clambered in front, arching his skinny body under bushes. His bony elbows winged skyward as he pressed his hands down and slung his lanky legs over the rough bark of low branches. I followed more tentatively, my toes always curling in fearful search of snakes.

A deeply carved path carried us from the edge of the bush in a winding upward movement through dusty grassland. The anthills stood as tall as my shoulder under the dry tan of thorn trees. The sun glared off their long white thorns, which made my eyes water and tingle in fear of their merciless thrust. I covered my eyes with my hands as the path wound too near the reaching, scratching branches.

And then I was bowled into the soft dust of the path by a yelling Michael, who had crept up on me while my eyes were closed. Sitting on my stomach, he howled, prising my fingers from my face. I squealed and fought to turn my face into the dust as he laughed and jousted with two thorns he had snapped from an overhanging branch.

'Stop it, Michael,' I shrieked, my squeals turning to dusty tears. He dropped the thorns then.

'Baby, baby,' he taunted. 'Scared of a little thorn.'

He tickled me, but desultorily, as if bored by my unchallenging response. He leapt from my stomach in one supple movement and trotted off along the path.

'C'mon, let's go see the farm.'

I snuffled myself upright, smearing my face with the flat of my hand. My nose I wiped on my T-shirt sleeve, tented towards my bent hand with a finger.

I ran then, following Michael who was making for the boundary fence. With his big toe balanced on the top wire, he teetered a moment on the poised, shivering strand before vaulting his legs over the top.

'Michael, no, you can't go over there,' I stage-whispered in awed fear. Indecisively I clung to the fence, watching his ragged lope across the grass. 'Michael,' I called, louder this time. There was no one to be seen on the other side, but the stillness seemed eerie to me and probably added to my panicky *grils*. I was fearful of being left alone on my side of the fence, and of what would happen to Michael should he go on without me. But my stomach coiled and shrank at the thought of the unknown on the other side. Our farm, our heart-warming soul sanctuary, no longer reached across that sinister stretch of diamond mesh.

The anxiety – for Michael, for me – drove me to clamber the fence and race after him. I had to get him back, to pull him away before he could meet anyone, before he could do any harm.

'Mi-chael.' It was a breathless cry which wavered as my feet pounded and slapped the rising dust. He stopped suddenly, just ahead of me, and laughed as my driving momentum flung my body against his.

'What's the matter, idiot? Are you scared? D'you think the neighbours are witches . . .' He lifted clawed hands to his hideously pulled face. With his forefingers, he exposed the raw redness beneath his lower eyelids.

'Stop it, Michael. You look ugly. Stop it,' I repeated as he brought his red-eyed grimace closer to my face.

'And I'm not scared of them. I just think we could get into trouble.'

'Cowardy custard!' he sung. 'Nyeah nyeah nah *neh* neh. Scared of a little trou-ble. The neighbours make you *skri-ik*. Yellow, yellow be-lly. Ching chong China-man, born in a bath . . .'

'I'm not scared,' I broke in. 'I just don't want to get into trouble for what you go and do. What do you want here?'

'I'm just looking around, that's all. C'mon, let's explore. No one'll catch us. It's OK.'

Ahead, Michael's intent eyes were fixed on a pair of wind-blown gum trees, exposed in their ragged soli-tude, somehow painful in their peeling raw trunks and alien height.

The trees screened a huddle of corrugated iron *pon-doks*, not from wind, which whined gently from the side, but from view. The shanties – squat, unwilling structures, forced into a semblance of huts – were imprisoned from wind-borne escape by the rocks which balanced on their flat roofs. Windows were small severed squares in the rusted sides. Patching their gap-edged corners were flattened cardboard boxes and the startling red of Coca-Cola signs. Doors stood to one side of jagged openings – sharp-toothed metal sheets whose drag marks showed their purpose in the dirt.

Plastic bags and paper scraps danced lazily along the ground in the desolate breeze. I could hear a wailing sound, that scary relentless wailing of a baby that can't be comforted. And beyond that, silence. I looked up at the gum trees and thought that they were wrong, they gave no comfort to the people who had to live in their shade. Not even the birds, greedy for trees and bushes to perch in, were clamouring to sit in their lonely, swishing branches.

'Where are the children?' I whispered to Michael. 'Where do they play?'

'Dunno, but it's not here.'

The doeked head of a woman bent to peer at us through the ragged hole which served as her door. Clinging to her skirt was a large-eyed child, about Michael's age, I thought. They stared at us a moment before the woman pulled the child back into the pitch dark of the hut.

'*Molo*,' called Michael. There was no reply.

I felt a thread of fear snaking through my stomach at the thought of approaching these huts, whose harshness held nothing homely or clean, or decent. Deep down I knew that it wasn't their fault, and that maybe it was temporary – maybe, just maybe the new farmer would still build nice warm mud-packed huts, and that perhaps they could still paper the walls with magazine pages and cover the floor with mats.

But none the less I feared these people and their sinister silence. Who were they, these people who could live in this coarse and inhospitable place? I couldn't then understand or work out for myself why those cavelike interiors filled me with dread. But years later, when I was awkwardly almost grown, I remembered unwillingly the day I saw those huts. And then, as if in image association, my mind moved on and played back all those tales I had heard of our city *boegieman*, the Valley bush-dweller. And I remembered the imagined dread of what he would do to small girls found wandering near his ragged, dark shelter.

'Let's get out of here,' I whispered to Michael.

'*Ja,*' he said, nonchalantly flicking at a small stone with his big toe. 'There's nothing to see here anyway.'

We ran, flying side by side across the rough ground. We were running to get away, to shake the fear from our stomachs in the hair-flattening breeze. We didn't talk about it – we never did in our family – but I could see the tension in his face, in the intensity of his headlong rush.

Movement in the distance, made suddenly distinct by the speed of our dash, turned us at last. We veered across the tufted ground, homing for the comfort of familiar figures. We ran, slowing into the balm of familiarity caused by two boys, digging rhythmically at a shallow depression in the ground.

They didn't look up as we approached, William's son and Albert's son, digging together in the shared harmony of their low-voiced chant.

'Hello,' I said. 'Hello, Johannes. Didn't you recognize me the other day, across the fence? I was with my older brother, Neil.'

Sweating, intent faces still fixed themselves on their spades' harsh stabs at the entrails of the earth – the small trailing roots, sticks and dangling severed worms.

'Don't you remember us, Johannes? You used to have pictures taken with us on Christmas Day in your new clothes . . . with the other children . . . when you were still on Ouma's farm . . .?'

'What do you want, Missie!' William's son stopped digging, his scowl glistening as he leant his bare arms and heaving chest over the spade's handle.

'Just to say hello.' Michael had wandered off and I could see him now, winging his arms at shoulder height as he soared, twisted and wheeled away. I could hear his guttural mewing attempt at an eagle's cry.

'Is that hard, digging like that?' There was no reply as the violence of rhythmic thuds continued. Beaten and diminished by the fury of their blows, the ground rolled over and surrendered its inner contents.

'It looks hard to me. You don't mind it too much, do you? You must be strong to do it so easily. Ouma says hard work makes us strong. She says God likes us to work hard and keep busy.'

'*Ja*, your Ouma,' said William's son. 'She has a lot to say, but she's never dug a rubbish-place.'

I giggled at the outrageousness of the conjured picture. 'But she's a lady.'

The digging continued, the two dark heads runnelled by silvery rivulets. I watched them in silence, sitting in the dust in front of them. I traced my name in the dirt with my finger and wiped it away with the blade of my hand.

'You know, it isn't fair if you blame Ouma for selling the farm. They had to, and she's says it's hard for her too.' The silence dragged itself out. I would have to go on. I was agonizingly trying to draw a response from the harsh-faced young men, to force them to tell me everything was OK. I didn't want to feel bad about them any more. I was exhausted by the guilt and the sorrowing sympathy. I wanted them to feel OK, at peace with God whose plan this surely was. And I wanted them to exonerate me and my family.

'She feels sorry for Johannes's being beaten, but she says he must've done something to get him cross. She says you'll be OK with the new Master if you just work hard and stay away from troublemakers. She says new farmers have new ways . . .'

I was silenced by the virulent abruptness of Johannes's frozen stare and the stillness of his spade. So impervious had he seemed, I had begun to talk around him as if he were not there at all, as if he couldn't hear me.

'New ways, new ways!' He turned and spat in the dirt. 'These are not new ways. These are old ways – the ways of the past that must die. These are the old ways of dealing with the kaffir.'

He flung the word at me. I had never heard it used in the city, and to hear it now, used with such boiling hatred . . . On my haunches, I cringed from his loud, spit-whitened mouth, appalled by what I'd created with my chatter. Silly chatter. I burned with the awfulness of how silly and how childish I'd been in the face of this adult torment. For the first time I felt inside me the shallowness of my whole life, my knowledge and my little emotions. From the depths of his dark anguish I could smell the rank nearness of rage and hatred.

'These old ways . . .' His voice was quieter now but I shuffled my body away from him, clutching my knees in a convulsive foetal position. '. . . They should die. They are good for nothing but to die.'

I wanted to get away from this talk of death and ugliness. I wanted to get away from these fearful men that I'd thought of as boys. Farm boys who carried the warmth and comfort of home. The eternal carriers of children with burning feet, the lifters of small girls stuck on chicken *hoks*. I ran, desperately ignoring the paper thorns which clung to my feet, my breath sobbing as I cut across the diminishing grassland towards the dusty figure that was Michael.

At first, the sounds of wind and my own sobs camouflaged the outraged screams over my head. I ran, my throat aching with dry sobs, until I was halted by the sudden whizzing power of a just turned 'dart' brushing past my hair. I ducked, screaming as a second object sped lower, cutting so close to my ear that I felt it brush my flesh.

Hysterical with choked screams, I flung myself to the ground, futilely covering my head with my arms. By now I could hear the bleak screech of the birds above me. I knew what I'd done. I'd unwittingly thudded too near the nest of a pair of *kiewietjies* and now they would dive-bomb me. They would continue their attack until I left them alone. But what could I do? I couldn't run away. I couldn't even stand.

I scraped my face across the ground to peer under my arm for Michael. He was crouched, his arms flung over his head, and he wasn't even looking at me. I moved my face over to peep under my other arm. Johannes was digging, impaling the ground with his spade. William's son had stopped, shading his eyes with one hand, the other still holding his spade. He took a step, then stopped and gave a desultory dig, watching me.

The dive-bombing continued, so close I could imagine the rocketing weight of impact. I shrieked in panic as I felt the rough brush of feathers, the rush of passing air. And then he came, William's son, dropping his spade and running, ducking and weaving as he moved within range of the *kiewietjies*. He threw himself on me. I squeezed my eyes closed as I felt myself lifted, my cheek pressed roughly against his sweat-filled shirt.

When he put me down the screech of the birds was

distant. Michael was running wildly, skirting the territory they guarded with such fury.

My face was wet and gravelly, smeared with snot, tears and dust. I could see the damp brown imprint of it on John's shirt.

'Thanks,' I gasped, finding breathing difficult in the struggle to control my sobs.

'Leave us alone now, Missie. We have work to do. Go home. You have no business here.'

He turned and strode away, leaving me to wait for Michael.

When he finally reached me his eyes were huge and he was out of breath. 'You OK, Kitty?' he said, with the baby nickname he'd given me and seldom used now that he was almost grown.

The silence of our sudden closeness was shattered by cackles of raucous laughter. We both turned, our faces still stiff with shock. Two children were dragging a go-cart from the direction of the *pondoks*. Both barefoot, both dressed in khaki shorts and shirts, one was ragged, one starched. One was black, the other white. The white boy's hair was beige stubble front to back, side to side.

They pointed and cackled, slapping their knees and imitating my cowering before the *kiewietjies*. Slowly my shaking transformed from fear to fury. How dare they laugh at me. How dare they. Let them just try and stay calm being dive-bombed by *kiewietjies*.

'Ignore them,' said Michael. 'What does he know, bladdy *plaasjapie*. And that *piccanin*'s got a bladdy cheek to laugh at us. Let's go. We'll get them back later.'

Elaborately hiding and crouching, we tracked the two boys. They chattered a mixture of Xhosa and

Afrikaans, dragging their pram-wheeled go-cart towards the slope near the pigsty and the square buildings. They didn't look behind them.

'Come, we'll get them back for laughing. Let's spy on them,' said Michael, leading me to the back of what I thought of as the dairy. Almost touching it was the second whitewashed shed. Michael stood between the two buildings, offering his laced hands as a stirrup. He hoisted me up the walls and I clambered to the flat roof by straddling the gap between the side-by-side buildings and sliding my feet up the two walls. Michael followed, his hands and feet prehensile as he scaled the wall with the ease and deftness of a monkey.

Flattened on the corrugated iron, we spied on them in the heat of mid-morning. It was exciting and shivery at first, to be there and hidden, watching their every move. But then we tired of it, endless racketing down the hill in the go-cart, taking turns to ride and drag it back up again past the pigsty. Our foreheads dripped and the roof began to burn our carelessly moved limbs.

Suddenly Michael leapt to his feet and stood upright, in plain sight. I watched him for a moment, and then joined him as he began his chant.

'Afrikaner *vrot* banana, Afrikaner *vrot* banana.'

My anger at the boy's laughter and contempt at his khaki clothes and bristled haircut erupted into a screeched chorus with Michael.

'Afrikaner *vrot* banana, Afrikaner *vrot* banana.'

We felt the slammed shudder of the door beneath us. Instantly silenced by the fury of the red-faced bulk glaring up at us, I saw before us the farmer's huge paunched body rippling in terrifying strength and size.

'Wat doen julle op my dak?' His voice crashed over

us. 'Weg met julle. Weg met julle voor ek my sjambok gaan kry. Get off my roof,' he repeated in English, 'or I'll be taking the sjambok to you.'

We scrambled in panic down the back wall, leaping the last few feet, falling and tumbling together in the dust. We ran then, vaulting over the fence and racing for the safety of our own farmyard. A small trickle of blood wormed down my thigh as I swung my legs.

We stopped at last in our yard. Suspended in anticlimax, we started to kick small stones to each other. We were giggling shakily as our toes sought and flicked the stones. Neither of us spoke, but we were both still scared.

'What d'you want to do now?' Michael asked, gazing at the ground. We both knew that we had to calm down before we returned to the house. That we were too shaken to show ourselves or they'd have the story out of us, and a truly awful punishment would follow.

'D'you want to go watch the "teenager" chickens?' I asked him. 'They're really funny. Especially if you feed them.'

We stood at the barrel *hok*, laughing at the frenetic flapping of the half-grown chickens.

'Watch here,' I said, showing off now in my knowledge of these 'teenager' fowls. Michael almost never took an interest in the chickens unless they were having their heads chopped off.

I pulled a handful of dried mealies from a sack leaning against the cage and threw it into the *hok*. In a splutter of flapping wings the chickens erupted, sweeping to and fro in greedy waves. In frantic pecking frenzy, they crowded and crushed against each other, flapping and squawking. We laughed.

'Throw some more,' said Michael.

I didn't actually see it happen, but I saw the bright speck of blood colour the foot of the speckled black-and-white. The chickens had been pecking wildly at the ground and one of them must have pecked his foot. It didn't look too serious though, just a small cut.

And then, to my horror, I saw another chicken peck at him, then another, then another till his feet were oozing and slimy with blood. They turned on his wings, his back and his head. Scrambling from the crush, the black-and-white ran from the mob to the edge of the *hok*. A surging wave of chickens followed, turned and swept after him as he fled back to the other end. They were hunting him down, maddened by the sight of blood. I screamed as they crushed him, pecking relentlessly at his sinking head and pulpy eye socket.

Trapped on the outside, I forced myself through the nausea to watch the carnage I had caused. I had let go my control of the farm. I had promised myself that I would hold things together. But I'd been showing off and I'd let go. This time I had done it myself. I had killed him.

When the chickens finally gave up, the black-and-white was a bloody heap, leaking a red stream towards us across the concrete floor.

1966 . . . Eight days to Christmas

Rivulets of watermelon juice raced around the mound of my belly and collided. Already stippled with water from my wet hair, my naked stomach ran with small streams, pinkish in the recessed light of morning.

It was early. Early enough to catch the phantom cleaners at work with their silent dusters. Early enough for just the glowing expectation of sun, setting each leaf of the wild fig darkly against the sky. The chickens clamoured and crowed and the generator rubbed and grated against the still warming air.

Carelessly dried from our early swim my father dripped, dabbing his nose on the towel slung around his neck. He was squatting flat-footed, I echoing his position, on the lawn in front of the stoep. Through the window I could hear Ouma's radio tuned to the Afrikaans station.

Dad sliced through the reddened flesh of the melon with the precision of a flourished scimitar. His blade split the circle in two and he handed, in silence, another piece into my reaching hand. The sticky sliding of a pip made its way slowly down my chest.

We were joined at last by the boys, wet and shaggy as

dogs, shaking themselves and raking us with flying droplets. In their prosaic, chattering presence, they proclaimed the ordinariness of day, and scattered the last spirit-wisps of the ephemeral earliness of morning.

Soon we'd be called in for porridge, hot and hon-eyed, on the starched cloth. We'd drink creamy-yellow milk and eat soft, sizzling eggs. I could smell the hungry waft of bacon through the open door.

'Hell, Dad, you should have seen it, Dad. It was unbelievable. Those chickens just fought it like any-thing, Dad. Wow, it was incredible. They fought it into the ground.'

Michael paused to slurp at his watermelon. Dad's unperturbed knife strokes and absent smile compelled him to continue.

'They even pecked its eyes, Dad. You should've seen the blood. Hey, Kati? There was stacks of blood. You tell him.'

I was watching with revulsion the thin pinkish stream of juice wandering and dribbling from my thigh. I placed the half-eaten slice back on the sloshing tray which held the melon.

'Had enough, Kati?' My father was looking at me, ignoring the background beat of Michael's 'Dad? Dad? Da-ad?'

'I'm just cold now, Daddy. I want to go get dressed.'

I wanted to remove my heavy eyes from his view. Hiding the guilt in their downcast depths, I could feel it swimming upward, ready to leap into the open before them all.

That was the worst of it, the guilt. The horror of that thin stream of blood had not been so much in the fact of a chicken's death, which, of course, I told myself in

mental flagellation, I knew to be the everyday forerun-
ner of gravied wings and drumsticks. But I'd never
been aware of it before, never considered the connection between clucking *hok* and carving knife. And at
least that death would be dispassionate – a detached
and impersonal execution.

The horror of this death was in the greed and gratifi-
cation of the hunt, of the maddened fever of following
and the abrupt turning of like upon like and fellow
upon fellow for some unfathomably small flaw. But
even that wasn't the worst. It was the guilt which
nibbled at my consciousness, desperate to burst into the
open. I pressed at it, feeling it and keeping it down. I
feared that Michael would tell them it was my fault –
that, in my showing off, I had destroyed a life. I didn't
know what they would say, how they would blame me.
But I was so scared that they would turn on me,
revulsion in their eyes.

'OK, go'n get dressed,' my father said. 'I suppose I
should've already told you to get out of your wet
cossie. Your mother would say that little strip of wet
material is terrible for the kidneys.'

'Not to mention the possible piles,' said Neil and
they both laughed.

I passed my parents' bedroom where my mother sat
in tableau on the bed, one knee drawn to her body as
she carefully painted each toenail. Her hair was newly
teased and puffed in the perfumed room.

I could hear Ouma's *'Dankie Here*, Amen' as I passed
into our room. Standing for a moment on the bed, I
watched the belted grind of the generator in the yard. It
was comforting in its repetitive familiarity – but suddenly threatening in its beckoning belt and the bared

teeth of its unguarded machinery.

That was the year, you see, in which I first noticed danger in the commonplace. When, for the first time, death seemed to reek from the livestock and hatred from my loved ones. When the certainty of the world unravelled, and when its familiar form turned slowly monstrous. But I had to carry on, to clutch at the sameness, to hold it all together.

With a growing desperation I felt I had to do as I'd always done, enjoy what I'd always enjoyed and play as I'd always played. This was my reeling incantation to the omens.

So I warmed my tummy with sweet Jungle Oats. I slurped at the glass of breakfast milk, dunked with home-made rusks and *soetkoekies*. And while sucking voluptuous crumbs from my fingers I sat with Michael, the last two to leave the table, while he retuned the transistor radio to Springbok. Dunking and sucking, we waited for 'Deathie'. The programme *Death Touched My Shoulder* could always make us *gril* pleasurably and squeal deliciously from the sanctuary of the breakfast table.

I was nibbling the crisped bacon rind from my mother's plate when I heard the knocker on the door. We stopped eating, Michael and I, halted by the strangeness of the sound. I don't think we'd ever heard it before. Visiting maids and boys from the District always came straight to the kitchen courtyard, calling to Dora or standing in the sun until noticed there. Visiting family were always expected, and were announced by echoing *yoo-oohs* and *Coo-ees*.

Michael turned down the volume and we listened as Ouma's quick steps tapped through the library to the front door. Our eyes crept over the scattered table and held as we heard the deep crack of the next-door farmer's voice greeting Ouma.

'Let's get out of here,' Michael muttered, scattering crumbs as he raced for the hidden recess behind the pantry door. I sat a moment, appalled, before I followed. I knew where he'd gone.

'I'd forgotten about him, after the chickens and everything,' I whispered to him. 'What d'you think he wants?'

'Us, of course. Don't you remember he said he'd take the sjambok to us? He wants to whip us. Those kind of people love to whip people.'

I felt my face pucker as I remember his bulk and his fearful voice. We heard the lounge door close and the muted voices murmuring. We heard the lounge door open again and my stomach cramped as I heard our names spoken on the way to the front door. The house sounded quiet as the front door shut out his deep rumble. I listened to Ouma's footsteps, waiting for the call that I was sure would come.

'Elaine, Elaine, kom na die sitkamer, asseblief. Ek wil nou graag met jou praat.'

We waited. Then my mother's heels tip-tapped along the wooden passage and the lounge door closed again.

'What d'you think's going on now?' I asked him, clutching his tensed forearm with the fingers of both hands.

'Shuh'we go'n listen?' he whispered back.

'No, Michael, no,' I said, watching his wide, dark eyes.

'Don't be a sissy,' he said suddenly, shaking himself and my hands from his arm. He stood up. 'The man's gone anyway. He can't sjambok us now. Anyway, I was just trying to make you *skrik*. Dad would never let him use his sjambok on us, idiot. Dad's easily as strong as him.'

The pantry felt very empty and very hot when he'd gone. Dora squashed her bulk into the narrow room, squeezing me behind the door. She clattered a bit on the shelves before squeezing herself out again. Quietly, I crept out, sidling down the silent passage towards the closed lounge. Michael was nowhere to be seen.

I crouched in the shelter of the doorway, leaning my hot face against the wood of the door. There was silence behind it, silence throughout the house.

'So it's come to this!' That was Ouma, her voice gruff and deep.

'I'll punish them, Ma.' Mom's voice sounded high in comparison, pleading almost.

'Is that all this means to you?' Ouma's voice cut through Mom's next soft murmur. 'A misdemeanour, a prank? To be punished, just like that?'

'Ma, don't make—'

'This can't be punished for. Can't you even see that? Can't you recognize the symptom for what it is?'

'Ma, it's nothing. All children—'

'Don't you dare tell me it's nothing.' Ouma's voice grew harsh and raspy as it burst through the barrier of her habitual quiet speech. I'd never before heard her shout . . . well, not in the house anyway. Maybe just at the dogs, or something. Her voice remained loud as she continued.

'Don't act stupid. It's not the roof-climbing I care about. Of course all children do that. It's not about that. It goes much deeper than that. It goes to the heart of you and me.'

'Oh Ma, I don't want to fight with you. It's Christmas. Can't we just forget about this and send them to their rooms for the rest of the day?' Her voice was very high and soft; she sounded almost like me. And her pleading was unmistakable now.

'Listen now, Elaine . . . Magtig, watter soort naam is die? Why must I force myself to call you that? When I choke on it every time it passes my lips. When you have a perfectly good name of your own. Helena, that's the name you were christened with, the name given to you in acceptance and love. Why must you *maar* reject it, and everything it stands for?'

'Ma, please . . .' I could hear her gasped breath through the door. 'I didn't reject it, I just didn't like the name. That's not a crime.'

'Not a crime, it's a symptom just like what your children did. And I can see exactly where they get it, where their attitudes spring from. It's plain what message passes from you to them.'

'I never ever—'

'You don't have to. It's there, it's quite plain in everything you do and say. There is nothing in those children, nothing at all of their *volk*. And nothing in them of me. I am an Afrikaner. I'm proud of it, proud of my people and my heritage. There's no pride in their nationhood. Nothing but scorn, for me and what I stand for. You and your children consider yourselves superior, above me with my simple farm ways. You think you're better, and so do your children.'

'Oh Ma, that's not true.' Her voice was shaking now, breaking off into a gasp. 'It was just mischief. Why must you always make things more?'

There was a pause, but my desperate ear could hear

even their breathing, even their heartbeats. I had to control this, stop it before it caused havoc, before it brought the farm crashing down around my listening ears. But I was helpless and I felt suddenly too small to hold back this tide of anger and hatred. To enter would make it worse. To run away would be to allow it to happen, to be too weak to hold up the crumbling walls. I squeezed my eyes together, pressing my cheek and ear painfully against the door.

'Please gentle Jesus, please God,' I whispered.

'And what, may I ask, have you – you with your superior citified ways – given those children to replace the heritage that should have been theirs? Nothing, nothing but second-hand snooty English ways that make them think they're better than everyone else. But give them nothing real – no place or values or culture.'

'We decided to bring them up English before they were born. You didn't say anything then.' There were tears in my mother's voice, but it was louder. I could hear it clearly through the wooden barrier.

'What could I say? And what difference did it make? You were already English. You'd already taken yourself beyond me and my help, with your fancy English husband and your fancy English home.'

'That is absolutely not true.'

'Just look at you.' Ouma sounded as though she were spitting the words from her lips, to have them gone from her flesh as rapidly as possible. 'With your teased hair and painted nails. And, *magtig*, you insist on wearing those short skirts on the farm – and in front of all the boys too. What do you think that looks like? What kind of values does that give your children, what kind of solidity for life?'

'These are my clothes, Ma!' She was shouting now, but her voice sounded thick. 'Not that you bother to see how people actually dress elsewhere in the world, but I'd just like to tell you that, no matter how you try and make out that I look cheap, wearing a miniskirt doesn't make you a slut. Everyone I know wears minis. It's the fashion. What's wrong with that?'

'Do you think I care what those *Engelse* in the cities do? Those people with no values and no morality? What kind of answer is that? Those are the same people who make demonstrations and take drugs. Is that then all right for you and your children too? Because *everyone* does it?'

'That's ridiculous!' There was a pause, an angry breathing silence.

'And what you seem to forget is, no matter how I dress and whatever my children say, I am still your daughter and they are still your only grandchildren. You'd better make do with us.'

'I forget nothing. But I know something else. Being a daughter means more than taking ... more than just taking the life that was given to you. And there's more to—'

'What! Is this it, then? Are you disowning me? Over something so absolutely stupid?'

'Being family involves more than passing on those big brown eyes, you know.' Ouma'd begun talking before Mom finished her sentence. She continued as if she'd never spoken. 'They mean building in your descendants the things that are important to your ancestors. That is what makes up a person and that's what makes a family.'

'Maybe it also means allowing a child to think for herself. Why are you always so sure you're right? Why does everyone else have to be just like you, or you want nothing to do with them?'

'Because I know what is important. I know that there is nothing . . . nothing left of me to continue through your children to their descendants. *Your* children. I can't say my grandchildren because there's nothing of me in them.'

A hot, welling wetness rose in my throat and burst silently from my eyes. I felt pleasure in the pain of my forehead pressing into the wood of the door. It was so much easier to bear.

I heard my mother's gasp and I heard her begin speaking. Quieter now she sounded, but her anger was louder. 'So you're even throwing up that relationship, disowning it because you don't approve of us. They're your *only* grandchildren, for God's sake.'

'Moenie die Here se naam ydellik gebruik nie . . . What I am saying to you is there's more to motherhood than a difficult birth. May God help me, but I still care for you, and your children, but being a mother means passing things on. I've passed nothing to you, you with your red nails and short skirts that offend me every time I see your legs. And the city talk that you and your family use. I'm not removing myself from you. You did that long ago. You did that when you removed everything of me from your heart.'

'Don't give me that! Don't you dare . . . You never loved me after Katerina died. You wanted her. I was never good enough for you. Well, I wish she was alive, I really wish she could have lived to disappoint you as much as everyone else does. Because she would have, you know. In the end, no one could ever live up to your expectations.'

'*Magtig*, Helena, don't you dare bring poor Katerina into this. And don't you dare throw her up into my face. I gave you everything, everything of the best.'

'Oh sure! Is that why you sent me off to boarding school as soon as I was remotely old enough to get rid of? And my name, as you well know, is Elaine.'

'*Magtig*, and now to have the things I've done for you thrown back in my face! You went to boarding school because your pa thought you should have the best. Because his precious only darling was too good for the District farm school. And you always thought you were too good for the local children.'

'Oh what rot! How dare you accuse me of snobbery? You sent me to boarding school because I was under your feet. I reminded you too much of the one who wasn't there. It wasn't my fault, you know, but you always made me feel guilty for being born just when she caught diphtheria.'

'I missed Katerina. How can a mother ever get over a loss like that? But it was you that always selfishly took that loss on to yourself. *Skaam jou!* You're still pouting jealously over a dead child. Well, we'll never know, will we? We'll never know, but maybe *she* would have remained true to her family.'

'It's not pouting – how dare you belittle what I feel. I know what I felt from you and I know what's fair. What isn't fair is that you throw Katerina up as a paragon to me and that you still blame me for becoming English. You call me a snob because of it . . .'

'If you aren't a snob then why have I said to you year after year: "Go and visit your friends in the District. Go

and see the children who were your first playmates."
And have you ever gone? Have you ever once inquired
after them or cared what happened to them?'

'That's not snobbery. That's because I have nothing in
common with them. I'm different, I'll admit. I am
English. But whose fault is that? Whose fault is it that I
was sent to a fancy English school? You can't get more
English than the school you sent me to. So what'd you
expect me to become? Why d'you send me off to
become English and then blame me for it?'

Ouma's voice dropped to a rasped murmur, but
every word cut quietly through the door to me. 'I didn't
send you there to become English. I sent you there
because it was considered the best education. But in
return I expected something from you. I expected you
at least to be true to your family and your religion. Not
to deny your roots and hold yourself above your family
and old friends. You sit there now and tell me that I
deserted you as a child. Well, let me tell you what I
know! It was in the end you that deserted us, and your
heritage. You betrayed me by removing yourself and
my grandchildren from me.'

'You're calling me a traitor? Me?'

'You used the word, but it fits. You betrayed me and
everything I stood for.'

'I'll never forgive you for that. Never. You've created
such a terrible thing out of something that didn't matter.' She was weeping now, I could hear the sobs.
Ouma's breath still came fast and hard – she never
cried.

'Don't try to pretend this was all my doing. This is
your doing – yours because of the ideas and values you
gave your children – and you must take the

consequences. You turned yourself into a little English lady. You should have known that doing that meant you had to give up something. Well, you've given up your forebears. And those forebears include me.'

The door burst open. My mother, sidestepping clumsily to avoid my crouched body, stumbled into the passage. One hand on the passage wall, she ignored me and blundered blindly towards her room with her other hand painfully clutching her eyes.

I lifted my agonized head. Ouma was standing absolutely still, gazing through the fly-screened window at the huge embrace of the wild fig tree. The light glowed and shone from her face as her head moved and she fumbled for a tissue in her bra. Her cheeks were wet.

As she passed me on her way to the kitchen she absently patted my head. How could she do that, after what had happened? Why didn't the earth crack open and swallow us all? I was waiting, teeth clenched, for the cataclysm, the crashing end of the world. This wasn't some peripheral edge-of-family fight. This was the mighty clash of the Titans of my life. The two great forces of the universe had battled it out and nothing could ever be the same.

I crept into my hot corner of the pantry. Crouching, too devastated to cry, I was waiting. I was waiting for a sign – I didn't know what – but a sign of what had happened. A sign that the family had crumbled and fallen. Would we leave now, today?

The sound of the shaken bell jerked my taut muscles and I gave a small, tense cry.

'Lunch, everyone.' It was Ouma's voice. But what was this? How could we eat?

'Yay, food!' I heard Michael's voice, but how could he

not know? How couldn't everyone know that this was the end of everything? I crept from my small spot, where the flies buzzed insistently around my damp head. I had to see what would happen. I had to be there to see the world fall apart. When I entered the dining room, everyone was seated except my mother and me.

'*Kom*, Kati, it's now time for the grace. Michael, today I think it's your turn.'

I took my seat silently and clutched my hands together. But I couldn't get my eyes to close. What could I thank Him for? I'd asked so hard and He hadn't stopped it.

'F'what we're 'bout t'receive . . .' Michael's voice clattered on as my mother entered from the passage. Her eyes were red and small but she was utterly composed. I glanced at Ouma, who briefly opened her eyes and nodded slightly. Then she closed them again.

'Amen.'

Ouma stood to serve and pass plates. Her brisk discussion of all that had to be done before Christmas rushed the table from its silence and dragged the family along. I was still waiting. Was she still ours? How could she be after that? Where would we belong? How could everything seem like before – the smell of roasted chicken, the *skree-bang* of the screen door, the drone of a tractor? Dora entered with pumpkin fritters, shaken by vast deferential laughter, full of her usual toothless bustle.

Ouma spoke and spoke. I couldn't take in what she was saying. Something to do with the baby chicks that had to come before Christmas Day . . . I don't know anymore.

'No gravy please, Ouma,' I whispered, surprised that

I could still speak and that I could sound so normal. But Ouma talked, her words pouring from her mouth, drowning the small sounds around the table.

My plate, when it appeared before me, was smothered in the farm's thick, oil-rich gravy. I stared at it as I heard Ouma's voice tumbling over the table. My tears felt as thick and as difficult to pass my throat as the film of oil on my plate. They welled and fell with a life of their own. Unable to stop them, I concentrated on my throat, on trying to swallow or take a breath.

The pouring tears began to water the gravy, breaking it down into curdled puddles as I became aware of the silence. Everyone was looking at me, I knew, but I couldn't look up. All I could do was try to breathe. I had to take a breath.

'*Magtig*, kind, wat is dit now?'

'She didn't want gravy, Ouma.' That was Michael.

'But for goodness' sake child, why didn't you say something? Why sit there weeping?'

She whisked the plate from before me and slid it in front of Michael. Briskly and in silence she dished up another plate. A loud click echoed off her palate as the new, gravy-free plate appeared before me.

I don't remember much more about that lunch. I think it must have been that lunchtime that Oupa reached across to my mom just before he lifted his knife and fork. I remember watching him ruffle her hair and tickle her neck in the babyish way he used for me. She gave a fragile smile and swayed delicately towards him as he squeezed her shoulders.

I think Dad and Neil discussed cricket, on and on about the teams – who was good and who was bad. Who should be in the team for Tests and who shouldn't. I do remember Neil rounding his cheeks to expostulate: 'Now he's rai-aly a sple-endid player,' in a Charles Fortune imitation.

After her gush of speech at the start of lunch Ouma was silent. She ate steadily, her eyes moving from speaker to speaker. Oh, I do remember that, while the cricket talk dribbled on and on across the table, her eyes shifted to Mom's face. I couldn't tell what was in them and I tensed, ready for the disaster to come. But the moment went by. Nothing happened. What were they all doing, those grown-ups? If something was going to happen, why didn't they just make it happen and have done? They shouldn't drag us on and on with everything just as it had been. Especially when I knew that it wasn't, when nothing could possibly be the same again.

I couldn't understand how everything could seem so normal. Or normal on the surface, I should say. I wouldn't have known the word surreal then, but I remember thinking of that lunchtime as quite ordinary in every way, except for one outrageously inappropriate thing which I couldn't quite put my finger on. Rather like a room full of people sitting down to dinner, all with no pants on.

'*My magtig*, Kati, why on earth did you make such a fuss about the gravy when you weren't going to eat anyway?' Ouma was scraping food scraps and stacking plates. 'Do-ora,' she called.

'*Ag*, Elaine.' She turned and paused, a knife poised against a plate. My mother had been heading for the door to the lounge, Neil and my dad following behind her. As she stopped and waited they passed around her, arms flailing in bowling demonstration.

My throat caught and imprisoned my breath. From the corner of my eye I could see Michael, impervious to the crashing end of the world, picking scraps of chicken from the plates and shoving them into his mouth.

'I thought we'd send across a plate of mince pies to the next-door farm . . . and maybe some *soetkoekies*. Will you help me bake some more this afternoon? Please?'

There was a moment's silence, which ticked through the still room like a metronome.

'*Ja*, Ma,' my mom said, and smiled slightly – her delicate English smile. Ouma reached out to her then with her smile, her robust farm smile, which lifted and rounded her reddened cheekbones above her face.

'*Ja*, well, that's settled then. And you two,' Ouma nodded towards Michael and me, 'you'll take the plate over. And you'll apologize to *Meneer* Van Rensburg. Properly, *hoor julle*?'

Michael and I were slow to cross the fence. I dragged along the dusty tracks, trailing long lines in the soil with my big toe. Michael was carrying the plate of mince pies, protected by Ouma's bead-edged doily. He swaggered ahead of me, but I saw his feet slow as we neared the fence.

The front door was a wooden slab with a square of distorting glass at grown-up-head level. By the time we reached it, the doily was dusted by brown fingermarks where it had been caught from slipping and reposi-tioned.

The man opened the door himself, his vast bulk blocking almost all view of the inside. For once Michael had nothing to say and the two of us stood side by side, gaping large-eyed. Past his trunk-like neck, I could just see a row of hooks against the wall, studded with hats and caps. In the centre flopped a large khaki sunhat, lined with green. From beneath it trailed the plaited snake of a leather sjambok.

'*Ja kinders, kom binne*,' he said, suddenly bending his pillowed waist slightly and flourishing his arm in an ironic bow. My heart hollowed as I trailed my feet after Michael's into the lounge. The boy was there, sitting on the floor with his back against his mother's plump, pantyhosed knees. Looking up from her magazine, she smiled as we entered. The boy's Ouma changed not at all as we dragged across the speckled carpet. Sternly upright, her hands clasped firmly in her lap, she held her thin mouth clenched.

'*Ja jong*,' the man said, his meaty arm thumping down across my bony shoulders. 'It's not so bad. Don't look like that – like a frightened rabbit. Haven't you ever been sent to apologize to anyone before? *Goeie magtig*, but I was always being sent off to say sorry to someone. And I usually got a good beating for my trouble too.'

He brayed laughter as my eyes burst anxiously from their downward cast and warily searched his face.

'*Ag*, I don't think we'll be beating anyone today. What d'you think, Magda?'

She clicked her tongue against her front teeth. 'Ag, Jannie, moenie die kinders so bang maak nie. Thank you, *my lamme*. Are those for us? Very kind of you.'

'So are you a boy or a girl?' the man asked, shaking me with the arm which still lay across my shoulders.

'She's a gi-irl,' said Michael, yelling through his and the boy's laughter.

'But I can do anything the same as a boy,' I said, my

fear forgotten in my indignation. 'I can cartwheel as well as Michael any day. And I'm never scared of any tree. I can even climb better than him.'

He propelled me forward with his forearm against my neck. 'Tell my boy your names. Kobus, stand up and shake hands like a man. And practise your English now, boy. Say hello nicely in English to our small English guests.'

He gave another bellow of laughter and cuffed his huge banana fingers against my ear and cheek. The boy smiled shyly and shook hands with Michael. His mother came through with glasses of Coke, which we drank in Kobus's room.

'D'you want to see my silkworms?' he asked. He wasn't so bad when he smiled. He had large new teeth like Michael and he spoke English fine. He didn't stutter or stumble over the words. 'I really like the bioscope,' he told us. 'So my English got good.' After a while I hardly noticed his hair, bristling across his pink scalp.

He gave us each some worms in shoeboxes burrowed from his mother's powder-scented cupboard. After that, we walked to a part of the farm which looked familiar to me again. There we picked leaves and ripe mulberries to squelch into our mouths.

When we returned to his farmhouse, the sun was splaying gold directly along the surface of the Zuur-veld. Deep shadow crept into the hollows and held the easterly sides of trees and small rises. Kobus's mother said she thought we'd better be going. The man saw us off at the door, which looked naked without a proper stoep.

'*Ja*, well, we're going to the coast on Monday, for the

day.' The man's eye wrinkles were white lines in his reddish-brown face. His eyes sparkled and his tobacco-coloured teeth were like a row of dried mealies. 'Would you like to come with us? We're going in the *bakkie*.'

1989 . . . 17 November

They don't read, those wispy pony-tailed ones with their books clutched close to their faces, their heads drawn close in the togetherness of titters.

I don't care any more. All I care about is that this is the final period, and this my last library class of the day. Not that they ever really touched me, those shallow-faced girls who bob from their chairs in blonde bounces, chattering outside the door with squeals of exaggerated vivacity.

But I used to care a little, enough to try tempting them into reading anyway. I suppose I can't really say it was for them. That was the time I still thought I could make my job as school librarian more interesting than the book-stacking drudgery that it is. It was the time I thought perhaps one could find some small satisfaction in this place of literature and young minds.

I thought that if I just got them interested in a book or two, I would give them some spark that could warm their ever-intensifying search for husbands, homes and dirty nappies. That was when I tentatively offered them slim Barbara Cartlands, and those untaxing teenage love stories which I ordered by the prolific crateful for the school. I thought the anguished stories of love lost and ecstatically found on the final page might just reach the romance that those girls giggled and yearned for.

But it seems the stories are tame compared to their own real-life forays into the world of romance. And it seems the headmistress is now ashamed to show the library to her VIP visitors – her term for all those balding, small-eyed men, puffed by their paunchy lifestyles and self-satisfied patronage. She says the 'shelves and shelves of your cheap romances' now desecrate this sanctified place of musty-paged learning.

At least that gives me some job satisfaction, seeing that tight-faced, tight-arsed woman backing desperately against my romance shelf, eyes darting wildly while she tries to spread her body all over the titles and distract her visitors' fascinated gaze.

Oh, thanks for small mercies. There's the final bell. Before it finishes its ring the girls are lurching and slouching from the library, clattering books over the reading tables with eye-rolling smirks. Sullenly dropping their eyes to avoid mine, they leave without a 'Good afternoon, Miss' or a 'Thank you' between them. Saving themselves for gum-chewing and *skinder* in the toilet. I suppose I could insist. I know I have the threat of detention after school – a great and awesome power, which carries the greater threat of missing the boys' school at the bus stop. But I don't care enough about them or their smutty little lives to bother.

I push through the perfume-sharing clumps of girls outside the cloakroom to reach the teachers' toilet booth. Bending forward to fluff out wafts of waved hair – intimidated into bobbles all morning – a group of ultra-cool girls smooth each others' overly short gym

slips and examine their mascara. These ones I dislike
the most. They barely shift their feet to allow me to
pass, these narrow-eyed girls, who whisper in their
smug containment in the 'in-group'. Two of them,
thinking my eyes are elsewhere, make smoking gestures with their hands, jerking their chins towards the
door.

Oh Jesus Christ, I forgot. I can't even leave now. I'm
on after-school library duty today. I sit for a while in the
cool toilet booth, my forehead pressed to the shiny
utilitarian green of the wall. I think I'll wait for the
crush to pass before I return to my dreary post. I hear
the cool girls' superior sweep from the room and a
group of gigglers replaces them.

'Do you think she actually does it?'

That's one of the girls who mouthed and sniggered
through my last library class, but I can't place which
one. Hand-smothered giggles mask the next murmured
comment. It amuses me that they have such a vast
preoccupation with sex, as though they're the earliest
explorers to quest for the orgasmic grail.

'She's married to some lawyer. She must do it. Men
don't stand for wives who don't put out.'

'Aha, but she's got no children. She looks like she's
sewn herself up down there so he can't get to it. You
never know, maybe he gets it somewhere else.'

'D'you think she ever sucks him off?'

'Oh, gross.'

I wonder if their shrieked horror is due to the act
itself, or to the thought of my doing it. Anyway, what
do I care? They'll reach their own disillusionment in the
years of fumbled, sweaty embraces to come. And in the
welcoming response that'll be expected of them – as it's

been expected of all those women before them – to that dark fingering of breasts and pressing penis.

There's such a sense of déjà vu to this, sitting in the loo to avoid the bitchy girls. This school, at which I punish myself by teaching, reminds me so much of my own. That all-girls' production line for young ladies of the colonies, where they gnawed at all our wayward little lives and spat out nicely brought up children like these, with no individuality and little creativity of their own. Here is another institution where all unladylike signs of anger are ruthlessly put down. Where all that pent-up adolescent aggression oozes out in malevolent bitchiness from those narrow blue eyes and tossed blonde hair. And, of course, now we also have those token few dark heads that we never had at a school like this, even five years ago. At first they were so easy to spot, clustered together in their awed sparsity. But lately, I've noticed, they've learnt to roll bored eyes with the rest of them and desperately chatter their entrée into in-groups, moulding themselves and their views to match the privileged ennui and passionate banality of the others.

Back in the library, I sit in my silent chair watching the still columns of sunlight grow from the long tables up to the high windows. I am avoiding those spitefully flung books, which still have to be gathered, sorted and put away.

My solitude is shattered by the scuffing of deliberately casual shoes on the lino'd floor. These ones keep their hair seriously scraped from their foreheads, winsomely allowing just the odd tendril to wisp past their make-up-free cheeks. Ignoring me, they lope for the serious shelves, sniffing as they glance disdainfully in passing at my collection of love stories.

They raid my neat shelves, swapping, discussing and adding to their piles of Shakespeare and Zen Buddhism. I'm used to these ones. They'll leave again in a minute with artfully tippling piles weighing down their arms, while their nearly empty satchels hold only biology, or possibly geography books. This is adornment by book, the jewellery of the adolescent intellectual. Perhaps they're off to attract their male counterparts at the bus stop, those careful James Dean copies with their bravely carried cheekbones and the cultivated fire of garrets in their eyes. They were around in my day too – I wonder if they still roll their Texans up in their T-shirt sleeves? But in my day their hair, candle-greased behind the ears for school, was combed out to flop over the forehead for the bus stop. Or perhaps these girls are off to dangle on each others' beds in wallowed knee-hugging and the enjoyment of their delicately agonized images of themselves.

I see them approaching me now, clutching handfuls of Sartre and Camus while free hands gesture impatiently or earnestly brush at straying strands of hair.

'Oh, rats,' I say, feigning terror. 'It's a *plague* of existentialists.'

They gaze at me wonderingly, my little conceit going right over their heads, even with the heavy emphasis I give it to help them a bit. But I stamp their books with added dash, my small enjoyment imbuing a touch of energy to the rest of my solitary afternoon of classifying and stacking.

I finish at five, when I lock the library for the night. My footsteps echo through the pillared courtyard as I make for my car, where I sit a minute behind the wheel and begin intently picking and ripping at my nails. Too late. Oh shit, I should have left early and gone home to shower. I'd put it right out of my mind, on purpose I suppose, Joe's bloody Christmas drinks party at the office. Oh well, fuck it, why should I care? I'm dressed, after all. They must bloody well take me as I am, even if I'm not one of those simperingly moist-lipped attorney's wives, so thrilled with their marvellous maids and over-therapized children.

I drive easily into town, where backed-up cars and fleeing pedestrians escape in opposite directions for the townships and suburbs. Town at night, it has the look of crisis – much as a threatened nuclear explosion might. First you get the desperate mass of humanity fighting and hooting to break out of the maelstrom. And then, with the falling of night, darkened desolation. Cars appear furtive, and only the odd human figure is still about, scuttling into a deserted alleyway.

The lift pings me to the plush-carpeted floor of Establishment Law. I can hear the desultory murmur of tasteful conversation from the boardroom, passing the loo as a cluster of secretaries bursts into the corridor, pouring their giggles into the red-nailed receptacles of their hands.

The senior partner greets me at the door, his head bobbing baldly in time with his courtly handshake.

'Your old man's really doing great shakes in our Labour department. Really. Very well indeed . . . Excuse me, won't you?' His eyes are already focused somewhere over my left shoulder. He gives me that patronizing little pat which I've noticed he reserves for the 'firm's wives' and breezes past me. I suppose that's a great relief to him – to have escaped so easily from conversation with a non-lawyer. Oh my God, we're scarcely human. And one as dowdy as I among these flitting cocktail sequins and little black minis, or more accurately – Jesus, look at that one – very wide black belts.

There's Joe, over at the far side by the windows. He's cradling his drink in his two large hands, his thumbs caressing the rim and his eyes intently downcast. He's the guy who's usually more gregarious than a Dale Carnegie get-together. And there – he hasn't noticed me yet – he looks kind of scrunched into himself, with his shoulders hunched over to protect his drink.

'Hi,' he mutters. His voice sounds unused and slightly rough. He clears his throat and turns away to order me a drink from the bar. Avoiding my touch, avoiding my eyes, he places the clinking whisky in my hand.

'Joe, what's the matter?'

There's something odd or incongruous about my question. As I'm asking, it strikes me as out of place in some way. And then I get it. Of course. How many times has Joe used those words over the years, used them pleadingly, to prise at what he thinks is my hidden pain? And have I ever asked them of him? I can't actually remember having done so. I've always been so closed in on myself.

But lately, I feel more . . . what is it? I suppose it's more needy for his openness, the other side of my coin. I mock him to death, but I've grown to depend on his rush of Pollyanna emotions to counter my bile-driven silence. I've become used to the bolster of his balancing self. So this silence of his, this new reserve, is uncomfortable for me. And now, now that I've finally brought

myself to ask him, I wait for the expected arterial gush
of feelings.

'Nothing particularly.' He shrugs and straightens
himself, looking around the room. Watching his face, I
see his eyes sent out in search of escape. They come to a
stop suddenly and he nods. His buddy appears at my
side, obviously in response to Joe's eye-sent invitation.

'Howzit, Kate! Straight from school?'

'Don't tell me it shows?' I strike my arm across my
forehead and gaze at him with exaggerated horror.

He has a deep gurgling laughter in his throat. 'Well,
Kati my dear,' he says leering down at me. 'You sometimes have that deliciously school-marmish look about
you. It's a definite turn-on, you know. But I'm sure that
couldn't be calculated. No-oo. Wouldn't that be a mor-
tal sin for a feminist – like dressing up as a nun or a
schoolgirl just to drive the men wild?'

'Well I wouldn't really know, Paul. Why don't you
ask that perky young thing I saw dangling from your
arm earlier? Ask her whether dressing up in bright-
young-attorney-with-a-social-conscience clothes quali-
fies. And I know she'll definitely be an authority. I
noticed immediately how proudly she wears her badge
of feminist membership on her legs. Or is it perhaps her
hair shirt of feminism?'

'Ooh, touché.' His gurgle breaks into a surprisingly
high-toned burst of laughter. He blushes slightly,
whether from the exertion of his laughter or my comments about his girlfriend, I can't say. Joe smiles
absently, caressing and clutching his glass again. Paul
turns to him suddenly.

'What's up, Joe? How'd your urgent go this morning?'

'What urgent?' I ask.

'Oh, didn't he mention it? His union clients were hit with an urgent application yesterday to interdict them from picketing outside head office.'

'Why didn't you tell me, Joe?'

'Why should I? I knew just what you'd say.' I'm taken aback by his sudden bitterness.

Paul, either insensitive to our small aside or wanting to defuse the building tension, ploughs straight in. 'So how was the consultation yesterday? I saw all your guys trailing into the conference room as I was clearing up to go home. Late, were they?'

'*Ja*, a bit. Didn't really matter.'

'Oh? So what defence d'you finally use? Were any of the ideas we kicked around any good?'

'Jeez man, Paul, not a thing worked. That bloody consultation knocked every bloody idea we had right into the ground. Every one of management's allegations that I put to them, they had some story.'

'You mean they weren't there, it was the other guys?'

'No, I could've at least worked with that. I mean they didn't care, they said it was all true. They thought it was all OK. You remember, there was that allegation that one of the temporary workers was beaten to a pulp round the side of the building?'

'Mm, I remember the one.'

'So I say: "What about this then? What've you got to tell me about it? I'm sure management must've been exaggerating? Or maybe it was some *skollies* around the side, unconnected with the strike? Or perhaps he taunted someone . . . whatever." "No," they say. So I'm taken aback. So I say: "You mean you admit to doing it?" And they say: "*Ja*, well, how else are we expected to win this strike? How else do we stop scabs?"

'Jeez, Paul, they actually think they have an entitlement to beat people up and threaten violence. They say that otherwise the power's all on the other side. How else can they win?'

'So what'd they have to say about the death threats to managers?'

'Well, they said: "Never mind what we did, look at how bad management is. Look at them, they won't offer what we want. They won't even budge from their original offer. So we have to act like this." Can you believe it, Paul?'

'*Ag*, Joe, what'd you actually expect?'

'I'm so fucking stupid. Here I actually thought I was making some difference. I thought the right was all on one side, that it was a right-and-wrong battle. I thought it was black and white, no greys.'

'So did you end up not opposing the application?'

'How could we? Every allegation management made was true. They admitted it. They couldn't give me one defence we could possibly use in court. So now they're interdicted from showing their lousy faces within one kilometre of the building.'

Joe's face has sagged like a bundle of white washing that's lost all its starch. But his darting eyes tear at one. Paul smiles gently at him.

'Well, I suppose the only thing you could've done is get some kamikaze counsel to argue lack of urgency.'

Joe coughs out a dry laugh. '*Ja* well I considered it, but I soon thought better of trying a stunt like that.'

'What judge did you draw?'

'Smit.'

'Yes, I suppose there's no way that would've flown,

considering the circumstances. Oh well, you win some, you lose some, Joe.'

'But I didn't expect it to be like this. With everyone so dirty. And the taint on all sides.'

'So, welcome to the morally complex field of labour law. So you're no longer a knight on a white charger. Welcome to the club. Don't take it so hard, china. You had to get there sooner or later. Law's not like that, you know. Even labour law's about arguments, not right and wrong. Isn't that so, Thami?'

He grins and squeezes the shoulder of the tall black newcomer to the firm, edging him into our group, probably so that he can escape Joe's despair and make it back to his young articled clerk. I can see his eyes covertly following her progress across the room as she is pressed backward in the crush by the intent conversation of the senior partner.

'Hi, Thami.' Joe raises his eyes in a quick smile and instantly drops them to his drink again. I haven't met him before, this new acquisition of the firm, this badge of their good faith that they wear so righteously, and with such pride. Oh, they have of course had the odd Indian and woman attorney for some time now. But this, this good-looking product of a 'white university', is the firm's very first truly black attorney. And oh, how they fawn around him here, offering him drinks and haw-hawing their red faces chummily into his quiet dignity.

'How do you do?' he says softly, bending his head towards my proffered hand in a gesture of attractively old-fashioned courtliness. 'You must be Joe's wife. How very nice to meet you. What was that you were saying, Paul? I didn't catch your comment.'

'No, I was just telling Joe here that he can't expect all his union clients to be brave and noble fighters of the struggle – it's a morally complex field, same as any other.'

'Jesus, Paul,' says Joe, his mouth wincing now in humiliation. 'I know that. My feelings are a little more complex than that.'

'Yes, I think I understand what you are feeling,' Thami says, his face serious. But his demeanour . . . at first I can't quite work out what it is about him . . . We are all three listening intently, but in our slouched cluster we are being more polite than we were before. I suppose you could say we are being too nice, all of a sudden.

I stare at Thami, trying to pin down what it is that he brought into the group. And then I glimpse the small quirk of anxiety which catches at his mouth. He's not a diffident man. I can see that he glows with the confidence of someone who has done well despite the odds. He has the attractive shine of someone with pride in himself, his abilities, his intellect. That's not it.

I think it's us. I think he's not that sure of our friendship, how deep it goes in this chattering white group. I have a feeling he's not sure at what level of informality to pitch himself. At this point I am, like him, a little outside the familiar circle. And looking inward, it seems to me that, though he's made it into the firm and the law, he hasn't yet broken into the easy buddy banter of the people in it. Aha, a kindred spirit! I could fling myself on his neck.

Thami's quiet voice pulls me back to the edge of the group. 'I think it is always . . . if you'll forgive my speaking this way, Joe . . . I think perhaps sometimes people . . . well-intentioned white people, more particularly . . .' He clears his throat. Slowly he unfolds his white handkerchief, dabs at his nose and mouth and refolds it. 'I think it is easy for those people to be disappointed, or disillusioned – I've seen this many times, even with the white Left at university – with people they perceive as noble figureheads of a movement they admire.

'I think . . .' He pauses a moment, gazing up at the ceiling. 'You know I think we have had too many "mystical figures of the revolution" . . .' he makes the quote marks in the air with his index fingers '. . . and perhaps not enough real mixing of real people. You know, Joe . . .' And suddenly he does look diffident, unsure of himself in making the comment he is about to make. 'I, well, some people could say there's still an element of racism there somewhere – in a converse way – in expecting black public figures to behave with overdrawn nobility and being disappointed when they do not. But you know . . .'

He smiles suddenly, a white wave of warmth and goodwill. 'But I would certainly rather there were more people with your level of integrity and idealism, for the future. I think we will get the genuine mixing right eventually, too.' His smile shrinks, leaving his face dark and serious again. 'But what I said does not mean I care for the level of violence that has characterized the strike with which you are involved. Perhaps I can understand, but I cannot like it. And it has been terribly bad for the community. It has divided neighbours and pulled people in the same community into violently opposed camps.'

'Anyway, Joe,' Paul says, snatching at the first clear

pause in the conversation, 'I must be going.' He slaps Joe between the shoulder blades and cuffs his chin with the back of his hand. 'You be OK, now?' He clears his throat, embarrassed by his own concern. 'By the way, where are you guys going for Christmas? You heading for the coast?'

'No, I don't think so,' says Joe, giving him a small smile of thanks and reassurance. 'We'll probably just hang around here. I've got stacks of work still, anyway.'

'OK, well, see you guys soon. Must get together sometime. Maybe we could go out and eat sometime. Could you cope with my feminist clerk, Kate?' He gives a last rumbling laugh as he squeezes me under his arm and rushes off to rescue the clerk, whose face I can just make out behind the leaning shoulders of the senior partner.

Thami doesn't seem to expect any response from Joe. And it doesn't look as though he's likely to get one. He also takes his leave, and I watch as he politely squeezes his way through the crowd to say his goodbyes and thank yous.

'So why didn't you tell me about the application?' I ask, bringing my gaze back to Joe's crumpled face.

'Why? So you could ram it down my throat?'

'But that's never bothered you before. You always give me your Pollyanna impression anyway.'

'That's exactly what I mean. But this time I couldn't face it. D'you want to know why? Because everything you could possibly have said to me I've already said to myself. "Naive fucking idiot. What did you expect?" You could've told me what they were like, couldn't you? You would've thrown all my words back in my face, wouldn't you? Oh, how you would've enjoyed laughing at how I'd believed in the union's moral higher ground, in their discipline and everything.'

His anger and hurt splatter like shotgun pellets all over me, over himself, his clients.

'Jesus, Joe, how can you be so hurt about what these total strangers do? What did you expect? They're in it for themselves, not for you. They're not your friends. They don't owe you your illusions.'

He turns away from me to the deserted, yellow-lit street below us, and downs his drink.

'Anyway,' he says, gazing blankly out of the window, 'they say they're getting things better under control now ... And maybe management will take notice. They're also to blame. How can they just stand by without budging while emotions are running so high and things like this are going on? Shows you, doesn't it?'

'Maybe it does. But now tell me, Joe, why'd you tell Paul we weren't going anywhere for Christmas?'

'Well, what does it matter? What does it matter where we go or, in the final analysis, what we do?'

1966 . . . Six days to Christmas

My life, my childhood, the child that I was, all these were held that day in the palm of God's Eastern Cape hand.

There in the creases of His weathered flesh, we began that wind-whipped flight to the coast. Half nervous, half thrilled, I felt the wind spike my short hair in forbidden abandon with the speed of that disapproved-of *bakkie*.

In our desperation to win approval for this trip – 'Oh please, plea-ease Dad, you're always saying we should practise our Afrikaans and make friends with them, plea case!' – Michael and I had tacitly agreed to stay away from all mention of the *bakkie*. My mother believed that only rough children rode in the back of *bakkies* and that, almost inevitably, they were, periodically and accidentally, flung out and killed.

We had left early, in a landscape silent but for the clamour of chickens. I was lifted carelessly over the tailboard, feeling momentarily the rough scrub of the farmer's khaki on my cheek. Kobus, with a foot on the tyre, vaulted over the side and stood behind the cab. Michael and I sat gingerly on the wheel humps, clinging to the rust-flecked sides with outstretched arms.

The *bakkie* revved raucously and, in response to its strident call, a small dust-plumed figure darted across the veld and raced towards us. The farmer, his elbow resting on the open window, moved the *bakkie* gently forward.

'*Kom, kaffirtjie, kom,*' he muttered as the small dark figure flung itself at the side of the *bakkie* and scrambled, cat-agile, over the side.

'Kom staan hier langs my, Jonas.' Kobus's words were whipped from his mouth and flung back at us as the *bakkie* took off over the spattering gravel.

Nothing, for Michael and me, was as exhilarating as this wild rush of wind and sunlight. Rutted gravel roads danced our small bodies to the rhythm of that freedom as we crouched out of the still chill breath of early morning.

I stretched my neck backward to feel the warming sun on my face. Growing brave, Michael scrambled his way to stand alongside Kobus and the tough, laughing *piccanin*. Shouts of elation churned from our stomachs and whipped from our mouths as we struggled – Michael and I, more than the blasé farmboys – to hold on to the excitement, to keep the moment of flying joy within us.

The wind whirled us through the olive-drab land, where the gravel crunched and twisted through wild clusters of gnome-like trees. Shrubs sheltered their bandy, gnarled limbs alongside them and stretched out beard-stiff leaves.

I'd grown up with that stubby vegetation – didn't recognize how unmistakable it was, how it could grow into a child's heart and root there. And whether one saw it afterwards with revulsion or joy, it never left one, that look of God's dust-dry place. It was part of Him and it was part of me. I would never be free of it and He, He is still free to do with it as He pleases, to puppeteer with wicked delight the dangling desires and wanton acts of the people who live there. There they hunch, joined by an unseverable umbilical cord to their uncompromising land. As all-embracing as the wild fig tree, as generous as the baking sun, as harsh as the unremitting drought and as stunted as the repressed grey bushes.

Shot through with the proud flame of the aloe, the land tipped rough-bearded into tangled valleys, musky with the smell of the fallen leaves and old man's beard. Before me were the thin stalks of the boys' legs, grey with grazes. And between them, through the dirty window, I could see the khaki hulk of the farmer seeming to fill the cab.

'See the sea, see the sea,' yelled Michael, and I scrambled upright to shove a place for myself between Michael, who still smelt of Ouma's washing powder, and the wood-smoke smell of Jonas's ragged shirt.

Gently rounding over soft, furred hills, the gravel wound us down to the sea. There below us it stretched, ship-dotted to the horizon. Like the crocheted edge of a blanket, it wavered and looped into bays and inlets to each side of us. Sandy stretches frilled along its edge, brought to sudden halts by the ungiving thrust of harsh dark cliffs.

At the foot of the hills, we passed the general store and bounced along the back of the straggling strip of 'shacks' to the end of the grey-packed road. The last shack was theirs, clinging sag-roofed to the edge of the hillside. Leaping from the *bakkie*, we followed the two boys across the front of the shack and stopped for a moment to gaze at the hulking rise of gentle green which marked the end of the scattered village. Softly grassed and furred with heather, the hill crept roundly to its crest before it was sliced off to fall sheer into the sea. Blackened rocks jaggedly replaced the delicate grassy slopes.

There, on that day, I can remember so clearly how I licked at the smell of the sea lapping around my face. And how it washed to my stomach and my charged legs, and then I couldn't hold myself from running, followed closely by whooping boys, down the rough wooden stairs to the beach. I could feel the salt on my eyelashes as, irresistibly, I plunged knee-deep into the water, to be rocked and swirled by the foaming waves. Warm it felt, unbelievably warm and clear and thick with life. The air around my head felt clammy, rich and nourishing.

Warm with promise and delight, the sun sprinkled sparks across the water and the passing ships held exotic imaginings of faraway destinations. There was nothing, nothing on earth like this wild sea, so cleansing in its freshness, so rich with abundant life.

'*Kom, Ouens.* First come up here and change into your costumes. You don't want to get your shorts wet.'

The farmer's voice, deadened by the thick salty air, just reached the edge of the booming sea. Roughly we scrambled back up the steps, legs tangling in giggled attempts to trip each other. At the top of the steps, Jonas veered off and threw himself down on the grass to wait.

'*Hlala phantsi*, OK, Jonas? *Siyeza. Ons sal'ie lank wees nie*,' Kobus called over his shoulder as we raced each other up the slope.

The Innocence of Roast Chicken

The shack was everything I knew a seaside shack should be. Right across the front ran a rough concrete stoep, which the spray would just reach on wild, overcast evenings. This led us through the single door into a large central room. Here, the sun glared through the small wooden windows, whose salt-grimed glass obscured the sea. The scuffed, threadbare carpet held a thin covering of sand and a musky, slightly damp smell of sea and bait. Fishing rods stood in a corner next to a framed picture of palm trees, which someone had painstakingly formed out of painted seashells. Two walls were covered, floor to ceiling, in shelves stuffed with comics, magazines and piles of musty old books, which might have been there through several owners and paged excitedly by countless children before us.

The two boys, still shoving and wrestling each other, shuffled raucously into one of the small bedrooms leading off the lounge. I, exploring cautiously, found another, where I uncoiled my 'cossie' from my rolled-up towel on the humped single bed. The room had the familiar shack smell of musty old cupboards, dusty carpets and salty damp.

And the rest of that sun-flecked morning. I can remember scrambling over rocks and ledges after Kobus's father, so large and sure-footed in his *takkies* and fishing tackle. I can remember how I needed to grab every vivid sensation – the stiff-fingered starfish picked off their rocks, the coral-red of the anemones which nibbled at tentative fingers lagging in rock pools.

I remember reaching the long flat ledge of his fishing spot and the brown mushy smell of his bait. The whirring *zwee-ee* of his line cast far into the heaving sea and his straddled stance as he held it firm. Calling the two boys – Kobus and Michael – he held each in turn in the hollow of his arms and bent chest to hold the rod. He held it firm for them while it whipped and tugged at their small hands, fighting the churning swell.

The three boys acted tough with each other, each daring the others to leap over chasms, climb the cliff face or crawl into cramped crawl spaces and caves. Standing on the ledge, they wrestled awkwardly with each other. Kobus and Jonas chattered and moved together in a rough companionship of tangled Afrikaans and Xhosa. Michael, caught outside this tough farm brotherhood, tried to break in by posturing and challenging. The other boys crowed and responded in good-natured shoving acceptance. I was a girl and automatically excluded, brought into their games only as a foil to their toughness, as arm-twisted prisoner or rescued princess.

But I treasured the shared exhilaration over the small octopus which brought us all together in the shallows of the jutting rock shelf. I remember the swelling joy of the boys' acceptance and approval as I spotted it. And how we lay together at the lapping water's edge, shouting and shrieking as we tried to reach it with the net and haul it up the rocks. Jonas, so tough and unflinching before, leapt away from the shifting creature with cackles of laughter. Oh, how inexpressibly brave I felt as I allowed its soft, sticky clutch on my wincing hand before releasing it to swirl away through the water.

'Kom bietjie hier julle,' said Kobus's father, bending his rugged mouth into a half-smile as he reeled in his empty hook for the umpteenth time. 'There's a *lekker* bed of oysters just round this rock here. I know from last time.'

There we squatted on the ledge with the sea spraying at our backs, stiff now with salt and sun. Kobus's father held a screwdriver in his huge fingers, deftly flicking the top shells off the oysters. The first he savoured himself, the second he motioned me to scrape from its bed with my fingers. Washed off in the rock pool, that oyster tasted of the sea, of the fresh breeze and the swooping gulls.

Replete with oysters, we trudged and scrambled back along the rocky edge of the sea to the shack. Thick smoke rose from the grass in front of the stoep, where an African tended a fire in a half-barrel *braai*.

'Ja dankie ou, Fred. Het jy pap gemaak?'

'Ja, Baas. Dis klaar, Baas. Da-aar in die kombuis.'

The farmer fetched a beer, which he slurped from the bottle as he took over tending the fire. Jonas disappeared, slinking around the side of the house to the small *kaia*, where he would eat with the chattering maids.

Kobus's father started another beer, throwing his first bottle on the lawn before drawing coils of *boerewors* from his cooler bag. We sprawled on the grass beside the *braai*, our stomachs working as the waft of meat sizzled through our nostrils.

We sat lazily into the afternoon gorging ourselves on sausage and pap. Several more beer bottles joined the first as we wiped our dripping fingers on the grass and lay with our arms behind our heads, watching the clouds.

'Oh look, loo-ook at them!' Michael shrieked, his practised grown-up growl breaking into a squeal. And

209

there they were – dolphins, dozens of leaping, carousing creatures of the wild sea, and of this magic place. Caught in the splash of sunlight, they gleamed in flying formation and danced for us in dazzling display.

We sat on, as a soft mist wisped past the cliffs to envelop the afternoon, wrapping us in a delicious dampness that you could lick off your upper lip. Pulling on our shirts, we called Jonas and leapt for the beach. The wafting mistiness filled me with the dank energy of all moist afternoons. I wanted to cartwheel, I wanted to fly with the keening seagulls.

'I c'n cartwheel further than you boys can,' I yelled, and Michael spurted into a run to join me as I flew into leaping dives across the damp sand.

'Ag nee,' I heard Kobus complain behind me. 'Ek wil dit nie doen nie. It's for girls. My pa se gimnastiek is sissy. Dis soos ballet.'

Michael stopped, his eyes following me for a moment. '*Ag*, no, I don't think I really want to. I can beat you any time I like anyway. That's really *pikkie* stuff.'

He turned to join Kobus as Jonas leapt from the last step and raced raggedly across the sand waving a 'catty' in the air. I stopped and watched the three head off behind a rock, throwing themselves flat and leopard-crawling around it. Taking turns with the 'catty', they ducked and raised themselves, pinging pebbles off a rock with *crack crack whee-oo* sound effects.

I wandered away to play an intense solitary game, leaping from rock to lumbering rock, the queen of the creatures and the magic waters at my feet. In the cooling damp I watched the rushing suck of the tide-change, and shivered at the menacing flotillas of bluebottles languidly floating to shore.

I laid myself full length on a flattened rock, like a fish on a plate, to yearn and daydream. The mist was beginning to obscure the village, which from my rock looked like a pugnacious lower jaw, thrust forward to show its row of discoloured teeth.

And then, as suddenly, the sun thrust through and the mist snaked away, leaving the late afternoon sunlight to glimmer over the very tip of the green hills. I sat cross-legged on my rock as the day lowered itself around me. To one side of me the village and sea were a lifeless grey. In the other direction, the sun's last flaming sparks lit sudden flares on the tips of luminous, white-crested waves. Serene and unhurried, the sun began to slip away behind the misty, blackened rocks. There was nothing dramatic about the sky. For a moment or two it was delicately pinked and pastelled, the sea still alive with a thousand splashes of light, and then it was dark in the shadow of the leaning cliffs.

The murkiness clenched a sudden band of anxiety around my stomach. 'Michael, Michael, where are you? Michael, we have to go home. We're going to get into terrible trouble. Look how dark it is.'

'It's OK, stupid. We're with Mr Van Rensburg. We can't help it if they leave here late.' The boys were all laughing at me, but I didn't care. I wanted the day to end right. Nothing else should happen. No more anger, please God, no more anger! I was climbing over the rocks to the sand where I could now make out their three dim faces.

'Anyway, sissy, it's not so very late – these cliffs make it dark early here. We'll leave just now, hey, Kobus?'

'*Ja*, just now. But my pa, he . . . hy drink nog. Moenie

enigiets vir hom sê nie. He'll go when he's ready.'

'Michael, you know it won't matter that it isn't our fault. We'll still get into trouble. You know how angry they get. They'll say we should've told him we have to be in before dark.'

'Well we can't say anything. Kobus says he gets really cross if they rush him when he's still drinking. Anyway, Kati, it's OK. Don't be such a sissy. I'll tell them it wasn't your fault. I'll say we did tell him, but he left when he wanted anyway.'

Subdued now, we climbed to the top of the steps where we crouched with Kobus, listening for the clink of the last bottle to join the pile on the lawn. I could just make out Jonas, squatting silently alongside the back tyre of the *bakkie*.

'Nou ja, ek voel nou lus vir my kos. Kom julle, is julle gereed om to waai?'

'Ja, Pa. Ons is almal hier, Pa. Ons wag net vir, Pa.'

'Goed,' he said, affectionately cuffing Kobus on the side of the head as he passed him. 'Dis mos 'n kind se plig om vir sy beters te wag.'

The *bakkie* careered and sputtered and slid up the gravel hill road, while the four of us crouched in the back. No one yelled this time, and not even the two farmboys stood up to lean against the cab. At the top of the hill we looked down to see a pool of darkness drowning the village. But ahead, out of the valley, a second sunset lit our journey.

'Isn't this a different way, Kobus?' I broke the silence in the back. 'I don't remember this road.'

'*Ja*, my pa always likes to take this way when we go home. It's where his *maats* go sometimes in the night.'

We hit the outskirts of the small village at speed,

roaring past the silent old houses and the new squat buildings in the main street. Some of the old houses still had their dignity intact in their wooden sash windows and *broekie*-lace verandas, while others were wrested from distinction by curlicued burglar bars and brand-new steel windows. We slid to a halt outside a small square hotel, where the farmer slammed from the cab.

'Wag hier 'n bietjie,' he growled. None of us said a word.

He stumbled slightly on the bottom step leading into the men's bar. '*Fok die donderse* . . .' just reached us before he ducked to miss the doorway and disappeared inside. We waited without speaking as the darkness became profound and lapped closely around us in the *bakkie*. It seemed a long time to us then, but maybe it wasn't. How can a child without a watch tell how slowly time passes in the anxious darkness?

The darkness was filled at last by the strident yells and riotous laughter of large, blundering men. In their loud bulk and sweating faces, they were utterly scary to me. And so alien to everything I knew to be right about life and the way things should be. Kobus put his head down silently, while Jonas shrank into the corner, almost disappearing into his own still darkness.

'Nou ja, Ouens, ons het 'n paar fancy-pantsy Engelse saam. Hierdie klein buggers dink hulle is baie refined, weet julle. Hulle het daar op my dak gestaan en "Afri-kaner vrot banana" geshout. So, wat dink julle? Hulle moet mos baie tough wees, nê?'

They moved around the *bakkie*, their breathy laughter and heaving stomachs crowding in on us. Michael put his arm around my shoulders, but his eyes were huge.

'You're scaring my sister,' he said tremulously, his

voice squeaking over the rough growls around us.
'Leave us alone. We should be at home, anyway. I'll tell
my dad if you don't take us home.'

The men roared with laughter, bumping and shuffling among themselves.

'O fok, hier's tough klein bugger,' one of them yelled.
'You're a fighter, hey? How 'bout standing up to an
Afrikaner – let's see who's tougher.'

'Kobus,' his father roared. 'Opstaan, laat sien hoe lyk
jy teen die klein Engelsman.'

Kobus remained seated, his eyes on his sandy feet.

'Leave us alone,' yelled Michael. The men laughed
more raucously as his father leant in and yanked Kobus
upright by the arm.

'Staan, kind. Stand and fight. Are you a girl or what?
Is jy bang? If you're scared then you're not my son.'

Kobus, his eyes watering and his mouth set firmly,
swung an ineffectual fist at Michael, who was now also
standing. Michael made no move to defend himself. He
pushed the flat of his palms out in front of his chest and
shook his head.

'No, no, Kobus, this is stupid. Tell him we can't do
this. I can't fight you for nothing. And we haven't got
gloves or anything – we can't box like this.'

Kobus's fist slid past Michael's chin. All the men
were yelling and I crouched, terrified, alongside the
silent Jonas. Kobus was snivelling now, smearing tears
and snot from his face with his fists, which then
dropped to his sides. The men lost interest suddenly.

'Ag fok, ek het *mosa* old woman vir 'n seun,' Kobus's
father said as they straggled away, mumbling about
their suppers. He made a lunging movement at Kobus.
'As ek sê jy moet veg, dan veg jy!'

But, as the slammed doors of trucks and station wagons swallowed the other men, he lost his impetus and, muttering to himself, stumbled into the cab of the *bakkie*. The gravel spattered wildly through the darkened veld, sliding us around bends and bouncing us into the air as we flew over humps in the road. As the *bakkie* skidded to a revving halt outside their farmhouse, Michael and I leapt over the back and began running.

'Bai'dank 'Meneer Van Rensburg,' we both gasped as we ran for the fence. At a sprint, we headed for the gentle yellow lights we could see glowing from our farm. We could smell the soup and mealies as we reached the stoep. Ouma opened the door as our feet touched the step. She stood, serene and backlit, watching our heaving bodies for a moment before she smiled.

'Well, you're a little late, but you were with the Van Rensburgs so I suppose you were safe. I expect you couldn't tell the family when to leave. Kom nou binne, kinders. Your supper is waiting for you.'

1966 . . . Five days to Christmas

'Dora, Dora, there's someone out here wanting you.'

The woman squatted in the kitchen courtyard, silently drawing a small tin of snuff from her bosom and placing a lump of the grey powder, with delicate thumb and forefinger, behind her yellowed teeth.

Dora heaved her body upright from the blue kitchen chair as I raced inside, the *skree-bang* of the screen door echoing my entrance. With instant garrulous chatter, Dora called to the woman from behind the mesh of the screen door, inviting her to enter. The woman unhurriedly rose, brushing at her long skirt and gathering her blanket around her waist. She brought with her the smell of the outdoors and of wood fires as she sat at the kitchen table, her calm hands lying serene in her lap.

Dora clicked on in her fast Xhosa, shelling peas and rising occasionally to check the pots on the stove. I sat quietly alongside them, resting my chin and temple on my two hands. I was savouring the familiar rattle of their speech, enjoying the smell of the huts – that little touch of the wild outside in the ordinariness of the kitchen.

The radio blared African music. I know my mother

217

couldn't bear its 'repetitive beat'. To me it was alien, yet so familiar – a part of every kitchen and maid's room of my childhood.

I couldn't begin to follow the rat-a-tat of their frenzied conversation, so I sighed in the fly-buzzing heat, swinging backward in my chair and kicking the table legs.

'Can I see your *True Africa* please, Dora?' I asked, swinging the chair back on to four legs and cutting into Dora's speech. She pushed the comic across the table to me, without looking at me or pausing in her breathless talk. Michael and I, forbidden to read comics – except for the British Bunter variety – found *True Africa*, the African photo comic for adults, utterly fascinating and exotic. My mother was repelled by its alien stories of love and violence in a world entirely composed of black people. For us, it embodied forbidden Thursday afternoons couched over comics in paraffin-scented maids' rooms, while drinks were passed around and boyfriends visited.

I settled now at the table to read 'Chunky Charlie', hearing in the background the *skree-bang* as another maid entered to place an unplucked chicken on the table. I looked around when I heard a scuffle and saw the dogs, reaching well up her thighs, push past her through the door, buckling her knees as they panted and pawed their way to the cool of the kitchen floor.

'Hau, Do-ra,' said the woman at the table, her voice rising on Dora's name. 'Hai hai, *Bambinja*.'

She half rose from her chair, shuffling clumsily to keep herself between the kitchen chair and table, shaking her hands ineffectually before her face. Dora, a placating hand motioning her down again, heaved her chest into a cackle of laughter.

'She very scared of the dogs,' she said, looking at me. 'She say there's no big dogs like this on her farm.' I laughed with Dora.

'You mustn't worry,' I said to the woman. 'They're fine. They never bite anyone. They're friendly dogs.'

'Never mind, Missie,' Dora said. 'She no understand English. She just a raw girl from the Transkei. You want some samp and beans?'

'Oh *ja*, Dora. You know I love your samp and beans.'

Dora dished the steaming sticky food for the three of us. For me, she used a porridge bowl from the pantry. For herself and her friend she reached under the sink for two enamel dishes.

'Go ask now if your brothers they want some.'

'OK.' I was unwilling to drag myself from the comfortable kitchen, from Chunky Charlie and the bright yellow spot of melting butter slipping down a small, glutinous heap of samp.

'Mi-ichael.' The lounge was empty and silent, the Christmas balls glinting from the tree in the mote-freckled sunlight from the window. Oupa sat in his library, a stream of smoke trailing past his squinted eyes. Intent on a ledger before him on the table, he didn't look up.

'Oupa, have you seen Michael and Neil?'

'Michael I haven't seen all morning. Neil I think is on the stoep. And your mom and dad, I think they're outside somewhere. I know your Ouma is out supervising something to do with the new pigs. Why, don't you want me? Looks like I'm the only one available. What do you want them for?'

'Samp 'n' beans.'

'Ugh, no, I'm certainly not available for that. Well, go and ask Neil then. I think he's still there.' He was smiling his soft smile, the look suffused with love and the gentleness of his character.

Neil lay full length on a towel just beyond the stoep. He had stretched out his Brylcreemed body in the full glare of the sun. As I stepped from the stoep, I could smell the heated hair oil which all the big kids cadged from their dads to speed a kif tan. Neil's head was buried in his pillowed arms. I wasn't sure, for a moment, what I should do. If he was sleeping he'd be furious at being woken. But he might be more furious at missing samp and beans, which wasn't made every day, after all.

My eye was caught by my strolling mom and dad, wandering through the flowers at the far end of the lawn near the wild fig. I could see he was leading her gently along the paths, his hands on her shoulders. And she, like the defensive buds around her, was unfurling her delicate petals for him, as she did at home. She was laughing and leaning on him, resting her head briefly on his shoulder. Sometimes he reminded me of that reaching wild fig, stretching its thick branches there above their heads. Rooted and raised so firmly in the dry soil of the region, he was all-enveloping in his protective warmth. He loved us to be flowers, his girls, and he sheltered us from the harsh facts and glaring details of our lives. I watched them as he took her hand, brushed it gently and walked off with it clutched firmly inside his own.

When I could no longer see them, I looked back at Neil and considered.

'Neil.' I called him softly, hoping that if he were

awake he would respond in some way and that, if he weren't, I had called too quietly to disturb him.

'Buzz off, brat.' He hadn't moved and his voice muffled through the restraining hold of his arms.

'Neil, d'you want samp 'n' beans?'

'No, of course I bloody don't want samp and beans. I'm not a baby any more to sit in the kitchen scoffing that stodgy stuff. I'll wait for my proper lunch, thank you very much.'

The kitchen was silent with chewing. Dora usually contorted her face while eating, moving her food around her mouth to catch her few teeth. But samp and beans she mushed with her gums, her lips and cheeks collapsing as she squelched them together. The dogs lay unmoving, side by side, just their ears flicking at the flies which hovered and landed.

I slid into my chair without speaking and began spooning my food fast into my mouth. My other elbow rested on the table, my left hand cushioning my head to read the folded-over comic. Engrossed, I hadn't realized anyone had moved until Dora called me. Both she and her friend were standing, their dishes scraped clean. Hearing the scraping of chairs and unaccustomed movement, the dogs had also lumbered to their feet.

'Missie, you can hold Kati for her to go. I hold Mikey. She scared to go with the dogs there. Come, we see her go and wave goodbye.'

I stretched my arm out sideways to clutch at the lolling dog's enormous collar. Docilely, she walked alongside me to the open screen door. The maid who was plucking the chicken in the scullery area looked at me in amusement as I passed her.

'I don't really have to hold Kati,' I told her earnestly, while Dora and her friend wandered slowly into the courtyard. I didn't want my panting, wrunkly dog, my namesake, to be misunderstood. 'It's just Dora's friend's scared. Mikey's sometimes a bit naughty. He once chased a horse and the horse bucked the rider right off its back. William had to race over and hold him tight with both arms while the horse galloped off again.'

As I chattered on, the maid plucked the chicken with small, deft movements. She was smiling. Dora was standing in the glaring courtyard, holding Mikey with one hand while she gesticulated with the other in final chatter and long farewell.

'Bye,' I called as I saw Dora's hand raised in a wave and her friend begin to walk through the courtyard to the yard on the other side.

'But Kati, Kati's never been naughty like that, you know. She'd never harm a fly. Look, you see, you don't have to really hold her tight. I can just keep my hand loosely on her collar. She'll sit here without moving. I c'n even tell her to sit while I feed meerkats.'

My resting hand felt the shiver of tension run through the dog and I laughed, thinking it was the mention of meerkats that caused it. Looking up, I saw that Dora's friend had started to run as she passed through the far door of the courtyard, in a straight line with the kitchen where I stood.

As I watched her, I felt Kati stretch from her tensed sitting position in a single leaping burst of energy. My hand clutched convulsively at her collar as she bounded, dragging me hard on to my knees, before ripping herself clear of me.

The world was suddenly filled with screams. I heard the maid scream in piercing bursts behind me, Dora's long wail, my own cracked whimper. And I heard the woman, Dora's friend, scream high and clear as she fell to her knees and clutched her elbows and hands protectively around her head and face.

I watched in slow, burning horror as Kati, beloved Kati, burst at her, again and again. And then suddenly the courtyard was filled with people. William was there, twisting the collar and dragging the dog away. The woman was crouched on the ground, her back to me in a keening backward and forward rocking motion. Her arms were still around her head. As William dragged the growling dog past me, I could see its pink, foaming saliva flecked on bared teeth and brown muzzle.

Oupa was at the woman's side, lifting her up by the arm. She was keening still, a high, horrifying sound in the sudden still.

'Don't look, little one. Don't look at her.' I could hear Neil's voice as he gathered me into his arms and began to carry me into the house. But I was stricken with shaking paralysis and my head turned to fix groping eyes on the woman.

Oupa was leading her step by step towards an upturned box against the kitchen wall. She held her doek up on one side of her head with both hands. Blood smeared her hands and cheeks and dripped from her chin above the blackened hole where her ear should have been. Dark fleshy chunks clung to the side of her head.

I began to pant in hot heaves that tasted of vomit. My body shook in rigid tremors as Neil held me firmly on one hip while he reached for the pot of rooibos which boiled perennially on the stove.

'O my magtig!' I could hear Ouma's voice from the courtyard. 'Het jy gehardloop? Hoekom het jy gehardloop? Why did you run, stupid girl? O magtig, now what shall we do? Dora, gaan nou dadelik vir die jong Miesies en Master roep.'

I heard my parents running around the side of the house to the courtyard as Neil lowered himself on to the kitchen table, holding me on his lap so that he could feed me sugared tea. Through the screen door I heard my mother's horrified 'Oh my God, what happened?'

'Keep quiet, Elaine,' Ouma's voice cut in. 'Jim, you'll have to drive her. Try old Doc Williams first. He's retired but he's not far. You know the farm. See if he can't *mos* sew her up. Otherwise you'll have to take her to Casualty in Grahamstown.'

I was unable to swallow the tea as the sounds from the courtyard trailed away to the yard where the cars were kept. I couldn't swallow at all, couldn't make those burning threads of shock go down my throat. Lifting me again, Neil carried me through to Oupa's bed, where he stroked my stinging scalp. I closed my eyes for a while.

'Shame, my darling. That was an awful thing for you to see.' I opened my eyes to see Oupa reaching lovingly for my icy hand. Behind him, Ouma's face was a mix of shock, distress and bursting irritation.

'*Ag*, man, how many times must I tell these people not to run?' she said as she walked to the window, staring out at the lawn. Oupa slipped a series of white sugar pills into my mouth, where they lay dissolving on my tongue. He always kept these tiny pills about him, sweet and comforting, to feed to himself and his loved ones in moments of upset and stress.

'But why, Ouma?' my voice scratched out. 'Why did the dog do that?'

'*Ag, my kind*, she wasn't one of our girls. The dog knew that. The dog knows the smell of all our people.'

'But it's never bitten anyone, never, even when Mr Van Rensburg was here. He's not from here and the dog didn't bite him.'

'Natives have a different smell about them. Dogs pick that up. It makes them wary. And the silly girl ran. That's the worst thing she could've done.'

'It's OK now, old thing,' said Neil, coming in with more tea. 'You're looking a bit better. Not so green about the gills.'

'I'd better go and see about Dora. She must settle down now. Nothing else can be done here,' said Ouma, turning from the window.

'She'll be all right, you know,' said Oupa softly. 'It looked very ugly but it wasn't really a serious injury. She'll be right as rain by tomorrow. She just needs to be fixed up a bit by the doctors.'

'But her ear . . .' I started to weep, in great shaking sobs.

'Poor child, it's an awful thing for you to have seen. But . . .' Oupa gave a deep sigh, '. . . these things happen, you know. I'm just sorry you had to see it.'

'But you don't understand, Oupa. It was because of me.'

'Oh now, what nonsense is this?'

'It happened because of me. I wasn't holding Kati properly. I thought she'd sit, like with the meerkats.'

'You're just a little girl. You couldn't have held that

great beast by yourself. Dora was stupid to have expected you to.'

'But it's because I loosened my hand. If I'd held tightly, the dog mightn't have gone.'

'You don't know that. You can't possibly say that dog wouldn't have gone for the girl, even if you'd been holding tightly. And quite frankly, it's probably a good thing you weren't. The dog might have dragged you with it, right into that mêlée.'

'No, no, the dog thought I was telling it to go. It's my fault.'

'Now, don't be silly. Take this pill. It'll make you sleepy. Neil, please fetch my copy of *Bosman* from the library. I'll read to you for a while, till you drop off, take your mind off it. Nothing like this can be your fault at your age, don't you realize that?'

I closed my eyes again, tasting the bitter gall of guilt in the back of my throat. I swallowed again and again, but it wouldn't go away.

'Rooineks, said Oom Schalk Lourens, are queer. For instance, there was that day when my nephew Hannes and I had dealings with a couple of Englishmen near Dewetsdorp. It was shortly after Sanna's Post, and Hannes and I were lying behind a rock watching the road . . .'

1989 . . . 3rd December

'Well, let's hope the aborigines don't get too uppity down under, or you'll be forced to move to Canada.'

I couldn't help that remark. I've just had enough. After this entire afternoon of warm wine and singed meat under the aching heat of their patio awning, I've had absolutely enough of Louise's smug sense that she's right about everything, that she can sashay off to live in Australia without a hint of moral condemnation around her.

'That's a remarkably snotty remark, Kate, even for you,' says Louise, placing her wineglass deliberately on the patio table and fixing me with her earnest gaze. 'You've known me for a long time – since varsity in fact. You've always known my views. I think it's particularly offensive of you to imply that I'm a racist.'

Oh, that's just too much. She thinks that her way-back-in-the-dim-distant-past lefty image gives her some kind of immune status, a passport to do as she pleases because she's proved her bona fides. My God, she's all outraged virtue, look at her. It doesn't even occur to her that, in the light of the fact that she's about to bolt, she marks herself very clearly as a hypocrite.

'Well, Louise dear, it seems to me that must be the reason you're suddenly emigrating, right on the threshold of change. After all, you stayed firmly put through all the oppressive times, shouting your mouth off.'

Louise opens her mouth to speak, but doesn't know what to say. She glances sideways at her friend, who is, besides us, the only guest at this Sunday afternoon *braai*. It was arranged, clearly, to break the news to Joe and me that they've sold the house, resigned their jobs, packed their bags; everything, in fact, except waved to us from the airport.

Obviously Louise invited this other woman as moral support. Both she and Louise work for one of the abounding acronymic non-governmental organizations, or ngo's as they rather preciously call them. She's made it perfectly plain to me already today that, as part of Louise's in-group, she's known about their plans for some time.

Christine, I think she said her name was. I didn't quite catch it. I was too busy being irritated by her hiking boots and black jeans – Jesus, it must be thirty-five degrees out here – and the way she swings her chair around to face me so that she can deliberately fold her arms above her head. Misreading me entirely, she clearly thinks she can shock this prissy school-marm by making a big show of the black bushes of hair protruding from the cut-off sleeves of her black T-shirt.

Exchanging pitying glances with Louise, she says to me now: 'Oh, that's fucking ridiculous. No one who really knows Louise would ever call her a racist. I can't believe you said that to her. I don't have kids, so I don't have Louise's pressures, but I know her reasons for going would always be moral.'

Oh well, of course. That's what this one's role is. Louise has always managed to surround herself with a coterie of ideologically sycophantic little arse-creepers. Well, I'll say this for her. She's succeeded in keeping it up, even through her great moral turnaround.

'Funnily enough, I've known Louise a lot longer than you have. But I do find it faintly amusing that you bunch – which ngo are you again: TRIC, FINC or PRIC? – that you bunch turn around so neatly on all your previous beliefs and still make it sound like you're treading the moral higher ground.'

'Actually, the reason we've decided to leave . . .' says Louise, tilting her uncompromisingly make-up-free face, the better to justify her greatest compromise, '. . . is the kids. The level of violence is such that I just can't justify our staying merely on some spurious ideological ground. And I can't actually see it improving through change. By all accounts, it's going to get worse.'

'Well, to quote you, Louise: "You can't make an omelette without breaking eggs." Isn't that what you used to say?'

'Oh don't be such a little bitch. I never expected it to be like this. We expected violence against the state, against the oppressors. We never conceived of the country just plunging into senseless crime and this . . . this violence against everyone.'

'What, you were working all those years for the glorious revolution, and you didn't expect it to affect you? Funny, I can see you now, fervent fist in the air, proclaiming: "Come the revolution, this and that." Oh, and weren't you the person who used to scorn people who used their jobs and their families and security as excuses for not getting involved?'

'Well, your priorities change when you have kids. We're not leaving for ourselves. We're leaving for the kids.'

To underline her point, underscore the difference between us, she stands suddenly and yells at the two splashing, screaming brats in the pool. 'Get out of there now, you two. Go'n change, please, straight into your pyjamas.'

Whinges and echoing whines of 'But why, Maw?' and 'It's so e-early, Maw,' float up from the water. Louise sits down again. She's done her motherhood thing. The children ignore her and continue their game. They know her well enough, I suppose, to have worked out for themselves that she's a person of instant responses and enthusiasms. She never follows anything through. Never did. She takes a sip from her wineglass – it's been sitting there so long, glowing in the lowered sun, it must be lukewarm by now.

'I personally would love to stay,' she continues, with a quick glance at her husband Peter. He shifts slightly in his chair and gazes absently at the sky. He's not going to be drawn into this discussion. 'I think things are going to be very interesting. I envy you actually. But I've had these kids. Now I owe it to them to give them the chance to grow up in a normalized society . . .'

Oh Jesus Christ, a 'normalized society'. Do people really talk this way, in real life?

'. . . where they can walk home from school without fear. But I wouldn't expect you to understand that level of unselfishness. You've never stopped staring self-absorbedly at yourself long enough to think about another human being, let alone one who's totally dependent on you for its security.'

'Ooh, we're getting heavily personal now, are we?' I force a laugh and trickle the last of the sun-warmed bottle of wine into my *braai*-smeared wineglass. Oh shit, not even the smallest block of ice left in the ice bucket. I swallow it back. No use sipping it. No one's making the slightest move to open another bottle. I suppose that's a hint. I wonder what the time is. Must be five at least.

Joe, slouched in his white patio chair with eyes half closed against the sun, rouses himself suddenly.

'*Ja* well, I think it's time we were going. If, that is, you women have finished tearing each other to pieces. Kate, it's nearly five. I've still got a lot of things to go through before tomorrow.'

Louise doesn't respond. She is breathing heavily, her eyes downcast and blinking fast.

Her young friend leans over to her, a hand on her arm, playing up the role of confidante for all it's worth. 'You must understand, Louise, the dynamics at work here . . .'

I can't believe this. Dynamics? What is this – a first-year sociology tutorial?

'. . . Your old friends feel hurt and bereft at your leaving. So they find it hard to appreciate your personal morality and they're taking their grief out on you.'

'Oh for Christ's sake!' I've had enough. 'Let's go, Joe. I've had enough justification rhetoric to last me a lifetime. Have a nice life in Australia, Louise. I truly hope you manage to cope with two kids and no house-hold help.'

'I understand your feelings of hurt, Kate, really I do. I'm sorry I never told you before, but we had to sort everything out first and make sure we could get in. I'd like you to know that I'm still your friend. And I won't take anything to heart that you've said today.'

'Oh please, Louise, preserve me from your patronizing friendship. Don't do me any favours. I don't need them, I promise you. We'll get along just fine back here without people like you.'

Louise sighs and shrugs, throwing herself back into her patio chair with folded arms and a mouth struggling between a pout and a caring curve. Peter rises to let us out.

'Thanks for the lunch, Louise,' I say as we step through the sliding doors into the house. 'It was certainly . . . informative. On many levels.'

'So, Joe,' says Peter quietly from behind us, as we negotiate the passage single-file. I can see he finds the silence uncomfortable, but he's clearly determined not to get into discussion over the merits of their leaving. I don't think he feels the same compulsion to justify their decision that his wife does. He wants to get out of here. The darkies are taking over, affirmative action rules, his kids will have to fight to get into university. That's that. But that's the last thing he wants to have to admit to us.

'So, Joe, how're the talks going? Haven't you been sitting in with your union guys in their newest round of negotiations?'

'Well, let's just say they're talking. What more can I say?'

'As bad as that, hey? Well I must say, it just underlines our decision . . .' He says this with some satisfaction. He clears his throat and stops, his hand on the front door. Glancing warily at me he turns back to Joe: 'You know, it makes me feel we must be doing the right thing when someone as optimistic as you can't bring himself . . . I mean, no longer feels excited enough to give us the blow-by-blow on what's happening in the country.'

Joe doesn't speak. What's the matter with him? He just stands there, his hands hanging at his sides, waiting for Peter to open the door. 'Well anyway,' says Peter, also looking curiously at Joe as he leads us through the door and down the drive, 'I'm sorry the women seem to be so uptight with each other. But I'm sure they'll get over it. I hope we see you before we leave. Nice having you, Joe. And you, Kate.'

He removes his hand from Joe's shoulder to manipulate the remote control button which will open the electric gate. Then he waves, backing swiftly up the drive to the house.

'Well,' I say to Joe as he starts the car, 'you were remarkably quiet about their leaving. You who've always had such a lot to say about people fleeing on the verge of change!'

'*Ag*, Kate,' he says on a sigh, 'somehow I don't feel quite easy any more about criticizing people for becoming disillusioned.'

'Not so long ago you would've been at their throats all day like a terrier, Mr Black-and-White. Mr Principle, that's how you always styled yourself before. Anyway, don't fool yourself. They aren't the types to be affected by your current attitude of disillusionment.'

'Why? You can't blame people for being disillusioned.'

'Oh Joe, don't be so naive. Louise never had the idealistic fervour of your brand of liberalism. She was a Stalinist. She was of the omelette-and-breaking-eggs persuasion, the end justifies the means and all that. I just find it all helluva amusing that, just as the supposed great change is about to happen, just as the people are really about to govern – and without even the upheaval of her much vaunted true revolution – she's up and leaving.'

'Well, you don't know what's really going on with them. You're not in the same position as they are, so it's hard to appreciate how they must really feel.'

'Oh yes, and now it's for the kids, always the kids, the new lefty excuse. You know what I find so particularly startling about this whole thing? Louise always shouted everyone down, even back in varsity days. She always told everyone what they should believe. And now, now that she's done the amazing turnaround, does she recant? No, now she still believes she's right. She just thinks she's mellowed a bit – she can't even see that she's turned her back on her principles. And she's still telling us what to think. Now she's saying people with kids who aren't leaving the country are selfish bastards who put ideology above morals!'

'*Ja* well, now you've had your little rave, maybe you'll feel better.'

'Jesus Christ, what's happening to me? I sound almost like you. This is your fault, Joe. I'm having an identity crisis because you've forgotten your role in life. You're the one who's supposed to be raving about the principles of the thing. I'm the one who's supposed to snort and ask what you really expected of cheap rat lefties, who gnaw and chew at the fabric of things and then leave the sinking state.'

I'm making him smile. At least that's something. He hasn't smiled in weeks. But why do I care? Jesus, I

The Innocence of Roast Chicken

really am teetering. He's forcing me out of my glass jar through sheer despair. And now he's setting out to build his own glass jar. I can see all the signs. I should know – I'm the expert glass jar builder.

But I can't allow him to. This just can't go on. As things stand, life can still continue with me safe in my own jar. But I need the balance, the support he's always afforded me. We can't both sit silent and unreachable in the back of our separate glass cages. I have to get him out of it somehow, he's making me feel quite unsteady. Kind of panicky.

'It's clear to me,' I continue, 'that I'm being forced to play some of your part because you've forgotten your script. Buck up, Joe, I depend on you for my role, to prompt me, feed me my lines. I can't go on being your understudy ad nauseam.'

Joe gives a slight chortle, but subsides again into that sagging silence I've been living with for weeks. It makes me decidedly uneasy. We park the car and unlock the house without a word. I head for the fridge. I could do with some nice cold wine, after that luke-warm stuff we've been drinking all afternoon. Joe makes for the answering machine and presses the replay button.

'Hey, Com Joe,' the message crackles into the kitchen, forcing Joe to bend lower to catch the words. 'It looks like a few more breakaway scabs are intending to go back to work tomorrow. But management shouldn't be allowed to use that to intimidate us in talks. Can we come see you early tomorrow? We need to talk about how we can convince them we intend to intensify the strike.' Click, *be-eep*.

Joe sighs, his expression unchanged. He pages

through his Filofax and, with his left index finger marking the spot, dials. He stands there for a long time, staring at the bright calendar on the wall. I'm about to go over and click my fingers in front of his staring eyes when he gives a small shake of his head and replaces the receiver.

'Not there, hey?'

'No, but that's usually the case. They leave me some urgent message about something that I'm going to have to prepare right away, and then they're not there to give me instructions.'

'So, Joe, you've been remarkably quiet lately about how this new round of talks is going. Surely there must be some progress? A few weeks ago, no thrust or parry would have gone undescribed to anyone who was willing to lend you even half an ear.'

'*Ja*, and no mocking jibe would've gone unexpressed by you.'

I sigh and unfold the *Sunday Star*, which lies still unread on the kitchen table. My eyes travel listlessly over the stories of hope and optimism and impending releases, and fix halfway down the front page on the headline:

FOUR BURNT TO DEATH IN
FOOD STRIKE VIOLENCE

Labour Reporter

Witbank – Four people have been burnt to death this week in the violence which has flared up over the Eastern Transvaal food factory strike.

One man, found 'necklaced' not far from the factory gate, is not yet formally identified, but is believed to be one of the hundreds of non-union employees who kept working during the past few weeks of industrial unrest.

The other three victims of violence – including a child – were not involved in the strike. One of these was Mr Bernard Mhlangu, who ran a trading store near Bronkhorstspruit and sold staple foods to the local community. Neighbours and family believe he was killed for not adhering to the boycott of staple foods produced by the South African Multi-Products Company (SAMPCO).

The boycott was announced recently by factory strikers, whose industrial action has so far achieved little in terms of compromise. No breakthrough appears to be in sight in deadlocked talks with management.

Mrs Mhlangu shouted at reporters: 'He died for what? For providing bread for his family? For selling food to the people? What was he supposed to do? Join the factory boycott and let us all starve?' she wept. 'Why must he die?'

Mr George Thembali, shopkeeper of Volksrust, said: 'My wife and child have been murdered for no reason at all. These *tsotsis* must pay for what they did. My life is also hard. If I sold no SAMPCO foods, my family would starve. And now they are dead anyway – burnt in my home.'

SAMPCO management said they would issue a statement as soon as they had details of the deaths at the retail outlets.

A union leader told this newspaper: 'We cannot stop the violence if it is not our members who are creating violence. This is just a strategy to discredit us in the community.'

Asked about plans to end the strike, he said: 'Any strike is a life and death affair for workers, who depend solely on selling their labour. The strike goes on . . . what other options have we?'

Observers, however, see signs of crumbling in union ranks. More workers, desperate for pay and mindful of Christmas bonuses and the need for jobs next year, are expected to join the trickle back to work which began last week.

Despite this the violence escalates. Last night the scenes of horror at the factory and in nearby communities were described as . . .

'Shit Joe, did you know about this thing on the front page? What does this take the death toll to now – fifteen?'

'You know very well it is. Why bother to ask me?'

He gives a small barking laugh, devoid of humour. 'I don't trust you, Kate. I know you're trying to tempt me into confiding in you so you can laugh and sneer at my past pretensions and my idealistic stupidity. But don't worry. I may be a late learner, but I'm coming around to your way of thinking. You always believed in the "All people are pigs" principle, didn't you? Well, I'm getting there, fast.'

'Oh Joe, I'm just trying to find out from you what's really going on. And you have to admit, I haven't said one word to you about the violence in the last couple of weeks. It's been hard, I'll admit, but I've taken a deep breath and held it. Not one snotty word have you heard from me. Not once have I reminded you of your past conversations, all liberally scattered with phrases like "moral higher ground" or "disciplined membership".'

'Gee, thanks for your deep consideration, Kate. I'm sure I can appreciate it. Particularly when I can see it in your face – that amusement as you stick your tongue in your cheek and raise your eyebrows – while you osten- tatiously turn the page of the newspaper without a word. Gee, you're so kind.'

'No but seriously, Joe. There's a cross-refer here to the leader page. D'you want to hear what the guy says?'

He doesn't reply, but I read it aloud anyway. What the hell. He should know what's being written.

STRIKE VIOLENCE: WHO'S TO BLAME?

By Derek Davis
Labour Correspondent

There is irony as well as stark tragedy in the confrontation between the South African Multi- Products Company (SAMPCO) and its unionized employees.

The 'necklacing' of a young man, thought by strikers to be a scab worker, and the 'torching' of at least four trading stores and shopkeepers' homes (the reports of violence from the Eastern Transvaal are still coming in) cast a bloody and black pall over burgeoning negotiating systems in this country. The strike at SAMPCO is only one of many which have suddenly erupted. But this one is terrorizing an entire community. The death and violence must not be allowed to obscure the facts.

The facts are:

*The union has been regarded as one of the most enlightened to come forward since the Wiehahn reforms of impossibly harsh labour laws some years ago.
*SAMPCO has been a pioneer in the painful process of recognizing – some say yielding to – the new unions.
*SAMPCO has a virtual monopoly in the manufacture and distribution of three staple foods in the rural areas from Witbank to the Natal coast and from Vereeniging to Lesotho. (But they claim that they dominate a regional market only because, by dispensing with advertising and packaging and unnecessary overheads, they supply basic foods to the poorest market more cheaply than anyone else. They allege that excessive demands for increased wages will raise food prices in these poor communities.)

But the welfare of innocent people seems furthest

from everybody's mind as wary cooperation between management and the union turns to disillusion and bitterness.

The hitherto pragmatic union is now saying that SAMPCO is 'an all-white capitalistic, monopolistic commercial conglomerate which exploits the workers and "the people".'

Setting aside the emotive factors in these labels, there remains some truth in their accusations. SAMPCO *is* white-controlled, capitalistic and a semi-monopoly. It is part of a major conglomerate. It is a financially healthy concern, and this is reflected in its remarkably buoyant share price.

Why does the company not pay its workers more?

Joint MDs Dennis Johnson and Johan du Preez have argued all along that its wage offer – which would bring the basic minimum to R5,45 an hour – is fair. They have claimed the strike to be contrived – aimed at recapturing the limelight from the released ANC leaders who were hailed as 'the people's' heroes at a mass rally recently. They claim they are paying higher wages than any similar commercial organization.

On the other hand, the union can be forgiven for becoming covetous in the light of pre-tax profits of R200 million for the last half-year, and a 25 per cent increase in dividends.

'The workers' wages are small while the company's profits are big,' says union secretary-general Terence Semani. He claims that his hard negotiating with senior management over the past 5 years has resulted in the boast now made by Messrs Johnson and du Preez that they pay higher wages than any other factory in the Eastern Transvaal.

The union also accuses middle management of being ruthless in singling out and victimizing shop stewards as 'troublemakers'. It claims that its members work in unhealthy conditions, and that their hours are abnormal because of the demands of this sector of the food industry.

On the contrary, say the joint MDs. The company has for years paid higher wages than its competitors and has done so out of a sense of fairness as well as good business. 'Our market is the one from which our employees are drawn. We know where our bread is buttered. We are intent on being enlightened employers. But when we offer a 15 per cent increase – the *increase* itself being the highest in the industry – the union rejects it out of hand and demands a ridiculous 35 per cent!'

But why this level of vicious and bloody violence?

The answers are too complex to canvas in detail here, but some observers believe that the basic cause is the union's frustration and anger. Frustration at being constantly and patronizingly outmanoeuvred by management. The union, in this strike, is pitted against a powerful, determined and sophisticated adversary.

Food distribution has suffered, but carefully laid contingency plans – involving stockpiling and the use of temporary labour – has meant production has remained largely unaffected. Some observers believe there can be no doubt that worker frustration at continued SAMPCO output is behind much of the violence which has marred this strike.

The cards have also been stacked against workers in their second-line strategy of a product boycott. SAMPCO's virtual monopoly in certain areas, and the fact that many black people depend on SAMPCO food sales for a living, have been potent obstacles.

On the other hand, the union claims it is not responsible for the violence at SAMPCO and in the Witbank community. It hints darkly that the factory is trying to turn the community against the union by assaulting and murdering innocent people. That's why masks and balaclavas have been seen on the killers.

But some of the neighbours and families of the victims say that it is union gangs who are creating terror by death.

The rights and wrongs, and the historical injustices involved in this vicious dispute, fade into insignificance once you look past the rhetoric and see the plight of the poor who live in the Witbank district. Whoever is killing and destroying, the fact is that the people who have had their homes burnt down and their loved ones murdered are innocent victims. Their plight is heart-rending. Yet even as the test of power seems to be ending, and workers trickle back to the factory, the violence escalates. If the union is not involved in the violence, then it ought to get involved in stopping it.

The same of course applies to SAMPCO, which must accept responsibility for the actions of even the lowliest in its (white) management ranks.

The red and black pall that hangs over Witbank tonight is something the whole nation should condemn. If it is caused by uncontrolled violence, then both sides should help to end it. If the violence is indeed orchestrated – orchestrated by some power clique in the union or in middle management using a would-be rival union – then it must be rooted out, now, before its poison infects our whole society.

When a breadwinner is kicked to death and incinerated in a ring of petrol; when a child is burnt to death by someone trying to make a political point, all of us are brutalized.

I clear my dry throat, and take a gulp of wine.
'What do you think of his analysis?' I ask of Joe's hunched back, watching it slowly move as he turns towards me. 'Is he talking shit or sense? . . . Don't look

at me like that, Joe. I'm interested. I may like to mock you a bit but that's because I've never had the same unrealistic expectations about people that you have. I'd just like to know what you think the union's role is in all this necklacing and stuff.'

'*Ja* well, the matter of violence came up on the first day of talks. I suppose I wasn't really even that surprised or shocked by the two attitudes – union's and management's – after the line everyone took in the interdict proceedings . . .' His voice trails away and he wanders listlessly over to the fridge. He opens the door and stares into it.

'And so, what'd they say?'

Joe closes the fridge again. 'Well . . .' he turns to gaze out at the shadows '. . . I suppose I now realize how scummy all sides turn out to be in a vicious struggle like this.'

'Well,' I snap, irritation breaking through my concern, 'it's taken you long enough.'

He pauses for so long that I think I've closed him up again. But, as if I haven't spoken, he continues at last. 'Until that interdict came up, I suppose I expected someone to care that people were dying. But they don't, you know. They just use it as a prod on the other side. Both sides use the same prod and everyone refuses to accept the smallest jot of responsibility.'

'But you still haven't told me what they said . . . about the violence this week.'

'Well, there sat management, pretending to the most awful shock, but really smiling at the moral higher ground they perceived it was giving them. "We must state," they said at the start, "how we condemn these actions of strike supporters. We have always held the utmost concern and care for those dealers who stock our products." Oh please, really! A more cynical statement it would be hard to devise, especially considering they've absolutely refused to compromise or negotiate at all, throughout . . .'

'Well, that's predictable, I suppose. But what did the union say?'

'. . . So, while I was still boiling with indignation over management's statement, in comes the union with a bland refusal to accept any responsibility either. "Oh," they say. "We can't be held responsible for the responses of the community. For the legitimate anger generated in the community. We can't do anything about it. The ball is in management's court. It's easy for them to fix, they just have to meet our demands. That'll stop the violence." '

'And what about their claim to the press that the violence was orchestrated by management?'

'Oh that! That never came up at all. I think that was just a little snippet to give them some martyred-victim-of-the-struggle status in the community. I don't think anyone even seriously believes it. No, in talks the violence was just something to be used, something that would "stop just like that" . . .' he clicks his fingers in front of my face, '. . . "if management would only shift from their position".'

'So's that been more or less the tone of the entire week of talks, so far?'

'Ja, neither side will move. No one really cares about the injuries and deaths. That's just part of the chips that both sides use to bargain with . . . You know, Kate, I don't know why I bother.'

'Well, neither do I if you're so put out just because

human beings don't live up to your fairy-tale expectations. I'm not going to tell you why you should bother.
Don't expect that of me. I can't give you your faith
back. I've never had any. But I'm sure you, the great
idealist, still believe there's some good in the cause,
even beyond all the scumminess you've only just
noticed. Only don't ever expect that from me. That's
not my role.'

'No, you can't give me back my faith. But you know
something I've just realized? You can't bear for me to be
without it. You've never had any faith, in anything.
That's true! But you can't handle me being without.
You've sucked off my faith and idealism all these years,
dragging me down with you. But you still expect me to
carry the full burden of keeping it alive. You can't get
off your butt, there in the protected haven of your own
selfish, cut-off little world, and help me now that I need
it.'

'Well, I can't see what I can do for you, Joe. I can't
give you what I don't have.'

Joe turns abruptly back to the window. He stands
there a moment with his hands clenched, breathing
heavily. He lifts one tensed arm and briefly hits the
window frame with the side of his large fist.

'I don't know,' he says, his voice strangling with the
effort of trying to control his emotions. 'But all these
years I've believed that you'd surprise yourself at the
resources you'd find, if you dug deep enough. If only
for your own survival. But really, if this's the way you
want it, then fine. Watch me go down. But bear this
thought in your shuttered little mind. Can you survive
without my hope and idealism to support you?'

'Well . . .' with a forced high-pitched titter, 'I've

always wondered how *you've* managed to survive with your dangerous level of optimism, with that raw sensitivity to everything and your unreal belief in people.'

Turning suddenly towards me, he erupts: 'You're a damaged half-person. By what, I've never discovered. You latched on to me because I've always been damaged in the opposite way. I was damaged by being unformed, by being the overprotected child, by believing in Father Christmas too long. We're two damaged halves that sucked off each other for our survival. Can you afford to let me lose everything, to sink into your abyss, without supporting me in some way, without giving me any help?'

'This conversation is futile, Joe. There's no point to it. I don't even know what you expect of me, and I'm sure that, if I did, I wouldn't be able to give it anyway.' I pause, trying to find some way out of this dangerous maze.

'Tell me some more about the talks. I'm interested, really.'

'Well, I don't know what more I can tell you.' He sighs and sinks to a kitchen chair, his elbows on the scrubbed wood of the table. He rubs both large hands over his face, distorting his eyes into slits before letting them go. 'Both sides sit there taking extreme positions and bristle at each other. Neither side will give an inch in case the other side thinks they're showing weakness.'

He pauses, gazing at me with those raw, aching eyes of his. I think he's finished talking, as I sip my ice-cold wine and lean against the wall. But, after a long silence, he continues.

'It's dragged on so long now that the rank and file is tiring. It's nearly Christmas time. They need money.

They don't need to lose their jobs, which looks like the conclusion to this unless things end soon. And some are, understandably, caving in and going back to work . . . you heard that, didn't you, on the answering machine. Anyway, management's using this in the most cynical way. "Oh," they told us last week, "but we're so pleased that some strikers are beginning to realize how good we are, how fair our original offer was." That just makes me boil. But the union's no better. "We'll never give in. We can make this strike last for ever. We can destroy the company." And, I suppose, what they don't add: "We can make the strike-breakers extremely sorry they were even born. And then blame it on management." '

'So it looks like this could drag on long past Christmas? For ever, in fact?'

'*Ag*, that's what they say. I don't believe it. I think the situation's against it. The strike's actually crumbling as we speak. People seem to be drifting back to work in greater numbers. Union leadership and management are caught in this bind of posturing. But actually the rank and file realize it can't go on for ever. They can't sustain it.'

'And you, Joe? Can you sustain this work?'

'I don't know any more, Kate. I just don't know about anything. I don't even know what I believe any more. I feel like everything's crumbling, all at the same time . . .'

He stands suddenly, almost toppling his chair, and makes for the kitchen door. I think that's the end of it. But at the door, he pauses.

'. . . Us too,' he says, turning his dissolving face towards me. 'I don't know how we can hold things tógether. It was always me, you know, me with my hopeless optimism thinking you'd get better, that we'd come right in the end . . .'

I will not look up at him. I am intent on my tearing nails, and the scrumpled newspaper in front of me, as he says: '. . . I haven't the strength to hold things together any more. I don't even think I've the strength to believe in anything. What can we do, Kate? What is there left for me here?'

1966 . . . One day to Christmas

The heat began to grow in the day's embryo. I could feel it even there, surrounded by the dark smell of fecund fruit. I could taste it, the day's heat still to come, in the juice dripping from my sucked peach, plucked with the chill still on it.

I was walking the ritual route, through the orchard to the swimming place, baptizing the day with a ceremonial swim, early enough to catch it fresh, dust-free and unspoilt. It was my own small offering to Jesus, an unspoken prayer for the day, that special day, the day before Christmas.

It wasn't too late. There was still time before Christmas. And this was the day of waiting, of anticipation. You could hold it in your hands and feel the possibilities for Christmas to come. Now perhaps God would make everything well. Now was the time for Him to heal the farm, heal this day of promise – for Him, if only for Him, and the celebration it pleased Him that we should hold. Surely God knew that for us this was a time of birth, not death and violence; a time of rejoicing, not mourning. He would make it OK for us to glory in the story of His baby.

I stepped from the musky dank of fallen fruit into the

glowing hope of the sun. My feet, hard from years of gravel roads and thorny grass, planted themselves on the settled grey of chill ground, producing small blossoms of dust. I could hear the strident boast of the cocks parading before the day. And the first *zing* of insects, triumphant in the early sunlight.

The water was still, darkened by shadow, and I could lower myself gently into its wallowing caress almost without ripple. I hadn't swum for days and days, not since that day . . . but I didn't want to think about it on this morning of such taut-strung hope.

For days I had had nothing to do with the farm. I had crouched in Oupa's library, mooning in my self-pity. And angry, so angry at life, even with God. But most of all I was angry with this farm, this living, breathing organism that had worked so hard all my life to convince me of its perfection, and then laughed as it ripped it all away. And underneath there were no banks of flowers, soft animals and unconditional love. Behind that curtain of deceitful perfection lay entrails, the smell of death, hateful feelings and flesh ripped dark and bloody . . . Oh Jesus, gentle Jesus, hold me from thinking of it. Hold me from seeing it every time I close my eyes.

Each day since I had fought and fought myself to keep the nausea away from my mind, and each time I looked at something it was coloured suddenly by a wash of dark blood. It lapped over the flower garden, swelled and submerged the sinking fig tree; it covered the chicken *hoks* and smeared the wooden stoep.

But now this water would wash it away. The clear chilling freshness of God's special place at this, His very special time, when the morning was still new, this would cleanse my mind and prepare the day to come.

And it seemed that it did, as the day rose in its fulsome heat and a small blossom of joy appeared suddenly in the very pit of my stomach. The smell of bacon sizzled from the kitchen and the jar of *soetkoekies* stood in its rightful place.

'The baby chicks are expected today. You can come and watch as William unpacks them if you like.' Ouma stood at the breakfast table, brushing her curls back with both harassed hands. She was staring at me closely, anxious lines puckering her forehead. This was the only way she knew to reach me. I had watched her detachedly these last few days, sorry for her brusque struggle to help me, but tied by my anger and my self-pity, unable to reach back in acceptance of her small consecrated gestures of Christmas cake and *koek-susters*.

'Oh Ouma, I'd really *smaak* that. It's them I love best of all the animals.'

She smiled suddenly, dropping her raking hands. As usual her tightened face was sweetened and rounded all at once by her slow smile. She ran a hand across my hair.

'That's my girl,' she said. And then she turned, bustling to the kitchen.

'Dora, Dora, make sure the Christmas pud is boiled today, *sien jy*, and the chickens must be plucked, and the meringues. I'll come in and make the meringues this morning. William, Wil-liam . . .'

Her voice faded behind the screen door's *skree-bang*. The rest of the family ate in silence. Looking at me, my father drew in a breath to speak. Oh please, I thought, don't let him ask me. I turned to Oupa and caught the slight shake and frown he sent across the table to my dad. And then he smiled at me and covered my clenched hand with his.

'How're you getting on with *King Solomon's Mines*? Enjoying it?'

'*Ja*, Oupa, it's great. You know, it's kind of like the kind of story you can really get inside. And you can forget everything, I mean, where you are and everything, while you're reading.'

'Well, that's as it should be. That's the best kind of book, isn't it? I think you'll find you'll want to look for books that can do that for you periodically all your life. In fact, I think if a person were to live buried in and surrounded by books, it would be the perfect haven, the best possible sanctuary that life could provide.'

And later, from the low embracing branches of the wild fig tree, it seemed as if God had heard me. The breeze shuffled and shushed through the large leaves and riffled the pages of my book in the growing day. And when I looked up from the cool of my place to the shimmering heat across the lawn, Oupa waved and nodded to me from his smoke-wisped place on the stoep.

I watched as Kobus, trailed by Jonas, scuffed bent-headed to the edge of the stoep. They waited, kicking at tufts of grass with their bare feet. When Michael raced out to join them, they whooped off together around the side of the house, arms windmilling through the wild heat.

I waited there in the arms of the tree, sitting motionless even as the faint growl of the truck reached me – I knew it was still valleys away. Only when I heard it revving and gear-straining to make it over the rutted

254

farm road into the yard, did I leap down.

And they were there, boxes and boxes of deafening cheeps carried swiftly hand-to-hand into their window-less hut. I sat in the fragrance of fresh sawdust, watching the frenetic yellow darting of frantic fluff. Unpacked, they huddled on to each other under the yellow light of the central warmer.

Ouma and William communicated silently, reading each other's lips and signing with their hands. The noise was deafening, one loud continuous high-pitched barrage of melded cheeps. Coiled among them, I could feel their pattering feet and brushing wisps of down against my bare crossed legs. I could catch and cradle them in my hands, hearing their cheeps separate from the beating chirrup in the room as I lifted them to my cheek. Released, each scurried into the whirling mass of pressing yellow bodies and its tiny sound merged again into the whole.

I sat there a long time after the others had gone, feeling the gentle newness of the chicks, the fresh unspoilt innocence of birth and the softness of the farm envelop me in its brushing yellow warmth. I sat, strok-ing the writhing mass of wriggling down, feeling it separate into tiny living beings as they pattered across my legs to disappear again on the moving floor. I sat, feeling the heat build from the central warmer, until Ouma appeared in the doorway with her peremptory beckoning arm and summoned me to lunch.

All she was feeling at that moment – exasperation, love, and relief at my recovery – leapt from her simple heart and scrummed there across her plain farm face as we walked hand in hand back to the house.

'I love you, Ouma.'

'Ja, my kind, ek's ook baie lief vir jou.'

'Where are you taking me, Ouma? Aren't we going back for lunch?'

'*Ja*, but first I thought it was time for you to choose your own chicken. I thought you'd *maar* enjoy that.'

She led me to the *hok* of scrawny-necked teenage chickens, where their silly frenzy made me laugh again. I couldn't stay cross with them, they were such idiotic, lovable creatures.

'So which one do you want, *my kind*?'

My own chicken, mine! For Christmas obviously. I could take it home, let it run around the garden. I could feed it myself and find its eggs. I could eat my own eggs for breakfast.

'Oh that one, Ouma. Thanks, Ouma, thank you. I just love that one, with the black speckle on her wing.'

I'll call her Sheba, I thought as we walked hand in hand to the house. She looks like a queen. A name like that would make a chicken proud.

The family was seated as we appeared. All except Michael, who scrapped and scrambled his panting way into the dining room, only to be sent to the bathroom with me to wash our grimy hands and faces.

'So, sis, what'cha been doing? You know what? We've been go-carting down the farm roads by the back there. It's just so *lekker* you can't believe it. It's kif, like flying. Wanna come after lunch?'

'*Ja*, I think so. Will you go with me the first time?'

'*Ja* OK. But don't act like a sissy in front of Kobus. I said you were OK, almost like a boy, so he said OK, you could come with us.'

Lunch gulped its way into our two dusty, impatient bodies as the family ate slowly in the heat of the soporific afternoon, their easy chat a low desultory buzz. We escaped as soon as we could, Michael and I, cadging a whole bowl of peeled prickly pears from the fridge.

'*Ag*, please, Dora, please. There's still time to peel more for tomorrow. Shh, don't tell Ouma, hey. Or I'll smack your bottom, smack smack smack,' said Michael, clutching Dora around her vast, chuckling middle and swiping his small hands at her swaying behind.

'Hai hai hai, *klein* Ma-aster,' she said, wiping her mirth-filled eyes with the edge of her doek. Shaking her head she held the bowl in front of us.

'And who will peel more, and *pluk* them from the *bosse*? Your Ouma she want them for Christmas breakfast.'

'You, Dora, you will,' said Michael, shouting with laughter as he wrestled for the bowl which she held forward and then snatched beyond his reach. 'Because you love us. And you won't be so *mafuta* if you run up the hill one more time. Thanks, Dora. We love you, Dora.' He managed to scrabble his fingers on to the rim and we escaped the kitchen, giggling over our conquest.

We ran quickly through the closed courtyard, where Ouma had enclosed the dogs for the rest of our visit. I couldn't look at them as they lay panting in the thin shade at the edge of the house. I didn't think I could ever talk to them again, or pet their scrumpled muzzles. I hated them.

We scampered to the Forest, I galloping sideways in the relief of feeling whole again, Michael careful not to spill the prickly pears. We left the succulent bowl there, on a water-cooled rock at the edge of the stream. We scrambled through the bush and out into the blast of heat on the open veld. And then to the fence, alongside the pigsty and the sheds. There was no one to be seen and shadows were scarce. The flies buzzed and irritated the nostrils and the edge of the eyes while we waited there, next to the silent sty of sleeping pigs.

Ooh ooh ooh-we-ooh, *ooh ooh ooh-we-ooh*, whistled Michael into his cupped hands, imitating the call of a dove. It seemed not to carry in the dead air of the still afternoon, but then came an answering whistle from way behind the sheds.

Ooh ooh ooh-we-ooh.

And two khaki figures scrambled to the fence dragging a rough wooden go-cart, its wheels swiped from some old pram. Between the four of us, we pushed and heaved it over the fence and jogged with it to the steeply sloped road beyond the swimming place.

'I'll just take my sister the first time. Show her how it's done, OK?' said Michael, and he sat behind me, holding the rope. His knees poked their skinny grazes on each side of me as the other two shoved the cart. It bounded forward, creaking and bouncing through the deep water-hewn ruts in the road. As we hit the steepest section we raced faster and faster, crackling and skidding on the packed earth, falling into dongas as deeply striated as those of a dried river bed, righting ourselves and careening fearsomely down the last section towards the flat. I was clutching the splintered sides, gasping in fear and elation, when Michael's bare heels shot out and slid us to a slow halt at the bottom of the hill.

And then it was Kobus's turn, controlling the cart desperately through the deep, creaking ruts, his thin body bouncing into the air with bare, bent-up locust legs. He held it till just past the steepest section of the hill.

I saw the wobble take the wheels in front and shudder through the cart. Unable to move, we watched the slow swerve which overtook it. For countless seconds, the cart swerved wildly on the steep, riven road before it crashed into the bank. Kobus flew head first from the cart, landing with a thump alongside an antheap.

We ran down the hill to where he lay unmoving. My heart was pounding from my mouth in quick sobbing gasps as we reached the bottom. And then he moved, pulling his legs up to his stomach and kneeling, crouched over himself. He gave a small sound like a mew, and then a groan, which might have been a sob. Winded, he was gasping for air.

'You OK, Kobus?' asked Michael, not sure whether he should touch him or not. He squatted down alongside him.

Kobus gasped until he could take enough breath into his body. '*Ja*,' he rasped, breathing intently. We watched each breath struggle to enter his body. 'I'm OK now,' he gulped at last. 'I'm not a sissy. That often happens on these roads. The only thing is, I think the axle's now bent a bit. I don't think we can go any more today. Sorry, hey!'

'*Ag*, shame, Kobus. Is it broken?' I asked, relief filling me with billowing magnanimity.

'*Ag*, my pa'll help me fix it. But we can't ride any more today. I just have to get my breath, OK?'

'*Ja*, OK, Kobus.' We sat with him in silence while his rasped breathing became easier and finally quieted.

'So have you ever looked properly at these anthills? They're quite *lekker*, you know,' he said suddenly. Michael and I looked up at him from where we squatted flat-footed, pulling at the wild grass stalks. Jonas squatted a small distance away, leaning his back against the anthill.

And so we stood as Kobus and Jonas showed us the busy nest of large black ants. With his pocket hunting knife, Kobus hacked at the top of their heap, exposing their myriad frenzy. I found I could catch them between my fingers and watch their leg-waving fight.

'I've got a magnifying glass in my pocket, you know,' said Michael. 'Have you okes ever roasted these big ants? That's what Kate 'n' I do in PE. Wanna try? They taste kind of like salty.'

We caught the large, substantial bodies between our fingers, placing each in turn on the dry packed earth. Covering the creature with the magnifying glass, we watched the cruel gleam in the sun bake it in seconds. Showing off slightly, Michael and I nibbled at the crisped salty bodies before offering our next cooked offerings to the other two boys.

Jonas rubbed his teeth tentatively together on the very end of the bulbous abdomen. Then he spat, a great foaming glob, which wet the dry earth. Shaking his head with screwed-up face he objected: 'Uh uh, uh uh, uh uh.'

'*Ja dis lekker*,' said Kobus. Determined not to be outmanoeuvred in this showing-the-others-around contest, he added: '*Nou ja*, well let me now show you something else. You haven't seen anything.

'Come, Jonas. Let's show them what we do with the red ants. And watch it, those ants bite.'

'*Ja*, we know,' I said, blasé with my languid prior knowledge of red ants.

We searched among the squat anthill towers for a nest of the small vicious red ants. 'OK,' Kobus called to Michael when Jonas located one. 'Go stand by the black ants. And wait till I tell you.'

I stood with Michael, waiting while Kobus hacked the top from the heap. 'OK, now hold that piece of anthill fast. Now run across here with it as quick as you can.'

The two boys raced past each other, Kobus howling and laughing as the red ants attacked his hands. Each dropped his piece of anthill on to the open nest of the other ants.

'Hey Jeez, look at them fight,' said Michael as we watched the pitched battle of black ants against the intruders who had dropped in on them suddenly from the sky. A vanguard of ants stood and fought. As they died, rows of warriors stepped in to replace those that fell.

'Hey, Michael, look at this, it's kif. Really, come round the back here.'

Michael joined me at the back of the anthill, where a solid stream of nursemaid ants carried white eggs out of the rear entrance, while the warriors fought the intruders in front. After a while we swapped with the other two boys, watching the black ants battle for their home against their smaller, more vicious opponents.

I can't remember if we tired of them after a while, and I can't remember the end of those battles, those fights to the death of the vastly outnumbered reluctant intruders. I remember only that, beaten finally by the afternoon heat, we trailed off to the Forest, where our cool prickly pears waited on the water-washed rock. I remember that we sat there, cross-legged on the flat stones, Jonas squatting on the path, while we swopped competitive snake stories.

I had once felt a *skaapsteker* slither across my foot. 'Oh, that's nothing,' said Kobus, beating my story with his own, of climbing a tree and coming face to face with a boomslang. Michael had a boy in his class in Port Elizabeth who had once been bitten while bundu-bashing in the Valley. His whole leg had swelled up and gone blue, he said.

With the empty bowl, we wandered back to our farmhouse. Three of us stood in the yard, flicking stones at each other with our toes, while Michael ran into the kitchen with the bowl. 'So what shu'we do then?' asked Kobus when Michael returned. He had waited – wouldn't have asked such a question of me, a girl.

'Hello, children.' I heard my mother's call behind me and turned to see my father and her walking hand in hand towards us. 'I've just been to see the new chicks. Cute, aren't they, my darling?'

'*Ja*, Ma, I saw them this morning,' I answered.

Kobus and Jonas were overcome with hanging-head confusion as my parents approached. Kobus's blushing face gazed bobbingly at his tangling legs. My mother looked at him with faint amusement.

She never allowed us to behave like that. At home she always told us: 'There's no such thing as shy. I won't have my children behaving like rough farm children who've never seen people in their lives.'

'So, little boys . . .' Oh no, how could she call them 'little?' I sank with the embarrassment. I could see my mother had set out to torment them a little, poke at them for their quaint oddities, their veld ways. '. . . So are you all ready for Father Christmas? Have you written to him to tell him what you want?'

'Ma-a-a,' said Michael and I, but there was no deflecting her.

'Shoosh, you two. Can't I hold a discussion with your friends? Now then, what do you expect him to bring you?' She could have spoken to Kobus in Afrikaans, but she was being her English self, her delicate, citified, thoroughly modern self. She wanted to distance herself, to show him and his like what she was now – not some Afrikaans *plaasjapie*.

'Ma-aa,' said Michael. 'People our age don't believe in Father Christmas any more.'

'Oh, is that so?'

Turning her quizzical gaze on Kobus, she said: 'Well, I don't know about your family, little boy, but in mine, children who don't believe in Father Christmas don't get presents. How about you, Kati? You believe.'

I was torn. I did sort of half believe. Well, I had an idea Father Christmas was my dad, but I still wanted to believe. But I kept very quiet about it in public. I knew very well that, if I wanted to fit in with these big boys, I had to sneer at the very idea. But then, was she serious about the presents? Surely not. Anyway, I couldn't stand up to the humiliation an admission would draw me into.

'Ma-a,' I mumbled, kicking at stones and squirming with my feet. 'No one believes any more, Ma.' I could hear that, even to myself, my voice sounded doubtful.

'Well, I simply don't know how you can expect presents then. And stand up straight. Don't squirm about in that way. You're not a farm child. You're used to talking to adults. Look me straight in the eye when I talk to you.'

Then, leaving us all hot with embarrassment, she smiled beneficently upon us and wandered into the house, crooking her arm through my father's. We stared uncomfortably at our feet. Conversation had vanished.

'*Ja* well, I think I better be going home,' said Kobus.

'*Ja* OK, you okes,' muttered Michael. He was cross, and I could see he wanted them to go now. 'See you after Christmas then. Bye.'

'So you don't really believe in Father Christmas, do you?' Michael asked me. He needed to vent his crossness, to spoil something, get his own back.

'Naa,' I said. 'Well, not really. Do you really think he's not real?'

'I'll show you he's not real. Come!'

And he led me into the house, tiptoeing down the passage to the large wood-scented cupboard in my parents' bedroom. There he showed me the piles of odd-shaped gifts, brown-wrapped and Christmas-wrapped. I found I didn't really mind so very much. It hadn't spoilt the day. I didn't count this. I really knew about him all the time, I think. It didn't matter, God. You didn't break your promise, God, it was still OK.

Despite the slight disappointment, the size and shape of the gifts built a wavering excitement inside me. And we giggled, Michael and I, at the anticipation and the exhilaration of what we had done. We didn't mind; it was Christmas tomorrow, and God was making everything right. He was the fixer, the healer. Tomorrow would be wonderful.

In the evening after supper we sat on the cricket-singing stoep and sucked at cut slices of watermelon. Then my father, with his quiet smile, reached behind him for a large stick of biltong. He must have been hoarding it since we arrived. Without a word, he leant over to slide his penknife from his pocket and began to slice pieces off and throw one to each of us in turn. Michael and I gazed up at him hopefully, eagerly catching each small piece in our laps as it was thrown.

Then we balanced on the stoep rail, not wanting to let go of Christmas Eve. Clinging to the bones of the day, picked clean of heat and dust. If only I could catch one more glimpse of Snowball's father, that omen streak of white perfection. Then everything would be perfect for tomorrow. Christmas on the farm. It was my best thing in the world. It just had to be right.

1989 . . . 15th December

'The strike's over.'

'Jesus, you're pissed, Joe. I don't think I've ever seen you pissed before.'

'I said the strike's over.'

'I know. I heard it on the radio this afternoon.'

Joe drops his bulk into the delicate reproduction across from me. His whole body sags like a dropped sack of sand. He gazes at me in silence while our impossibly young waitress, the one with the perky blonde pony-tail, bobs eagerly across the crowded restaurant. She smiles at me, half in solidarity, half pityingly I think. Perhaps she thought I'd been stood up, all the time I was steadily making inroads into my Boschendal.

'Hi there, my name's Juliette. And I'm your waitress for the evening. Can I bring you something to drink, sir?'

'Bring a whisky.'

The room tinkles with gentle sounds. Softly chiming music, background to the tinkling laughter of the very wealthy. Crystal glasses chink quietly against each other while blocks of ice and languidly held knives and forks clink discreetly. It's a very expensive restaurant, but the food is orgasmic, as they say. Food is the one indulgence we've never stinted on. And, after all, we can afford it. We've no private schools, therapists and dancing classes to pay for.

'Well, Joe, you're fairly substantially late. Didn't we agree to meet at seven? Can I assume this means you've been celebrating the end of the strike? Or maybe drowning it out of your mind?' To myself, I mutter: *And you clearly are out of your mind, at this stage.*

'Oh what the fuck! Fuck the strike. Fuck the workers. Fuck this godawful country.'

The background music suddenly sounds very loud.

'Oh very profound, Joe. Well done. But judging by the silence you've created in this terribly refined atmosphere, I think we'd better be leaving.'

'Forget the whisky,' I tell Juliette as I hand her my credit card. She rather discreetly hustles us out of sight of the entrance. Her expression is now one of pure pity – my goodness, not only nearly stood up, but then joined by a drunken man. Just you wait, my girl, life will catch up with you one of these days.

I drive Joe home after manhandling him into my car. But judiciously, so that he thinks he's getting in himself and making his own decisions. Men are so pathetic about being helped. His car will just have to take its chances in the parking lot until tomorrow. We'll fetch it on the way home from our Saturday shopping expedition.

Joe stumbles into the house, presses the TV On switch and flops on the couch in the still darkened room. He catches only the very last item – a light-hearted one – of the TV1 news. And it's Friday, so it's in Afrikaans. Joe mutters to himself, turns it off and drops his body back on the couch. His hands are over his face, scrubbing at it, so it's a moment before I see that he's weeping. But not Joe's usual manly leaking at the eyes, with the break in his voice betraying his macho emotions.

Great heaving sobs begin to tear at his huge body. He removes his hands suddenly, uncaring of whether I'm watching or not. His mouth looks painful, a broken gash in his smeared, wet face.

His utter despair frightens me.

'*Ag*, come on, Joe.' I sit beside him. I don't know how to reach him. I have no practice at this. And how can anyone reach into a pit of such despair? I sit in silence, but for once it is, from my side anyway, a gentle silence.

'Can't you at least just tell me what it is you're taking so hard? Is it the settlement agreement?'

'It's everything, Kate, everything about the strike, the violence, the settlement, everything.'

'They said on 702 – I was listening in my car this afternoon – they said the union accepted management's original pre-strike offer. Is that what's got to you?'

'*Ag*, Kate . . .' He sighs.

It's an effort for him to speak. I feel this great, welling panic filling me with the desperate need to keep him talking, to keep his sinking soporific despair from pressing in around his head. I have to keep him at it, to keep him facing it and talking about it, rather like keeping a person pacing the floor after they've swallowed a bottle of sleeping tablets.

'Yes, Joe? What is it? Do you feel responsible? Is it the settlement that's depressing you?'

'No, it's not that. I just . . .' He sighs again, and then

looks up. 'It's just that everyone behaved so appallingly. There was no side you could look at and say they
had the moral upper hand or that they ended with right
on their side. It was supposed to be a battle for justice . . . and both sides turned it into a ratfight.'

'But you knew that already. You went through that
when all the violence was going on.'

'I know.' He is silent so long I can see the thick
choking clouds of his despair closing in on him again.

'But? But what, Joe?'

'Well, now it's over. Eleven weeks of turmoil, of lost
earnings, hungry children and struggling wives. Eleven
weeks and fifteen – was it fifteen? *Ja*, I think so – fifteen
people dead, and for what? What was it all for? They're
in exactly the position they would've been in if there'd
never been a strike. If people had never got beaten up,
necklaced or burnt in their homes by firebombs –
people utterly removed from the strike, mind you.
People who just happened to be the families of traders
who tried to make a living by selling boycotted goods.'

'Joe . . .' I struggle for something to say to him. I don't
usually express things, except to deride. I feel creaky
inside, rusted over in the path from my brain to my
aching throat. Before I can speak, Joe breaks in again.

'And d'you think anyone cares? Is anyone mourning
them and what happened in the name of the struggle,
the worker's right? No, fuck it, both sides are strutting
around claiming a victory.' His words are angry, but he
speaks them detachedly, one side of his mouth twisted
upward in a parody of amusement. 'Everyone's rushing around pompously proclaiming their cleverness
and strutting their power. No one cares, dammit, no
one gives a sweet fuck.'

'Well, let me give you the other side to this.' His bitterness is frightening. I can't leave him like this. If I can just get him to see the optimistic side to this – the Pollyanna principle I used to taunt when it was his normal state of mind. 'OK . . . OK, everyone behaved badly. But let's look at it closer. First let's take management. The offer they made at the start wasn't exactly a bad one, was it?'

'No, but Jesus, Kate, they were so inflexible. And their profits are published. The workers know how many millions they made last year. They're a bloody monopoly. They could've afforded more, and they could've moved just once from their inflexible stance, if only to save face for the union and allow it to settle, especially when they saw all the violence starting.'

'Well, OK. But in fact the workers ended up with an increase of fifteen per cent. If you think about it rationally, it's not bad in isolation. OK, now let's take the workers. It's their behaviour you're taking particularly hard, because it's them you really believed in.'

'What are you trying to do, Kate? Restore my faith or something? Tell me everything was OK in the struggle, that somehow there's some sort of moral victory in there?'

'No, I'm not sure what I'm doing. But I'm just trying to understand what it was you took so hard. Maybe get you to see things in perspective. You're too close at the moment, too bitter to see anything but the worst. OK? You believed they had the moral higher ground, you believed they could fight the good fight with disciplined union membership and minimal beastliness.'

I start to pace up and down the kilim in front of him. I can't keep still. This is about the hardest thing I've

271

ever done. Nothing that I've been before has prepared me for this. I just have to plunge in, I suppose.

'But look, they had a bloody sophisticated adversary. It must have appeared to the union guys that management was sneering and chortling while they made a big show of hardly being affected by the strike at all. First they managed to find enough scabs, and then it turns out they'd been stockpiling. And then of course, as you mentioned, they're a monopoly. The union thought a boycott would be their ultimate weapon. But how d'you expect a boycott to work when there's a monopoly? And especially when so many traders, small-time black traders too, are dependent on selling stuff like this to survive. Can you actually conceive of the level of frustration that must build?'

'I know that,' says Joe, crushing the sofa cushion between his two large hands. 'I'm not an idiot. Jeez, you must think me a stupid, naive fool. It's just that . . . their anger . . . frustration . . . whatever, doesn't make it right. It's just that no one seems to care. The people who were really involved . . . the people on the ground whose lives are affected, or even lost . . . they're just treated like bargaining chips. It's just that the violence wasn't the isolated sort of scuffling with scab workers, letting a bit of frustration out here and there. It was so horrific. So calculated. Burning alive the small traders who're struggling just as much as the strikers, if not more. It's just that they're all strutting around now claiming they've won and how clever they are.'

He looks up at me, his eyes imprisoning mine mid-pace.

'It's just that it was all for nothing. What was the point?'

'Well that, I suppose, is life, Joe. You can't go around always looking for the point to things.'

'But this was so clear-cut. I thought we had the moral higher ground. It was a good place for me to feel I was doing something for the struggle . . . please don't sneer, Kate. It just seemed that there was a point. It seemed the right thing to do.'

'Well now it's over, Joe. You have to put it behind you. It was a case for you, nothing more. You have to come right. You have to snap out of it. It's not your whole life, can't you see that?'

I can see him already shaking his head as I finish speaking.

'But it was more than a case to me. It was my first labour work and everything seemed to be falling together. The country seemed so hopeful, everything was happening at the same time. I even thought there, for a while, that you and I could come right. It was a symbol, you see, that's why I can't just shuck it off. It was a symbol for everything I believed in. It's not just the strike. I suddenly feel as if maybe people like Louise are right in leaving. For me this stupid strike represented all I hoped for in the country, and in the changes to come.'

He pauses, searching for the right words. But at least he's talking. At least he's not sinking into that awful silence. At least his speech is sounding vaguely passionate again.

'It seemed to me such a good fight to be part of. The struggle in the country, I mean. It was so unequivocal, all the jailed leaders were so right. I wanted them to be on the side of right. And I wanted to be there with them, also on the side of right, in my small lawyerly way.'

'For God's sake, Joe, life isn't like that. Neither is the country. In a struggle, or a war or a strike, it's easy to have sides, to see the right all on one side. It's like a great big war comic with lantern-jawed Germans strutting up and down shouting "*Achtung*" and "*Himmel*". This country's been a great big war comic for much too long. Everyone knew where right and wrong lay. It was easy – black and white, so to speak. But at the end, you have to face the fact that once we move from a struggle situation, we have to stop living in a war comic.'

I can see him sinking again, sagging into his seat with the heaviness of this new load of sadness he's carrying. I have to keep talking – I feel I'm losing him. I stand right in front of him, trying to keep him, hold his eyes hostage while I try to reach him.

'Joe, just look properly at this strike. Can't you see it as neutral? One lot made a reasonably fair offer. The other side thought it could be fairer, but they couldn't make an impact. So they got frustrated. So violence broke out. It's understandable in terms of human nature. You can see how it happened. Some things aren't just right or wrong, Joe.'

He looks up at me, and then his gaze wanders to the walls and then on to the intricate patterning of our pressed-steel ceiling. I can see his eyes wandering the curlicues, turning maze-like through their twists and curves. Is he listening? It's hard to tell. I can hear a harsh quality in my voice now, a straining for him to hear me, a desperation to pull him back from the pit he's falling into.

'Most things are merely neutral, Joe. And actually I think that's the most we can hope for. Maybe, just maybe, the world isn't split into the good and evil you try and see in everything. Maybe – Joe, dear God, listen to me! – maybe that's some weird Christocentric thing we've imposed on our lives. But it doesn't fit this place. Can't you see that? It doesn't help us make sense of the harshness of this country. Maybe a balance is the most we should hope for, to keep things neutral, to merge the good and evil that we've split into two, so they can do the least damage to each other. That's the balance of Africa.'

He hunches down into himself. He's trying to escape me, my words that beat at him. I still can't tell if he's listening to me, or even if he's capable of hearing. I feel exhausted by the effort. I'm fighting harder than I've ever fought for anything in my life.

I can't bear him to be like this. Not so much for him. It's for me! I can't survive without him. The way he was, I mean – not this. He was always raw and open to hurt, but now he is a crushed snail, the shell peeled away piece by piece. Without it, he'll either die or he'll have to weave himself into a cocoon, build himself his own glass jar. I should know. I've been like that, peeled and crushed, where every breath of air is painful. And I simply can't allow him to drop into the kind of prison I've been in my whole life. Joe's been my connection with the world outside my jar. He's been my counter-point, my balance, the other leg to my stool. Without him, I crash.

'Mm, well, that's that I suppose,' Joe says suddenly. 'I suppose you could've told me all along not to expect anything of people or causes. Why did I try? I should've listened to you. I should've taken it to heart when you used to say all people were pigs. How fucking naive I was. How stupid you must've thought me.'

'Joe . . .' I search for the words to reach him. I feel like a pale night creature, blindly creeping from its hole for the first time in years. Jeez, this is scary, and absurd. For fourteen years he's been begging, coaxing and sympathetically encouraging me to open my jar. And all that time he's failed. In the final analysis he had to nearly destroy himself with disillusionment and despair to do what he couldn't do all those years with love. Not that I'm altogether out of my jar. But suddenly I can feel myself. I can feel all kinds of things. When last did I feel this pity, and this strange unaccustomed yearning?

Emotionless, blunted by glass, I was free to sneer and indulge myself to my heart's content. Now, what is this, this aching caring for him? He whom I've scorned and laughed at, talked to, lived with and, yes, leant on all these years. But never loved. I always scorned love as a romantic myth. I used to say that people clung to each other because each took something from the other, used each other in a mutually acceptable way. But this strange, blind, mole-like creature, forced by danger and crisis to grope its way from safety into this new element, this creature feels pain in every part of it. It aches with sensation, stings with pity and sorrow and wrenches with a longing tenderness.

'Joe. Help me here! I'm trying, you know. At last I'm actually trying. Doesn't that mean something to you?'

'It's too late, Kate. Much too late. I no longer care. It's a great release in a way. I don't care about anything, not a thing.'

'Yes you do, deep down. You're not so locked in that you can't come out of it again.'

'But why on earth should I want to? Why should I want to return to feeling the way I did? It's too painful.

I can't survive like that, you know, Kate. No one can feel like I did, again and again, and live.'

He seems perfectly sober. He stands, absolutely steady now, and in control. Actually too much in control. He's curling away inside himself before my eyes. He disappears into the kitchen and returns with two wineglasses.

'Spritzer,' he says. 'I felt like some wine but I thought maybe we'd had enough. So I compromised.'

'Well, that's progress I s'pose,' I say, but without my usual acerbity, and with a small attempt at a chuckle. Joe leans his great body against the fireplace, his elbow on the mantelpiece.

'You know,' he says, and pauses to take a long sip. 'I'm tired. I'm exhausted by dealing with the country and all its ramifications, nastiness and violence. I'm tired of hoping all the time and then feeling disillusioned. Little bit by little bit it's all drained out of me. I know you think I overreacted to this strike . . .'

'Well maybe I just think you took it too hard. You've been disillusioned by things before.'

'*Ja*, I have. But you see, this was the culmination of everything for me. Everything led to this point, and, because I was involved, it symbolized my role in a new South Africa, the hope I felt and the way I expected things to slowly come right between people. Because it was my first labour work, it just turned into this big shining symbol. You know, I never told you this – I thought you'd sneer – but when I did law I thought I could use it to do something worthwhile, to work for what was right in this country. And slowly it dawned on me that things didn't always work out that way in the day-to-day grind of making a living. This desire of mine to get into labour work, it was my last hope, my last try, to get on to the side of right.'

'So what are you saying? What d'you want to do now?'

'I'm telling you that I'm tired of the struggle to live in this society and be moral. I can't do it any more, Kate. And I don't care to try. I don't know what you want to do, I don't even know how I feel about you or what you do, but I want simply to get out. I'm exhausted and I've had enough. I want to leave the country.'

'Oh, Joe . . .' As he speaks I feel my blind, squishy inner self oozing out, beyond all my efforts at control. Exposed all at once to the glare of this emotion, it tries to slip back into its dark imprisonment. But it is out. Even the air hurts. It aches to breathe.

'Oh Joe, you can't leave, any more than I can. You and I are rooted here . . .' I feel suddenly a wetness on my face. I jerk my hand upward to touch my cheek and find that I am weeping. It is so long since I cried, not since I was a small child – not since that year, in fact, when my life changed. I'd forgotten the feeling, what it felt like to cry. Joe is watching me, torn between detachment and wonder.

'What d'you mean?' he asks suddenly. 'You never cared for anything to do with this country. You always scorned everything in sight. And you've always put as much distance as you could between yourself and your Eastern Cape roots.'

'But that doesn't mean anything. I've never gone back to the Eastern Cape, you know that, but that doesn't mean I'm not part of it . . .' My throat aches with the effort of trying to express something I've never thought to put into words, something I've always resented and hated about myself and this hard country.

'It's . : . it's that my flesh comes from that dry earth, my blood flows because of those gnarled bushes, my sex smells of the musk of the old man's beard. Whether you love it or hate it, whether or not you ever go back, you and I are rooted in that thorny soil. Heart and soul, we're imprisoned by those twining branches of the wild fig tree – remember it? We're pierced and pinned by the acacia. We are part of it. We are this place. You and I couldn't leave. We're too thickly embedded. Leave, Joe, and you'll wither and die. You'll end up a dried old husk of a bitter exile. Your heart will die.'

'Why do you care, suddenly? Why after all these years that I've loved you and cared for you and tried to heal you? Why now? I could hate you for that, I really could. I tried so hard to make you care and now, now when I give up, then you suddenly decide it's time to burst open.'

I am weeping openly now, sobs forming cracks and dangerous fissures in my glass jar. It is all or nothing now. A different game, far more dangerous than before. I won't easily be able to escape, or disappear again. I somehow have to make this work.

'I suppose it's what you said, Joe. That we've always been two damaged halves. I always felt safe the way I was – comfortable. But I needed you, Joe. I needed you the way you were. You kept the world near, but far enough from me so I could handle it. I felt that without you I might have disappeared entirely into myself, become catatonic or something – and even that had a certain appeal. I sometimes sat, quite warm inside my . . . what I call my glass jar, and just rocked myself to and fro, to and fro. I could've done – and the world would've receded more and more. But I also had a resistance to it, to giving up. Perhaps deep down I wasn't quite ready to give up on the world. So I needed you.

'Joe, I knew you were reaching for me, trying to help me, but I couldn't feel anything. Now I can't tell you how much all those years of emotions feel piled upon me. Every piece of me aches with the sorrow of what I've done to you.'

'So what do you want us to do now? We can't go on like before, Kate. The curtain's ripped from side to side. We can never go back. I can't be the person I was a week ago, even for you.'

'The only way we could've survived here all those years was together, you know that, Joe? I'd have receded into myself. Or finally shrivelled up and died with the barrenness of my forcibly desiccated life. But you, you couldn't have survived without my balance either. We were complementary – two halves of a South African truth.'

I stand and walk to the window. God, it is so beautiful in the moonlight: the towering oak, the sheltering camphor trees, the tiny yellow-wood that Joe planted one summer. God, it hurts. It hurts so much to care. I wrap both arms around my clenched stomach and hunch there, my back to Joe.

'No one can survive this country with your level of hope and idealism. It'll let you down every time. Too much idealism is an affliction, just as much as my cynicism. This isn't the kind of place where it can flourish. This is no gentle green and pastoral land, nourishing hopes and quiet dreams. It's too harsh a place. Its people – and I'm talking all of us – we're all too rooted in the parched and thorn-scattered earth. The people of this country mirror the land, the environment which suckled them. It's not cruelty, unless you wish to impose that on it. Is there more cruelty in the lion eating the bushbuck, or dying because it cannot hunt? It's the way of the land. People here are too close to basic survival, too bound by the earth rules of life, to uphold soft pretensions.'

Joe looks at me for a long time. He has never before heard me articulate such feelings. I can't read his expression, but I'm all played out. I can say no more. And then he speaks.

'So, what do you want us to do? It doesn't seem like there's anything to be done about us, then. How are we to carry on?'

'I think we have to suck from each other, Joe. We have to teach each other. We have to become whole. We need a balance within ourselves. We can't leave, we need to survive.'

'You talk as if we can do it just like that. As if we can have some kind of cross-transfusion and everything will be OK.'

'I know it can't happen like that. It'll be hard. I can't tell you how hard.' I turn from the window. Each sob shoots an aching dart through my tense shoulders and chest. I want to touch Joe, but I have no practice in reaching out to him.

'It'll take us ages and ages and it'll hurt . . .' I'm heaving now – the child's dry, involuntary sobbing heaves. 'It hurts already. I can't tell you how it hurts.'

'Is it really worth it, Kati?'

'Is life worth it? No one told us we had a God-given right to happiness and an easy life.'

'Yes they did,' said Joe, with a small rough growl of laughter. 'My mother did. I swear she did. She told me I had to hope for things and have high-flown dreams and that I should search for happiness. She told me I had a right to be happy. And that I was lucky to be privileged because my life would always be eased by my background, my skin colour, my schooling and stuff. And she really believed that's how it should be.'

I laugh too, a tiny, hurting laugh which rips through my sobs. The idea is so absurd, in the circumstances. 'Well, I suppose you weren't alone there. I didn't have that sort of upbringing. It was blown up, ripped apart too early for those kind of expectations.'

'What was it, Kate? It's absurd that we could've lived together all these years and I feel I don't know the largest part of you. The thing that's made you – more than any other – into what you are.'

'So, Joe . . .' He thinks I'm changing the subject. His face hardens and he turns away to sit on the couch. I walk from the window and stand in front of him. 'So now the strike's finished, we can go on holiday. Are you still keen to go down to the Eastern Cape?'

'Is there a point, Kati?'

'There has to be a point. We can't not go. If we're to be whole, if we're both to survive, we both have to face what's made us what we are. At some stage it has to be done.'

'D'you think you can face it, Kati? I know it's hard for you. I mean, I can face what I am by laughing. As long as I can see the absurdity of my cotton-wool existence, I'll be OK . . . but you?'

'I can . . . I think, if you help me. And Joe?'

'Yes?'

'I . . . I love you.'

'*Ag*, Kati, love.' His voice cracks on the words.

'But first . . . you see, there's something else I have to do first. Before I have to face it, the place where it, where I, happened.' Joe remains silent. He's staring up at me, his eyes moist.

'I think that before I can face it, I must tell you something. Joe, let's go make ourselves some coffee. There's a story I have to tell you. And I've a feeling it's going to take a long time to tell.'

Joe stands, and we move slowly towards the kitchen. We still find it hard to touch each other, but there's a softness there between us now, and somehow I think perhaps we'll learn.

'Joe, I think I'm going to find this quite hard. Possibly the hardest thing I've ever done. I don't know how I'm going to find the words.'

'Just start slowly, Kati. Tell me in your own time.'

'Well, maybe first I could start by telling you how nice it was, how idyllic. What a perfect childhood I had before that time. I think that's what I'll do. The rest of the story'll come in its own time.'

1966 . . . Christmas Day

'Namhla sizalelw' umntwana,
Indla lifa yamadinga.'

The high harmony of women's voices shimmered through the early stillness, lilting me down from the drowsy dreams of wakening day. Gathering my scattered thoughts and limbs to me, I lay a moment wrapped in my sheets, straining to catch and hold this first glowing symbol of Christmas.

My inner eyelids were pinked with just woken light as the women's Christmas fervour gathered strength. Powerful with trilling ardour, their hymn suddenly broke through their quiet restraint and rode the wild morning air. Triumphantly it soared through the house and yard, shucking off the chitter of chickens and bucking the three of us finally from the last of our sweaty sleep.

We were silent, my brothers and I, for what on earth could be said! I could feel that no everyday words could compete, could even be used, in the presence of such a sign of God's glory and the magic of Christmas Day.

Michael sat up in bed and scrubbed his knuckles into

his eyes, trying as he did each morning to disperse some of his woundingly large-eyed vulnerability. Neil lay on his back, his arms tucked behind his head. He didn't want us to look at him. I could feel him resisting our eyes, willing us not to see his screen of strength fall.

His face contained . . . what was it? At the time, surreptitiously glancing through my lashes, I could sense the feelings he poured into the room like the soury-sweet pervasiveness of citrus, though I couldn't name them. But I held it – the look of his face and the odour of his emotions – locked inside me, as I did everything else about that day, that day which started as God's own.

It wasn't sadness, it was poignancy – painful poignancy – which emanated from him as he lay listening with such intensity. And as I squinted at him, I suddenly saw him as a grown-up. On that morning, I think, he passed from boyhood into his adult life and, in so doing, he felt the farm with different senses. He scattered the magic, as a poltergeist chaotically flings vases, and finally passed beyond the enchanted world of our childhood farm. In those few seconds, he lost the wonderment.

I couldn't have articulated that at the time, but I felt it. Those were the days when, though I did not know their names and seldom understood their source, I felt emotions and atmospheres with the shuddering strength of spells.

Now I can name them. With great skill I have learnt to use words as a talisman of protection. But if naming does give the user some small measure of strength against the sorcerous power of passions, it's too late now! It's too late for the child that I was. It's too late for the farm. You know, I still feel the helpless guilt of someone who should have seen what was coming – read the signs better. But I don't think any words could have deflected what happened later that day. Acts of love used for hate, godliness and the glory of Christmas turned to evil by the vileness of men and the callousness of God.

But then, then we were silently illuminated by the sunlight and the chimera of Christmas song. Filled with its joy, I reached to my bedside table for my glittering Advent calendar. Beneath the last unopened shutter I found a tiny baby Jesus, serenely asleep in the arms of a girl who looked not much older than I, with large blue eyes and a blue doek on her head.

Michael was the first to break from the spell of inactivity which hung over the room. I was behind him, in my shortie-pyjamas, as we broke into a run and raced through the kitchen. *Skree-bang*, we were in the crowded courtyard. Neil followed more slowly and went to stand, taller than my dad, alongside my bent-shouldered Oupa and smiling Ouma.

The women of the farm – our people – swayed together in the harmony that seemed to come from their hearts. Their hands, rough working hands, were clasped before them. Each had a doek upon her head. Blankets were tied around waists and babies blanketed to backs. Small children clutched at skirts and blankets, all awed eyes and solemn faces, in amongst their mothers.

'*Dankie, mense*,' said Ouma at last. 'Thank you for that hymn of praise. Just wait a little now, and you will all get your Christmas box. Neil, *asseblief, my kind*, those parcels in the kitchen.'

Neil carried the brown-wrapped food parcels – fat
with mealie-meal, tins of baked beans and meat – past
the *skree-bang* of the door and handed them, one by one,
to Ouma as she moved among the women.

'Ethel, how is your mother? I see she is not with us
this morning. Tell her I shall pray for her health.

'Maggie, thank you for the help this year. You've
been a good girl.'

'Lizzie, that baby's looking *lekker vet* now. Better
make sure you don't have any more, *hoor jy*?'

The women, shy-faced with their downcast smiles,
bobbed to Ouma and clapped courteous hands together
before taking the parcels with both hands.

'*Dankie, Miesies.*'

Dankie, Miesies.'

The women waited for Ouma to speak to each one of
them before pressing the children forward with small,
rough shoves. Squirming and giggly, they sniffed and
wriggled skinny legs as they accepted their Christmas
clothing – khaki shorts and shirts for the boys, shift
dresses for the girls. I felt warm with their gratitude,
benevolent beneath their smiles.

'Happy happy! Happy happy!' called the women,
high and clear.

'Happy Christmas, Happy Christmas,' we shouted,
smiling and waving as they turned and rhythmically
swayed from the courtyard with shuffled dance steps
and swinging arms.

> '*Kulowo mzi kaDavide,*
> *Kwisitali seenkomo . . .*'

'Happy Christmas, my darlings,' said my mother,

encompassing both Michael and me in the perfume of her bosom as she swooped to embrace us. The swinging orange flower clipped to her ear tapped against my temple as I hugged her. And then we were all hugging. Ouma and Mom clutched each other fiercely, their eyes so similar in their damp darkness.

'*Ag, my kind*, I think we must *mos* try harder to understand each other. We are flesh and blood.'

'Oh Ma, I really do love you . . .'

All that anger, all that hate-filled energy, with such power to destroy. And they could sweep it away, just like that. They could just say sorry, as if they'd torn a dress or something. Grown-ups were like that. They allowed all the dark creatures out of their lairs, fluttering their dank wings, because grown-ups didn't seem to understand their destructive danger. They thought they could call them back afterwards, send them home to their caves, not realizing how they gained a life of their own and multiplied on the outside. They had lost what I still had, a realization that bad feelings clustered around a house and a family, growing and sharpening gnashing, monstrous teeth. That, left there too long, they could make bad things happen.

'C'mon, Katie, c'mon.' Michael was dragging at my arm, pulling me through the kitchen which was sizzling with the smell of bacon.

'Happy Christmas, Dora,' we called, stretching our arms around her as she stood sweating in the glow of the coal stove. My face pressed into the soft jiggle of her flesh as her large chuckle shook through her body.

'Happy happy!' she called, in high-pitched counterpoint to her laugh. And then we pulled away and slipped past her bulky hips which nearly blocked the kitchen door. In the lounge, at the foot of the towering Christmas tree, were the most important things about today. There stood two ... Only two? Why only two? ... crisp white pillowcases, outlining bulges of throat-hollowed anticipation.

And there we all were, clustered, with the enveloping warmth of Christmas, at the foot of the tree. The grown-ups were already dressed and, after a couple of minutes, so was Neil, appearing in the doorway with newly combed hair. In my strawberry-patterned shortie-pyjamas I crouched beside my mother, clutching at the excitement in my belly with both arms. Mom, sitting on her legs on the carpet, reached for the pillow-slips and placed one in front of me and the other on Michael's lap.

Looking down into my face, she placed a finger under my anxious chin and answered my clinging eyes.

'Neil told us he was too old for a pillowslip this year. He's going to get presents from under the Christmas tree like the rest of us. But you two still believe in Father Christmas, don't you? Enough to get presents from him anyway – isn't that so?'

I smiled and ducked as she ruffled my short hair away from my forehead. I didn't care. I wasn't going to tell her I'd seen these 'humps' in the cupboard and that I didn't believe in Father Christmas at all now. She might become irritable and change her mind, as grown-ups sometimes did when children weren't exactly as they would like to see them. You never quite knew with grown-ups.

The lounge filled with discarded Christmas paper and rustling cries – squeals of joy from me and my mom, the boys' deeper 'Oh wow!' and my dad's quiet: 'Oh lovey. Just what I wanted.' Ouma and Oupa watched us all in silent happiness before exchanging small gifts – a new, leather-bound prayer book for her and, for him, Elizabeth Barrett Browning's *Sonnets from the Portuguese*.

Michael received the Size Twenty-six bicycle, with three speeds, that he'd been dying for. My dad had taken a picture of it and they'd wrapped up the photographs in his pillowslip with a bicycle bell, so he'd thought he wasn't getting it. It was waiting in his room back home in Port Elizabeth. Neil got a backpack for taking overseas with him when he went. Mom swung round and flung her arms around my dad when she unwrapped the delicate diamond drop earrings he had chosen for her. And I, I got the floppy doll that I'd wanted so badly all year. And it was the big kind, not the small monkey-faced type that my friend Penny got for her birthday. I'd been envious of hers, but that was only because I hadn't had a floppy doll at all.

Michael and I had to gather up the paper before we were sent off to wash and dress, starving by now because of the trailing waft of bacon which had tantalized us through the present-opening ceremony. We joined them on the stoep – Christmas breakfast was always eaten on the stoep – where the faintest breeze kept the heat moving across our faces. We sucked the cold from chilled prickly pears and nibbled at the crisped fat of farm-cured bacon before the grown-ups settled into their chairs and slurped at coffee. Ouma and Oupa dunked Dora's buttermilk rusks into their cups, but Mom refused to dunk, a quirk of the faintest distaste just there at the corners of her mouth.

After breakfast we moved back into the buzzing heat of the dark lounge. Michael and I suffered Ouma's Bible reading and prayers, wriggling our feet and stretching our eyes behind our hands. I gazed longingly at my confiscated floppy doll, lying on a chair across the room with her vacant, beautifully blue eyes closed. Michael poked at me a few times with a straightened finger, but soon lost interest when my mother's scowl reached him. Finally we stood to sing 'Hark the Herald Angels Sing', which we all knew off by heart. And then we were free.

I squeezed off a quick, silent prayer as Michael and I were heading for the door. 'Please, gentle Jesus, please say thank you to God for today. Please just let it stay like this, please, God.'

'What are you doing? Praying or something?' Michael had caught me.

'No, of course not. What makes you think I was praying?'

'You've got your eyes closed and your hands clutched up at your face. You tripped over the chair in the library. Of course you were praying.'

'I was not! I thought I was going to sneeze, that's all.'

'Ka-ti was pray-ing, Ka-ti was pray-ing,' chanted Michael as he darted around me, giving me little taps on the face and head at the longest reach of his arm, so that my hands ineffectually flapped at him, unable to slap him back.

Later I wondered if it could've been that which started what happened that day. If I, like Judas, hadn't set off some inexorable process towards violence and mangled horror. And, if I had, could I have stopped what happened if I'd acted differently? If I hadn't presumed, and begun to take His favour for granted again. Could I, could Judas, have done any different? But surely God, if there was one there that day, couldn't have been so angered by one small child's denial. Surely He was more of a grown-up, or, as I hoped, more than a grown-up.

Michael joined me under the wild fig for a while, being the daddy who went to work. Work was up the tree. I sat at home on the grass, feeding my baby from a magic milk bottle which appeared to empty but never did. He soon got bored – pelting me with twigs and practising his dove-call whistle – since he couldn't come home while I declared it to be daytime, and he wasn't sure what he was supposed to do at the office once he'd gone there. Coming down from the tree, he tried to make the game more interesting – 'I'm a boogieman now, OK? Pretend I'm not the dad, OK?' – and kidnapped my floppy doll. At first I chased him up the tree, calling for the police. But then he went too high for me to follow and I tired of the game too.

'Ah, Michael man, give her back. Ah please, Michael, ple-ease give her back, Michael. It's not fair . . .'

'Chi-ildren!' My mother's voice floated up to us in the cool branches. 'It's time for the pictures. Come down now.'

We scrambled and scraped down the tree to join the family on the lawn. As they did every year, William and Petrus had brought their younger children round to the front lawn before lunch. Looking clean and uncomfortably proud in their starched new outfits, they posed with us for Christmas photographs. I have such a clear picture of us, as we must have looked. Six young children from the Eastern Cape, from the same farm, who hardly knew each other – two of us white, four black. All of us barefoot. Against the swaying splash of Ouma's bright flowers we stood smiling together, the black children stiff in their Christmas clothes. One small black girl clutched a Christmas toy, an unbending trading-store doll, its hair and clothing painted, its skin white. We, Michael and I, held a shiny silver bicycle bell and a huge, beautiful doll with 'real' hair and closing eyes and baby clothes.

We were happy then, when the photographs were taken and the children trailed after their fathers back to the huts. How could we have been so happy? How could I not have seen how God had used me? How He'd tantalized and taunted me with Christmas as it should be, as it had always been?

It was time for lunch. Time for pulling crackers and wearing silly hats – which Michael and I wore around our skinny necks and my dad had to tear slightly to fit over his wide forehead. Time to swap cracker rings for small clown games, and for me to beg for dolls' rattles. For Michael to argue over who would pull the wish-bone.

'Ta-ra,' called my dad, making a big thing of Dora's giggling entrance with the two enormous chickens. And then Ouma appeared, smiling from the kitchen, with a plate.

'This is specially for you, Kati,' she said, pride in her surprise leaking from her every gesture.

'What, Ouma?'

I could see though. My mouth had turned bitter. But it couldn't be! Surely she couldn't have done that. I think that's when I realized that the day was going to go wrong. From here, from this moment, when things weren't as they should be, till . . . till the things that happened later.

'It's your little chicken, your very own Christmas chicken.' She placed the small-boned meat in front of me, hunched and brown now with cooking. There was no sign of the lively feathered creature who'd strutted its white body through the *hok* the day before.

'It's the chicken, *my lief*. The one you chose, remember?'

'I can't . . . I can't eat it.'

I choked on the saliva which was filling my mouth, and the table blurred.

'*My magtig*, now what's wrong? It's just a chicken.'

'Her name is Sheba. She's not just a chicken. Stop calling her a chicken.'

Darkness took me from behind then, sliding in on both sides of my head. I could hear Ouma's voice somewhere far away.

'*O my magtig*. But this is a *pieperige* child. She gave the chicken a name. On a chicken farm, where we eat chickens every day. It's just lucky she wasn't born on a farm. All right, take it away, Michael . . .'

'I'll eat it, Ouma . . .'

'No you will not, Michael. Don't cause more trouble than you can help. Give it to Dora. Tell her she can eat it.'

The helpless darkness receded as I stared at my empty Christmas place, littered with cracker debris. All that was left was that burning – the burning which couldn't be blinked or swallowed away.

'Settle down now, child. Don't take it so hard.'

Tick Tick Tick

In the dead of the silent afternoon, I curled myself into the cool castle under Oupa's desk in the library. The desk clock above my head moved the day onward with clumsy, clattering slowness.

This was always the worst part of Christmas Day – the time when the presents were played with, the food eaten, the crackers pulled and the paralysing heat lay upon stomachs laden with midday feasting.

But that afternoon it wasn't like that. I had none of the usual drowse of anticlimactic satiation. That day my body felt at war with itself. My belly hollowed and hankered for my uneaten ritual dinner, while my gut galled in rebellion at the thought of my Christmas pet – reduced now to sucked bones. And I was alert, aware even of the small sugar-ants pattering out from the skirting board to a sticky patch on the wooden floor.

Tick Tick Tick

On my knee I held *King Solomon's Mines*, a refuge from this place and this Christmas time. This Christmas which had seemed the same, but was now slightly askew. Just a little out of kilter, stirring the unease in my throat, the anxiety in the prickles around my hair-line.

I hadn't turned a page for a great many ticks. I was unwilling to let go of the house as if my vigilance, late though it was, gave me some control over the hovering demons and dank fluttering of unnamed darkness.

In the midst of the silent house, I had to stretch my senses outward to be aware of anything but the quiet and the clock. Desultory chickens clucked in the drowsy afternoon and somewhere far away – maybe the boys' huts – I could hear children singing. Every now and then I caught the ominous grate of the generator. I reached further outward, trying to sense all that was beyond my small boxed-in haven.

My father gave a loud snore from the bedroom, jarring the settled silence. And then it was quiet again.

Dora and the boys had gone off after lunch to their families. I never went near there, their huts or their separate lives, on Christmas afternoons. The garrulous swallowing of beer and loud-laughing celebrations scared me. I was used to everything about life, its merrymaking and its sadness, tuned to a lower pitch. I was used to a certain restraint, which blanketed and muffled all that we did and the way that we acted.

Tick Tick Tick

Allan Quatermain again began to ride the afternoon, but inexpertly, falling off and drifting out of my mind's eye. Each time it sucked more of my energy to pull him back into my consciousness and force him on his journey again. I sighed and tugged my eyes back on to the page . . .

What was it that roused us?

What was it that brought me sharply back to this place, and this time? It seemed the house grew tense around me – its bricks creaking with taut alertness, its floors stretched to high-strung rigidity. I heard no sound from the bedrooms, but I believed in that instant that everyone was awake. It seemed to me that we were waiting – for the inevitable, the predestined. For God's finishing of what He had begun with us that day, that holiday.

A wind had begun to blow, one of those rough, East Cape winds that begin suddenly and buffet the morning's heat from the afternoon. I could hear it shushing through the trees and beating at the roof which creaked in its coarse hands. It would be a dirty wind, the kind which swept dust into your eyes and grit-layered your hair. A window slammed; it must have been in our bedroom. The screen door, battered open with a drawn-out *skree-ee*, slammed shut again with a powerful *skree-ee-bang*.

I think I knew then, or it seems to me now that I knew then. I knew that God meant to toy with us that Christmas. It seemed to me that we all knew it. That we were all waiting for His move. Had we heard something, somewhere in the back of our unconscious senses? Or was it God who, anxious that we be aware of His machinations, had whispered in each of our ears?

And then I did hear something. I heard his panting footsteps – heavy, running footsteps which pounded across the stoep. I could hear the heaving of wheezed breath as he battered the door. Battered and battered, while I cowered and curled under the desk.

'Miesies, Miesies!' He was shouting, pausing to wheeze in more breath. 'Come, Miesies. Come quickly. Iets het gebeur, Miesies.'

I could hear the family now, beds creaking, voices murmuring, feet thudding on wooden floors. I heard the squeak in the hinge of Ouma's wardrobe.

'Ek kom! Magtig, wat is dit nou? Just wait a little. I'm coming.'

And then she padded through, zipping up her dress, her bunioned feet moving past me in her stockings. 'Is dit jy, John?' she called, opening the door. 'Wat doen jy hier?'

It was he, William's son. It was shocking to see him there. At the front door. I heard my mother gasp as she came through, her hair tumbled. 'What it is, John?' she almost whispered. 'What's brought you here to this side of the house? Is there trouble?'

William's son was heaving to catch his breath. Crouched below them, I could squint upward past the desk chair and see his mouth working as he struggled to manoeuvre his words past his wheezing chest and working throat.

'Speak, John!' said Ouma. 'What has happened? Is someone ill? Is it the politics? Have they come here? Have those political natives come here to the farms?'

'Miesies,' he said on a sob. 'There's big trouble, Miesies. Please, Miesies.'

'What is it, my boy?' That was my father's voice, somewhere near the inner door of the library. 'We can't help unless you tell us.' He sounded deep and calm. He would help, I felt sure. He could fix up most things.

'Master, it's the *ou Miesies*, on the other farm.'

'Yes my boy? Is the old lady ill? Is she hurt?' That was my dad again. He would find out what was wrong. He would do the right thing. I was sure he could make it better.

'*Ja*, Master. She's hurt, Master. She ... it was Johannes, Master. He didn't mean it, Master.' The young man – tall, proud, angry, as I'd known him – crumbled away, leaving the inner boy. His hands scratched and clawed

299

at his face. His eyes, the whites very bright in his dark, shadowed face, flew from wall to wall. He sobbed then suddenly.

'*O my magtig*,' said Ouma, her cupped hands moving in slow motion to her mouth. 'And I sent him there. He took my boys because I asked him to. O my magtig. Wat het hy gedoen, John?'

'He was drinking, Miesies. He gave us a *dop* after lunch, Miesies. The Baas he gave us very strong *dop* for Christmas. Johannes, he took more than anyone. It was the drink, Miesies. He was very angry from yesterday, but it was the drink that made him do it.'

No one spoke this time. Everyone waited for him to take his struggled breaths and heave out his dry sobs.

'She made him angry, Miesies. Yesterday the *ou Miesies* she say he pull up her new flowers. She call him a stupid *kaffir*. It was in front of Mary, Miesies. The girl he likes – she works in the house.'

He paused again for his breath to catch up with his runaway story. Again, no one said anything.

'The *ou Miesies*, she make him kneel on the grass and hold the flowers to his face. She say this is because he will know them the next time. And she call the Baas then, Miesies. She call the Baas and told him to sjambok Johannes while he was still holding the flowers. I could see Johannes, Miesies. I could see he look at Mary while he is sjambokked and the tears come to his eyes. I know then, Miesies. I know something break down in Johannes.'

'What did he do, John?' My mother's voice was a whisper. But it came to me distinctly behind my chair. 'What did he do after he'd been drinking? You must tell us. We can't help otherwise.'

'He take the *ou Miesies* . . . He take her when she go to

the dairy in the afternoon. She went to get the cream, for the tea. He must have followed her, Master. He was mad with the drink. They say . . . the Baas say he held her down on the ground and used her, Miesies.'

'You mean he raped her, John? He raped her? Is that what you mean?' My mother's voice shuddered with trapped hysteria.

Suddenly I could feel the dark beasts, baying and fluttering, their dank mustiness right here in the room with us. Finally we had let them in. For a long time they'd hunkered, cowardly, on the perimeter of the farm, and of our lives. Now they were upon us. No one could stop what was happening, and what was still to come. We had to ride with it, fly with the damp, scaly-winged creatures with the smell of death upon them.

That word, the word my mother had spoken, I didn't know it. But I could feel its reverberations in the room, the horror of its utterance, the spitting of its remains from my mother's lips. I could feel the end of things in the voicing of it, the shrivelling of childhood, the mutilation of innocence in the naming of it here.

Skree-bang. The screen door slammed the sound of women's weeping into the house. Dora's long wailing cry trailed from the kitchen and snaked its way down my goose-bumped back and into the pit of my vomitous entrails. My hair prickled in sharp needle stabs over my scalp.

'*Ja*, Miesies.' William's son was quieter now. 'He raped her. He used her hard, Miesies. The *ou Miesies* is hurt. Her leg is hurt . . . I think the hip, it broke.'

'Oh my God!' That was my mother. No one chastised her for using God's name. No one said anything. At last my Ouma spoke. Her voice was hollow.

'You must go to your mother, John. And to Johannes's mother. We will now do what must be done. Has the Baas taken the *ou Miesies* to the hospital?'

'Ja, Miesies, but I am feared about when he comes back, Miesies. He is mad, Miesies. Mad with the anger. And . . . and also with the Christmas drink, Miesies.'

'Well, you should be here with your mothers anyway, John. Go now . . . And John? . . . You know what he did was evil, *nê*? You know it's no excuse – his anger and the drink he took? The Baas has a right to his fury, and his grief. His own mother, John! You grew up with Johannes, he is like your brother – you feel bad for him. But John, you know he will go to jail when he is caught, *nê*? Maybe even hanged?'

'*Ja*, Miesies.' He turned, all the pride sunk out of him, all the vibrant angry youth beaten from his bent shoulders and grief-burnt eyes.

I crouched still, unseen under the desk. I could see Michael's vulnerable legs twining around each other against the library wall. I could feel that nobody knew what to say. The horror was too heavily upon them. Ouma spoke then, clearing her throat first and dabbing at her nose with a tissue from her sleeve. Ouma would cope, I could see that. She'd cope as she always did, by organizing.

'Jim, I think you must go over there and see what you can do to help, especially when Mr Van Rensburg returns. He might want to organize a search party or something. Elaine, you and I must see to our people. We must calm down the women before there is chaos. Johnnie . . .' She reached out and squeezed Oupa's shoulder – more for her own comfort, I thought, than to reassure him '. . . Johnnie, you can't help much at the other farm. Leave that *maar* for the younger men. I think the best help you can be is to stay here with the children. And to answer the phone.'

Compliant to her moulding, the family moved away. But they still walked dazedly, caught up in the web of misty revulsion which clung stickily to the walls of the house.

'Shall I come with you, Dad?' Neil asked as he came back through the library, the clink of car keys in his hand. Dad stopped, considered, and looked at Neil as he stood, large-shouldered and taller than Dad, in front of him.

'No, son . . . I think not. I don't think it would be a good idea. I think the family needs a man in the house now. A young man. I want you to take care of them, OK?'

'OK then, Dad . . . And Dad? Be careful, OK?'

I crept out when they'd all gone. Only Michael still clung to the inner door frame, tangling his legs and finally dropping into a flat-footed squat, his back to the frame. I watched as, one by one, he began to squash the ants carrying the grains of sticky stuff back towards the skirting board. The ants climbed unperturbed over their fallen companions. A few began to drag one of the corpses away – one minute a friend, the next, just food.

'Did you understand all that, Kitty? D'you know what he did?'

'Not really,' I whispered, squatting beside him. After a long while, Neil came and stood in the passage outside the door, rubbing his hand back and forth across his chin. He was checking us out, I thought, to see how much we knew and whether we were going to be OK.

'What does "rape" mean, Neil?' asked Michael

suddenly, his head shooting up to aim his huge dark eyes at his older brother.

'It's nothing either of you should know about. It's a terrible thing – not something men should allow to happen to their women. It's OK now. It'll all be sorted out. I think you should both try to forget about what's happened.'

We stared at the ants some more. We could hear Oupa talking to Neil in the lounge.

'D'you think we should see what's going on?' Michael asked me, without looking up from the dam of corpses he was creating to hold back the stream of ants.

'Don't know. I'm a bit scared.'

'*Ja*, that's OK. But I think we should see what's happening. Come, I'll look after you.'

We left quietly, skimming across the gusting veld with the silence of dusty feet on dusty ground. When we reached the fence nearest to the Van Rensburg house it was late afternoon. Darkness hollowed the ground where the sun could no longer stretch. Hadedas howled their possessed cry into the wind.

'Mr Van Rensburg's home again. There's his *bakkie*,' Michael said, twining his arms over the top of the fence and screwing up his eyes against the biting dust in the air. 'Dad's there too. See his car?'

We squatted there, watching the darkness scuttle over the bleak landscape. Finally vanquishing the glinting, speckled sunlight, it took over the squat house already haunted by its internal horror.

The yard was entirely in shadow when the *bakkies* began to arrive – dusty, revving beasts, bucking and straining over the ruts and water-washed striations of the farm road. One after the other, they roared and screeched into the yard, fury in the yowling of their engines and the smoke from their exhausts.

The men clustered in groups in the yard, hands on wide hips or clasped around shotguns pointing to the sky. They were sweating, red-faced men, with anger in their stillness, violence in their inactivity.

We could hear the mutter of their discussions and the crack of guns being opened and loaded. From the swamp of sickly light in the doorway, Mr Van Rensburg stepped into the shadows of the yard. The group of men swallowed him in murmured ingestion in the time it took for the wind to drop. It dropped suddenly – as the wind does sometimes in the Eastern Cape when the sun goes down. The spectral stillness enveloped the house and yard as the group scattered. The men strode intently to their *bakkies*, their tautly held ferocity given focus and purpose.

'Look, Kitty, there's Dad.'

For the first time ever, my dad looked unsure. He stopped at the edge of the yellowish light from the door and half turned, his eyes searching the inside of the house. He moved a step forward, towards the *bakkies* and the men, but his eyes remained inside. He looked distressed.

I watched him, dread creeping up my legs from the cooling earth. He was no longer my dad, not the dad I knew and depended on. In the spotlight of my anguish I could see he was no longer strong. My dad . . . what made him Dad was his strength, his eternal sureness. It was my mom who showed distress, worry, indecision. It was he who comforted, calmed, made everything clear. On this late afternoon, as the darkness slowly blotted out the sun, this last refuge was snatched away from me. The last small hideaway from the awfulness scuttling over my farm, from the evil overtaking us, was no longer firm. It creaked with the rickety danger of collapse.

'Kom now, Jim,' Mr Van Rensburg called through his open window. 'Jy behoort met die manne te kom. You don't want to stay with the women.'

His decision was made for him and he also stepped into the shadows, joining Mr Van Rensburg in the revving *bakkie*.

We waited a long time as the darkness slowly dropped. We didn't speak, Michael and I, but slowly walked up and down the fence, kicking at stones and running sticks along the mesh. There was no laughter in it, this clinking of sticks undertaken solemnly to feel our bodies still moving, our children's souls still alive.

I wonder how long we really waited there, that evening. It felt like the time it could take to end the world. The crickets began to chirrup their chorused joy as our two small figures paced alongside the fence, up and down, up and down. I don't remember whether we even wondered if we'd be missed. With Ouma and Mom with our people we probably wouldn't have been. But I'm not sure it would have entered our heads, or if we even cared.

We paced until Michael stopped and quivered, his small, animal head feeling the air, his nose sniffing. There across the farmlands I could see them too. Careering headlights throwing dust and revving petrol fumes into the still air. He began to run, desperation tightening the muscles of his whip-like legs. I followed him, adrenaline firing me across the ground, scarcely feeling the small stones and thorns which stabbed at my blindly running feet. We both wheezed with fear and urgency as we flung our bodies over the fence and ran for the congregated *bakkies*, their encircling headlights glaring off the dense wall of dust between them.

This is the hardest part. All these years my tongue has felt glued to my mouth to stop me from talking of this, of naming it, giving it power in my life again. But in a way, that Christmas Day has ruled my life. It took over, possessed me, made me into someone else. It sucked the spirit from me and left me an undead husk of a person with the juice poured out. I was scared to speak of it. I was frightened of releasing the demons from me on to the world. I couldn't let it happen again, you see. I had to cage the darkness inside me, never free it to devour those around me. And that very inability to speak of it soured my life and snatched the childhood from me for ever. And of course there was the guilt. The guilt that I couldn't have seen it coming, that I couldn't hold out my arms to protect what I loved. That I let it happen, kept silent and didn't do anything to stop what they did. It wasn't only what happened there, in that place I loved above any other, that evening. It was everything, the way every small thing that happened on the farm that year, in a way led inevitably to this – to a sudden and violent knowledge of brutality and a chaotic awareness of the savagery of humans and a God who could allow such things and such people to exist.

My mouth finds it hard to put such things into words. But I shall try.

We ran to the back of the two adjoining outbuildings, the dairy and the storeroom, and slid our feet up the walls. On the flat roof we crept forward with shuddering fear, our bodies moving to the edge in a compulsion of dread. Lying full length, we could look almost directly down on the milling men. At first I couldn't see what was happening in the swirling brown cloud. I thought for a moment with relief that they hadn't found him.

The men unwound a light from the storeroom, which they hooked to the bar at the back of Mr Van Rensburg's cab – and I saw him with a flashing start. Johannes crouched in the back, a wounded, cowering animal – his fierce anger gone in this last struggle for survival. He was taut with the shivering, frozen fear of a buck which gazes into the eyes of a lion. But these weren't lions, these men. At this moment they slunk forward from the shadows like a pack of hyenas, snatching at a weakened creature, taking pleasure in its torment.

Michael must have felt my body quiver as I caught sight of my dad on the edge of the group. Silently, he crept a small hand up and clamped it over my mouth.

The other men had the look of the hunt about them. I could see the cold savagery in their eyes, glowing almost red in the brilliance of the flashlight's glow. They were closing in. The evil was closing in, encircling and clamping down on this place as coldly as these men were approaching the back of the *bakkie*. But my dad stood there, indecision in every jerky motion of his head and arms. He didn't move away, he just stayed there on the edge of the group, not saying a word.

My body jerked as the loud click of a closing shotgun sounded, halting the crickets in their Christmas song. The gun was pointed at Johannes's juddering temple. Nobody touched him. This frightened me. Even in my innocence, I knew it would go better with him if they beat him now, if they shouted and swore. I remember that scene. Oh how I've tried to blot it out. On sweating, wakeful nights sometimes, all I can see is that circle of excited men, their breath coming fast, their faces hungry for hate and savagery.

'Opstaan, kaffir!' Mr Van Rensburg's pistol-shot voice jerked my body as though a shock had run through it. Michael tightened his grip on my mouth. We watched Johannes try to rise. His fear-numbed limbs wouldn't hold him and he collapsed. Lifting himself on painful hands and knees he tried again, and this time managed to stumble into a standing position. Again, the men held their taut fury intact. No one touched him.

'Trek uit jou broek!' His voice was low and quiet now. Johannes's shaking hands fumbled with his fly and dropped to his sides. He moaned, an aching, eerie wail.

'*Ag*, please, Baas. Take me to the police, Baas. Please.'

'Trek uit jou broek!' he said again, quieter than before. The gun pressed closer to his temple. I looked across at my dad, distress working his mouth and blinking eyes. And then he looked away across the veld where the moon lit a single horizon-held buck, and where the crickets sang still. When I looked back, Johannes had fumbled his pants off and dropped them.

The men were still deathly, savagely silent. I didn't want to look any more. The scene pierced my eyes and ate at my heart. I swear I didn't mean to look. But my eyes couldn't move away.

'Do you know what this is?' said Mr Van Rensburg, still in Afrikaans. I couldn't see what it was. It was shiny in the light, it glinted with the cruelty of the men.

I felt Michael gasp, almost in pain. He let my mouth go and coiled himself into a painful foetal position, his hands clasped between his legs.

Johannes was also clutching at himself, blubbering now in his terror of the mutilation and death to come.

'You've done it to pigs,' Mr Van Rensburg said. 'Now you'll do it to yourself, because you are a pig, *'n kaffir vark.*' He spat into the *bakkie.*

He pressed the castrating knife into the slack, slippery hand which was imploring him. Johannes let the knife fall with a loud clatter, holding his hands together in shaking prayer position.

'The police, Baas. Please, the police. No, Baas, no.'

I tried not to watch. I felt as condemned as he. I felt condemned to watch that knife cut into my insides and slice away my life. I tried to look where my dad was looking, out over the hopeful horizon. I didn't see who retrieved the knife and pressed it back into Johannes's hand.

I heard a click from the gun pressed against his head, and Johannes screamed.

'OK,' he said, shrieking his panic. 'OK.'

And then I watched, my eyes held by the horror of those glistening-eyed men surrounding the helpless creature. I watched his shaking hands move his penis aside and cut into the testicles which nestled below. Johannes was silent now as he operated on himself, alone in this ultimate pain. But I could hear Michael's hot breath coming in small quiet sobs.

When he was finished, Mr Van Rensburg lifted a stick from the ground and, with utter contempt, flicked two small objects from the bakkie floor. They fell in the dust.

That was the last time the family holidayed at the farm. We went to Cape Town the following year and spent Christmas Day in a hotel. Not long after, Oupa and Ouma moved to a flat in Grahamstown. They were just too old, they said, to cope with the farm any more.

From the time my Ouma moved into that flat, her mind began to fly from her, to whisk her back to the land she loved more than anything. When she died, unable to remember Oupa's name, something in Oupa gave in too. He died not long after.

It's funny, but I can't remember another detail about that night. I can't remember how we got home or whether anyone spoke to us. For a long time it seemed my eyes and my sanity were fastened on two small objects falling in the dust.

The next day, Boxing Day, was our last on the farm. I remember becoming aware that the men had driven Johannes to the police station and handed him over. But I can't remember who told me this. I think Ouma told me that he would live – and would probably still go to jail.

Mr Van Rensburg went to jail too. He was found

guilty on a charge of assault with intent. Neil attended the trial in the Grahamstown Supreme Court. He told me later that all the District *manne* had turned up in their *bakkies*. They'd raised money to pay the fine they were sure he'd get. When he was sent to jail with no option, Neil said he thought they'd used the money in the Cathcart Arms to drown their sorrows. He saw what I didn't want to ask, and told me Johannes was there to give evidence. He was serving ten years and seemed fine. He'd got plump in prison, he said.

My mother told me old Mrs Van Rensburg healed too, from 'that ugly incident' – physically at least.

It's strange, but a person can shrink and die inside and still carry on with the business of being a daughter, attending school, passing exams. I did go to boarding school, though. I said I needed the independence. I didn't change schools – merely moved out. I saw the family on alternate weekends. My father and I never spoke of what had happened to us. But he knew that I knew. My own guilt always stopped me from condemning him aloud, but he was never able to discipline me again, or tell me what to do.

I think he had nightmares. On my alternate weekends I sometimes heard his snore break into a strangled cry and I could hear my mother's quiet comfort. I wondered if he also felt haunted sometimes; if, when he closed his eyes, all he could see before him were those small objects lying in the dust.

I left the Eastern Cape as soon as I could. And I have never gone back . . . until now, that is.

Though I have felt tied to it all this time by a corrupted umbilical cord, I have hated it. I have hated its roughness, its frontier quality. I have hated its people and their rigid lives.

I never ever went back to the farm after that Boxing Day. I knew that it couldn't have remained the way it was. I know it should never have been the way it was. But sometimes in my dreams I can see the orange flutter of a hoopoe or the white omen streak of a wild cat. Sometimes I can taste a *soetkoekie*, dunked in condensed-milk coffee. And I can never feel the heat of the sun on my skin or hear the buzzing of a lazy fly without hearing the *skree-bang* of the screen door in the Eden of my childhood. The way it really was. The way it should always have been!

A selection of quality fiction from Headline

All Headline books are available at your local bookshop or newsagent, or can be ordered direct from the publisher. Just tick the titles you want and fill in the form below. Prices and availability subject to change without notice.

Headline Book Publishing, Cash Sales Department, Bookpoint, 39 Milton Park, Abingdon, OXON, OX14 4TD, UK. If you have a credit card you may order by telephone – 01235 400400.

Please enclose a cheque or postal order made payable to Bookpoint Ltd to the value of the cover price and allow the following for postage and packing:

UK & BFPO: £1.00 for the first book, 50p for the second book and 30p for each additional book ordered up to a maximum charge of £3.00.
OVERSEAS & EIRE: £2.00 for the first book, £1.00 for the second book and 50p for each additional book.

Name ....

Address ....

....

....

If you would prefer to pay by credit card, please complete:
Please debit my Visa/Access/Diner's Card/American Express (delete as applicable) card no:

Signature .... Expiry Date ....